NEVER HURT ME

Larry C. Rothman

This is dedicated to

all those for whom high school was not their best years...

ACKNOWLEDGMENTS

I wish to acknowledge my son, Jim, for his valuable research. He lives in Hollywood, Ca., working on his acting career. Having finished writing and starring in his third short film, he now writes scripts for feature films. His knowledge of the locale provided much detail for this novel. I will always cherish and hold dear to my heart his oft repeated encouragement; those three little words: "Just finish it!"

I wish to thank my daughter Amy, living near Olympia, Wa. with her husband Martin and son, Hunter. Amy's talented artistry would provide original, hand drawn illustrations as needed.

I also wish to thank Michael Jaffe, owner of Brookman Stamp Co. in Vancouver, Wa., for his technical (what's a JPEG and a PDF file?) support. His many tedious hours were instrumental in the completion of this book.

And finally my Mother, Eunice, without whom (for obvious reasons) this book would never have been written. Her support and encouragement along with her proofreading was invaluable.

This is a work of fiction; a product solely of the author's imagination. Any similarity to real persons, living or dead, is purely coincidental.

NEVER HURT ME

Larry C. Rothman

Gun raised, Sgt. Burke used his last ounce of strength to kick in the front door, a loud crack as it smacked the inside wall. If not for leaning against the doorjamb, he would be on his butt, his strength gone. But he could still pull a trigger.

Bright daylight flooded the cheaply furnished living room. To Burke's right against the wall was a cot and balled up blanket. A few magazines cluttered the floor next to a wooden table, growing splinters like hair, covered with cards and half filled ashtrays. There were only two chairs, 50's style and a single floor lamp, shade ripped, as the sole source of light for the dingy room.

To Burke's left was a worn-out, green upholstered couch, the middle of three seat cushions missing. Obviously, Goodwill was their boutique of choice. Peeling, floral print wallpaper, clinging to the walls for dear life, completed the décor.

At the sound of the shattered door the three men in the small, musty room turned to the source of the noise. Still leaning against the doorjamb, Burke quickly scanned the three for his first target, glad none were missing. The man on the left stood frozen, eyes wide, staring through long, stringy, dirty blonde hair in his face. The chunky, bald Mexican in the center, no shirt, turned to run down the hall. The one on the right reached for a shotgun. He was muscular, bare feet, jeans and sleeveless T-shirt showing tats covering both arms up to his neck. Also bald. In an instant Burke knew which targets were first, next and last. He also knew it was seldom that easy.

What happened next was a blur of action that seemed to fill an hour, although from first bullet to last took less than three minutes.

The .357 slug hit the man in the chest just as he reached the shotgun, lifting him bodily off his feet and slamming him into the wall behind him. He fell forward; his head slumped over, dead before he hit the floor.

Burke, still struggling to stay on his feet, swung his gun in the direction of the man fleeing down the hall, but growing less steady and weaker. Unable to raise the big gun higher, he hit the second man in the back of the thigh, bringing him down.

He now turned to face the man on his left who finally reacted and disappeared over the back of the couch. The third target's scraggy blonde head reappeared, and then a gun, which he fired, aimed chest high where Burke had been standing. But, no longer able to, Burke had slid to the floor, the slug hitting the wall 18" over his head. Judging by the man's head and neck exposed behind the couch, Burke returned fire from a seated position. The slug exploded through the couch's fabric, blowing a cloud of stuffing in the air, then through the padding and wood frame into the center of the man's chest. The victim jerked back, his arm flinging wide. The gun flew out of his hand careening off the wall at his right, landing on the arm of the couch and sliding to the floor.

Then all was silent. Just smoke and the smell of gunpowder and blood filling the room. Burke took a deep breath, held it and pulled himself across the floor to look around the edge of the couch. The corpse was lying on its side, a hole in its chest Burke could throw a football through without it getting wet.

Three shots: one down, two dead. Not bad. He wouldn't have to reload. Still on the floor, without the strength to get up, he dragged himself to the hall entrance to finish it, expecting trouble. His gun leading the way he looked down the hall for the Mexican fugitive he had dropped. But the hall was empty, a red smear on the threadbare carpet disappearing around the corner to the right.

Burke knew he had to get out of the house. With a kick of adrenaline he made it to his feet just in time to catch a glimpse of movement outside the window on his right. He turned to look as the barrel of a shotgun smashed through the glass and fired, hitting Burke in the left shoulder. What happened next was a blur of motion in which Sgt. Burke had no conscious involvement. The force of the blast spun Burke like a top, his gun arm hanging at his side. As he spun, centrifugal force flung his gun arm out and up and he fired wildly, hitting the wall. He continued spinning, making a complete 360°

turn. Gun and arm now parallel with the floor, he fired again, hitting the man outside the window just above his left ear, the angle of impact blowing away the top half of his head. Burke hadn't even aimed.

"Three for five. And that fourth shot shouldn't count. 'Course, I can't really take credit for the last kill; lucky shot. But dead is dead."

He bent the page down, closed the book, dropped it on the floor next to his bed and turned off the lamp.

"That Sergeant Burke is one gutsy S.O.B." he said to himself. "But like Dad used to say: 'Only in the movies and cheap novels'." He yawned and lay back in bed with his hands behind his head, staring up at the dark nothing.

"Slow and methodical," he thought to himself. "That's how to do it. Calm, cool. With a little panache' and a lot more subtlety. And Cold. Definitely cold. Slow and cold. Ice cold. That's the only way." With a self-satisfied smirk, he pronounced to the specters in the dark his favorite phrase, one he never got tired repeating: "'Revenge is a dish best served cold.' May I take your order, please?" He laughed out loud, yawned again, turned over and went to sleep.

Chapter One

L.A. was hot. The traffic was hopelessly clogged, as usual. The freeways, struggling to move, were like so many gigantic vines; writhing, twisting, determined to strangle the life out of the behemoth that was Los Angeles. There was no good season for L.A. traffic.

Looking down on the city from far above an observer would see an extraordinary sight. If he were on one of the endless flights leaving LAX on Century Blvd., bound for a northern destination, he would first head due west out over the calm Pacific Ocean. The starboard wing dips, the plane banking right in a wide, sweeping arc on its way north. He looks down to see white beaches, speeding surfers on white crested waves, then a deep, blue ocean under a clear azure sky punctuated by only a few puffs of white cloud.

As the passenger liner completes its 90° turn, not quite leveled off, our viewer looks down and back at the city, the tilt of the plane giving him an obligingly unobstructed view. He stares, shocked by what he sees far below. Los Angeles sits in a basin surrounded by hills. But he can't see L.A., reminding him of the old knock, knock joke:

"Who's there?"

"U.C.L.A."

"U.C.L.A. who?"

"You see L.A. when the smog clears."

But it never does. Beyond the hills to the horizon in all directions the sky is just clear blue air. But the air directly over the city, trapped by the surrounding hills, is not clear or blue, but a rusty orange, if it could even be called air at all. A rancid orange juice-colored poison cloud squatted on the city. Only the tops of the tallest buildings poke through the poison cloud, like the eerie, silent, street level scene of Harry Lime's fingers, in *The Third Man*, twisting like worms, up through the sewer grate, trapped, clutching for life just out of reach.

"People actually live down there?" our observer might think. Not all off them. Some regularly die during the worst L.A. smog alerts. Most of them just feel a sharp pain in their chest if they breathe deeper than a shallow inhale. Were our observer a Sci-Fi writer he could easily concoct a story of a generation of L.A. mutants, adapting to their environment, unable to live anywhere else. Perhaps they would explore space, at home on planets with an atmosphere poisonous to normal humans? Would they try and takeover the country and outlaw smog devices? Just an idea. Maybe it could spawn a TV series, there were plenty worse. Or maybe they would all just die breathing L.A.'s poison atmosphere. City of Angels. City of Ghosts.

Tucked away in an area of N. Hollywood away from the traffic and noise, a small and old residential community of small and old houses, was not being bothered by the smog. They were actually enjoying a rather pleasant early summer. But one resident, though safe form L.A.'s smog, had a much more immediate and deadly threat than that posed by L.A.'s poison air.

In a typical small house on a typical quiet street of the sedate neighborhood, not far from the glamour of Hollywood, a victim struggled, bound and gagged. The would-be killer pulled the window blinds of the small bedroom for added privacy. This only magnified the pungent odor from the clammy, sweat-soaked sheets and cut off the beams that had filtered in through the hydrangeas outside. The sound of children playing with a barking dog two houses away was muffled into a distant whisper. The much dimmer room turned the light blue wallpaper a deep purple.

"Let's throw some light on the subject." The intruder flipped on the overhead and vanity lamps, revealing a variety of make-up items. He also turned on the standing floor lamp in the far corner. The room was suddenly very bright.

"O.K., now let's get started." He barely glanced at the 5'2" 115 lbs. blonde tied wrists and ankles to four corners of the bed. Ten years ago her looks alone could easily attract attention. Even now, 15 lbs. heavier, her features had not changed much. But at the moment, there was nothing attractive about her. Her tan slacks, yellow blouse and tan running shoes, unchanged since morning, were crumpled and stained.

There was terror in her pretty blue eyes, her contorted face screaming fear. Her muscles, taut and tired, strained against the bonds. The terror carried her to the edge of panic. He barely glanced at her as he unzipped the duffle bag, took out what appeared to be a confusing assortment of small metal objects and then a small electric motor. He did glance at her as he kneeled by the side of the bed to assemble the parts into a working order.

"It's not so bad. Look at the bright side. You'll be getting what everybody wants: to die in their own bed." He found this rather funny and laughed. "Just not so soon? Well, we can't have everything."

Her eyes pleaded the "Why me?" she was unable to ask through the dishrag gag. She wished she could wipe the moisture oozing from her eyes, dripping from her small, round nose and drooling from the corners of her mouth. Her face had become a comic mask of wildly blended make-up, mascara and mucous. Exhausted, her muscles briefly relaxed and her eyes closed.

The sudden shrill whine of a power drill inches from her

head spiked the petite-plus blonde's panic to a crescendo, with a painful strain at the bindings, arch of her back and loss of bodily function control. But she felt no embarrassment. Her emotions had no room for it. The smell of powdered plaster, sawdust and perspiration almost masked it anyway.

Busily at work, contentedly humming a little tune, the killer at first did not notice her accident. He finished drilling the wall by her head and unplugged the drill.

"This shouldn't take long to set up." He put the drill back in the bag and turned to the small pile of chains, pulleys, ratchet, gears, levers and a small clock.

"Not only do you get to die in your own bed, you get to have the, honor?, okay, distinction of being the first to field test this, what is it? I never gave it a name. But I guess it doesn't need one. It's not like I'm going to apply for a patent. A patent!" He thought that was funny and got a pretty good nasally laugh.

"Nope, this is one of a kind. I designed it just for you. No one will get to appreciate my inventiveness. Is that a word? Maybe I just invented one. Only you and I will ever know how this thing works."

 A small pause. Then, in a low, threatening voice, "We both take it to the grave." Another small pause. Then an upbeat: "You first!" That made him laugh again. "Ha! I kill me!"

He drew sober; saw the irony in his last statement, then broke out again with uncontrollable high, nasally laughter, bringing tears. He was really enjoying himself. When he regained control he went to the foot of the bed, then went back for the drill.

"Forgot I needed it again. Like I said, first time in the field." When he plugged it in the drill roared to life and the hostage's body jumped straight up straining the bonds and sending stabs of pain crisscrossing through her from one lashing to the next.

"Oops, I forgot to turn it off. Guess I'm a little nervous myself, or just having too much fun. More practice might help, but, like I said, this is just for you."

As the drill bit chewed through the paper and plaster, dust and debris settled on the floor molding and carpet. When he finished drilling he got a hand vac out of the bag and cleaned the carpet under the holes.

"Neatness counts. Don't you hate it when people say those stupid little things? Whatdya call 'em? Hackneyed expressions, clichés? I hate them. Makes me want to pull wings off flies. But I don't do that anymore. Kid's stuff."

He started to arrange the pulleys and levers and chains.

"Now give me a few minutes and you'll see something really fun. My cool, little invention. Should be no problem here. I've assembled this and taken it apart many times."

He worked steadily, assembling the various parts. After about ten minutes he said, "Okay, all ready. Now this will be audience participation. I see we have a volunteer, the whole audience! No pushing and shoving. You'll all get a turn…"

The girl struggled harder, her eyes wide in anticipation and fear. He stared blankly, at nothing, paused, memories unfolding, then mumbled to himself "…you'll all get a turn."

She stared at him, her curiosity momentarily replacing some of her fear, as the stranger, who was he?, vaguely familiar, went unhurriedly to his work. First he mounted the clock, back removed, and attached two wires to the electric motor, to a pulley, gears and ratchet. As the clock advanced the hands on the face, the added two wires also ran the second motor, which drove the chain. He could regulate the rate the chain constricted by the lever action and ratchet the slack. The other end of the chain was connected to a reverse pulley constricting against the pull of the first one. In between enough pressure could be applied to crush a cocoanut or gently enough to crack an egg without breaking it. It all depended on how the operator regulated the constriction.

He now slipped the two chains, padded to avoid neck abrasion, over a twisting and shaking head and settled them loosely around the throat. The twenty-eight year-old blonde's adrenaline was running low, sapping her strength to resist, but fear still keeping her body taut.

As the killer leaned over the victim to adjust his homemade contraption, he thought he'd take advantage of the situation to breathe in the fragrance of what he supposed would be some pleasing perfume. That particular experience, being close enough to a female to get a strong whiff of perfume, was unknown to him. Instead of the pleasant aroma he hoped for, he became aware of her accident for the first time. Actually, this was a better turn of events. A pleasant unexpected twist. He smirked and looked directly at her. He wanted her to know he knew. Her death would have an added psychological dimension of humiliation.

"What a shame," he mocked. "Never outgrew bed-wetting. That must be very embarrassing. Do your friends know? I don't know if I can keep a secret like that."

She stared at him. Confused, exhausted, fading as the noose slowly tightened. Slowly, slowly tightened. Her eyes started to flicker; her breathing becoming more and more shallow. She was barely aware of the sights and sounds around her. The children outside playing, the dog barking, growing more and more distant, muffled.

Her vision becoming more blurred, hard to focus on the swimming room around her. The colors: blues and purples and yellows, muted, blending into a soup of no distinction. She stared at the only bright light left, the lamp near the foot of the bed. It was the sun, the center of her universe. Yet her curiosity was still an overarching presence. It still nagged at her.

He leaned over her now, his face very close to hers. She was able to shift her focus to him, his eyes. Something about his eyes. Strange, oddly familiar now. He continued talking.

"How should I spread the news about our little secret? Too bad I couldn't write your epitaph. Wouldn't that be great? Let's see, what should it say? Umm…

Here lies Shawna,

under a tree,

found murdered in bed,

but still took time to pee!"

That brought such a hacking spasm of laughter he reached into his pocket for his inhaler. The noose made one final constriction closing off the esophagus allowing no more air into the lungs. She held her last breath. Her eyes suddenly went wide in recognition, froze that way, and she lost consciousness. When she died, her eyes were still open wide, staring into nothing. The killer disassembled his contraption, packed it away and was gone.

Chapter Two

He woke up in his rented, Culver City duplex. No frills. Not even any pictures on the walls. Austere. That's how he liked it. Simple. Reminded him of his Army days long ago. No fuss. Even easier to clean, although 'clean' isn't exactly how most people would describe it. Still, it wasn't bad. Sure, the drab, green walls could use a little fresh paint, but after a few years, who notices? Could use a little dusting, but clutter was to a minimum, with the same amount of furniture: minimum. Not really much room for more than the minimum anyway. Austere. That's how he liked it.

Years ago he might have given a fleeting thought to how he could improve the looks of the place, make it look a little more, what? Friendly, homey? But he had to admit he had no creativity and was basically…, OK, lazy. At least when it came to home décor. Just wasn't interested. It was just a place to flop, so what was the big deal? It reminded him of what his Dad used to say before he left, working two jobs to support a wife and five kids. He used to say if it wasn't for the burden he had to carry, all he needed was a room and a cot. Looking at his place he understood what the old man was talking about. Sometimes he wondered if that's how the old man wound up. Probably. Wherever he was.

He knew where his Mom was, sort of. He was pretty young when his Dad left and he was told, he wasn't sure by whom, that his Mom had a "very delicate disposition". He didn't know what that meant at the time. He thought something to do with being sick because he did remember she was either sick or on the verge of being sick pretty much all the time. The strain of when his father left, so it went, along with the burden of four boys was more than she could handle. She went back to live with her sister, a widow; maybe in Nebraska or Iowa, maybe. Anyway, one of those corn states. He and his brothers and sister were all native Southern Californians and wouldn't have gone to live in a corn field, even if they were asked. He didn't think they were. Didn't really remember. At first it seemed strange that he never heard from his Mother all these years. Maybe it would have just brought up bad memories for her.

Case's two older brothers got their own apartment and shortly after joined the service, different branches he thought. Maybe the Marines and Air Force, or Navy. He wasn't sure. He and his younger brother had moved in with an uncle who happened to be a cop in Santa Monica. After a two year stint in the Army when he was seventeen, his uncle got him into police training. It turned out to be his calling. He got on the force, and with an analytical mind, he was exceptional at solving all kinds of puzzles. Details and bits of information just seemed to fall into place for him. He made detective grade quicker than lots of guys with much more experience. And that's a sure formula for friction on the force. And the rest is history.

He stretched, scratched, yawned and rolled over. So did the empty scotch bottle he shared his bed with, roll over, and clatter to the floor. Not a welcome sound to the brittleness in his head. More noisy than even the city traffic outside his curtained windows. Plain, drab? OK, drab curtained windows. Austere. That's how he liked it.

He swung his 51 year old legs over the side of the cot and fished around the floor for the fugitive bottle while he rubbed his head, mostly still covered with hair, and mostly still black with intrusions of gray. Yeah, a cot. But no, this wasn't for his love of austerity or nostalgia for his Army days. It just felt better than a mattress. Took up less room, too.

He looked at the travel alarm on the floor next to the cot. 10:29 A.M. So it wasn't the crack of dawn. He was on vacation. First one in almost 2 years. And it's only Tuesday, still most of the week left and the weekend before he had to go in.

He flipped the radio on for a little company. "...thirty A.M. on this sunny, getting warmer by the minute Los Angeles May 22nd Thursday morn. Great day for the beach if you're not already there. Don't forget your SPF 30, or whatever turns you brown", the rapid-fire DJ 'cleverly' driveled on.

"Thursday!? Doesn't that idiot even know what day it is? Overpaid drop out." But warm was right. It was already getting too hot in the small room. At least it was relatively smog-free air. He wasn't quite ready to open the window and let the outside in yet.

After a quick, hot shower he stood leaning with both hands on the sink staring in the mirror, trying to decide if he really needed a shave. He rubbed the stubble on his chin, a little coarse but not too heavy. The face looking back still showed traces of his boyish good looks. Besides a graying stubble, and hints of gray starting to lighten the once all black hair, there was little indication the man was a half century.

Homicide Det. Lawrence Case didn't give his appearance much thought, but as he noticed his hair beginning to change color, he realized he didn't mind it as much as he thought he would. If given a choice he'd rather have it gray than not at all. Which was where he could see he was headed as the thin spots in back encroached to meet the retreating line in front.

"It doesn't really matter," he thought. He was more concerned with staying fit as he looked at his mid-section. No six-pack, he admitted, but he was glad to see each morning when there was less than one inch of loose flesh to pinch around the middle. The speed bag, on a hook in the corner of the living room he worked out on most mornings, saw to that. It served double duty as it helped dispel some of life's frustrations.

Still, the bathroom sink was competing with him over majority ownership of his hair, and slowly winning.

"If the Lord really does count each hair on my head, that's becoming less and less impressive. Pretty soon I'll be able to do that myself." He looked up. "No offense."

The most striking feature of his whole 5'11" frame was his steel blue 20-20's. He'd take the bargain of being a Rogaine candidate to not, at past 50, ever owning a pair of glasses. And his eyes told anyone all they needed to know. No compromise of standards. His code. That's all he really had. His code and his job. He didn't know much, but he knew right and wrong. It's what kept him alive in the army and what kept him alive as a police detective. He was no saint, but he would not 'play ball', skim a little, compromise or sell out. Any cops who did were not cops at all as far as he was concerned. It was his one constant. His code. Period.

He tried forgetting there were fewer years ahead of him on the force than the 29 already behind, way less. He could take his pension at 30 if there was something else he wanted to do. But so far he couldn't think of anything to retire to and no one to retire with. Fine. He liked it that way. It made his life easier when life was simple, because murders weren't. That was his job. Solving them. With few distractions and demands, equally few cases remained unsolved.

Case knew at 51 he should have had more promotions, but that would mean a desk in front of him and a wall behind him. And Capt. Murdock knew Case would retire first. Besides, he was too valuable in the field, so Case's record gave him the juice to stay where he wanted, doing what he wanted. The brass could think what they wanted. It was too late to care. Is that why people called him "Hardcase"? He didn't mind the pun on his name. Kind of liked it.

He pulled on some blue jeans and a faded orange T-shirt he had been meaning to throw away and thought about breakfast.

"Pancakes down at Sandy's or cereal here?" He found a quarter in his pocket.

"Heads Sandy's, tails shredded wheat. Wait, better check the milk first."

He went to the ageing but working refrigerator and got the magnet-free door opened on the first try, hesitating a second to look at the lone picture taped to it.

"May 20th." He wasn't sure when he last turned the

pages on his desk top calendar sitting on the kitchen table. It could have been a couple days.

"If it is the 22nd like the guy said, it should still be OK." He closed the fridge door and flipped the quarter. "Tails. Best two out of three." It was tails again.

"Even though George couldn't come up heads, he couldn't tell a lie, either, and neither can I. I want pancakes." He stuffed his size 11's in the tennis shoes he was also meaning to throw away. "Why should George tell me what to do? He may have been the father of our country, but he wasn't my father."

He rubbed the stubble on his chin: coarse, but not too heavy. Not bad, didn't need a shave. It was only pancakes. He grabbed his wallet, keys, and money clip and then headed for the door. As if on cue, just as he grabbed the knob, the phone rang.

"What the…? Nobody has this number but the precinct and it's days before I go in. "As Detective Sergeant", he thought, " I should be smart enough to find out what day it is without letting on I don't know." He lifted the receiver on the phone on the floor by the cot.

"Make it short."

The clipped voice on the other end did. "Captain calling."

"Put 'im on."

With no pleasantries or preamble, Capt. Murdock got right to the point. "I know you're not due back until day after tomorrow…"

"Thursday! Crap! The dropout was right." Case thought.

"…but if you don't have big plans I want you in this morning. I'll make the two days up to you."

"Love to. But it just so happens my daily planner is booked for the next two days. I have 18 holes reserved this afternoon at the club, then later I'm taking the yacht out for a cruise to one or two of the islands, then tomorrow the Mayor's wife has an emergency hair appointment and I'm filling in for her at her mahjongg club."

"Sounds like fun. Be here in thirty minutes." And the line went dead.

Case pulled the quarter out of his jeans, turned it over and looked at the smirk on George's face. "So shredded wheat it is." The milk landed on the bite-size biscuits in about four coagulated lumps. It was not going to be a good day. At least the garbage disposal got to have breakfast.

Det. Sergeant Lawrence Case took twelve minutes to

shave and change into his work clothes: a decent Navy blue suit and grey tie and headed out the door. "A doughnut on La Cienega. Gotta keep up the image."

Case had no trouble, this time, starting his '88 Caprice with noticeably more fading blue paint than shiny brown rust, parked in the carport next to the duplex. He seldom drove it anywhere than to Police Headquarters downtown where he picked up an unmarked cruiser. Pulling into moderate traffic he flipped on the "all joke" weather station because the job of a weather forecaster was a joke in So. California. The weather was either sunny and 70° in Winter, whenever that was, or sunny and 77° the rest of the year. The real question was about the smog. Today was reporting a level 2 alert and warning the elderly to stay indoors. Many had died during level ones.

Case used the native's method for checking the smog. Los Angeleans learned how to breathe shallow. A deep breath, pulling L.A. "air" deep into the lungs felt the same as the first time inhaling a cigarette. There was a sharp stabbing in the chest. Depending on the toxic levels of the air, shallow breathing prevented most of the pain.

"Level two. Feels about right." he mused. "I still think that crackpot city councilman everybody laughed at had something. What L.A. needs are giant fans, mounted on the top of the hills circling L.A., to blow the poison cloud out to sea. We're just missing the river to turn the turbines to generate the power to run the fans."

Case liked to give free rein to his imagination to clear his mind before taking on a new murder case that he was sure was waiting for him. That was the only reason the Capt. seemed anxious to see him. He knew it wasn't his life-of-the-party personality. He skipped the doughnut and went straight downtown to the underground police parking garage. The attendant waved him through with hardly a glance at his badge. "Nice to be recognized, but lax in the security department", he thought.

Chapter Three

He took the elevator to the third floor, checked in and went to his desk. About 10 minutes later his partner of less than a month showed up.

"Hey, Case."

"Rod."

Det. Jr. Grade Manuel (Manny) Rodriguez hung up his coat and sat at his desk across from his twice-his-age partner.

Case hadn't 'broken him in' yet, still pretty sure he didn't want to. He remembered being assigned his new partner, just a few weeks ago. He didn't remember much but the conversation.

Case had rapped once on the Captain's door.

"Come!" was the one word order shouted from the other side of the door. Case opened it and went inside.

"Close the door and sit down. You have a new partner. Did I say get up?"

Case reluctantly sat back down, his objection never getting out of his half opened mouth.

"I know you don't want one and I don't care and I don't have time to listen to your side of it because you don't have a side of it. There's no discussion. I didn't call you in to have tea. I called you in to give you your partner's badge number." He motioned to a sheet of paper on his desk. "Now report to personnel."

"Captain..."

"Dismissed." The Captain went back to the paperwork he had been doing when Case came in.

"Captain," he repeated.

"What?" he answered without looking up.

"I don't need a partner. It'll just slo..."

The Captain slammed down his pen. "Dammit! Who do think you are, Dirty Harry? You're a cop who takes orders from his boss, one that doesn't like to repeat himself. I didn't ask him what's his favorite color of drapes, either. He has this assignment, just like you do, and you'll work with him. His name is Detective Manuel Rodriguez. He's a good cop. To show that I am reasonable, just for your sake, I will repeat myself: dismissed."

Case didn't waste any more breath. He picked up the

badge number and left the office, smart enough to only close the door firmly, but not slam it. Captain Murdock raised his eyes to watch Case pass a few desks.

"Dirty Harry," he repeated.

"Great day for baseball!" Rodriguez was saying.

"If you like baseball."

"Sa matter, don't you like baseball either? You gotta be a Dodger fan. All the way this year."

"Sure, OK."

"Hey Case, I know you know everything and everything, but c'mon, man. Solving murders and chasing bad guys can't be your whole life...what's left of it. What are you, about a hundred?"

"I'll dance on your grave, kid." Case changed the subject, sure that that one was over, since he won. "They must be getting backed-up to pull us both in with only two days left before we had to show."

"Yeah. The Captain said the top brass is cancelling all time off immediately. They want to get more cases cleared with budgets coming up next month. Bodies are piling up in the streets. You Gringos should visit south of the border and you wouldn't worry so much."

"They'll still be dead in two days. And the Captain told you all that?"

"Sure, what'd he tell you?"

"He said to tell your partner to quit talking so much, grab a file and get to work."

"OK, Amigo, so whata we got?"

Case looked at the files on his desk. Two murders last night: drive by shooting in Watts and in East L.A.

"Pick one," he said to Manny.

"Let's go to Watts. They have a great barbeque chicken joint. The best."

"Man, that's worse than the tacos and refried you're always scarfing."

"You just don't know how to eat."

"I know how not to eat. Your gut will be bigger than your sombrero before you're thirty."

"You call tuna, mac and cheese and carrots, just 'cause you don't know how to cook, eating? And with your support you can't afford restaurants every night."

"What do you know?" Case bristled.

"Wild guess. So how about it? You got an old lady some place with her hooks still in you? Maybe a kid or two you're paying tuition for?"

"Mind your own business." Case picked up a file.

"So, when are you going to come over and let Consuela make you a real meal? She still hasn't even met my partner. And don't worry, you won't scare the kids. I warned them. Once they get by your ugly looks, you're not so mean. They seen Beauty and the Beast a million times."

"Let's go. Tell the Capt. we're on our way. I'll meet you in the garage."

A few minutes later Case pulled the unmarked police cruiser into thickening traffic. They jumped on 101 then got off at Alameda St. and took it down to Slauson Ave.

"Why don't you come over for dinner this weekend?" Rodriguez pulled a picture of his family out of his wallet. "See? The kids are beautiful. I've taught them Gringos are people, too. They won't bite. I'm beginning to think you don't like Hispanics."

"Sure I do. Especially your names. I'm usually not good with names but I know if I say Felipe, Jose, Juan or Ricardo I'll be right three out of four times."

"Wise guy."

Actually Det. Case was as far from being a racist as possible. Growing up and attending only public schools in So. California, with an almost equal mix of nationalities and backgrounds, to Case, people were just people. The way he looked at it, they were either on the right side of the law or they weren't. Good or bad. It made life simple: avoid the good ones and lock up the bad ones.

Case turned left on Central Ave.

"So how about it?" Rodriguez asked.

"How about what?"

"Come over to dinner this weekend. I'll get some Buds. Dos Equis is not your style. We can catch a game on the tube. I got a huge flat screen. I know, you don't like baseball. What else? The fights, stock car, Oprah?"

That made Case laugh. "You know I don't socialize. I wouldn't know which fork to use."

"C'mon, man. It'll do you good. Stop thinking about the job for awhile."

"I'll check my appointments secretary. Then I gotta see if I have a clean shirt to wear."

"Consuela is expecting you to come over some time. She wants to meet you."

"So I'll think about."

"So you're going to think about it?"

"Yeah! Alright! I'll think about it. Man, now I know why I got divorced!"

The dispatcher called. Manny took it. They were to proceed to N. Hollywood.

"Hollywood? Get the Captain." Twenty seconds later Det. Case was talking to his boss.

"What's the problem?"

"We're two blocks from the Watts shooting. What do you want us up in North Hollywood for?"

"The Watts shooting is a drive-by. Uniforms report the victim's a Skull and witnesses, that'll talk, put the perps in the Royal Tres. The uniforms can handle it. There's a reported death in North Hollywood. No apparent disturbance or motive but definitely not natural. I want you to check it out. And Case…"

"Yeah?"

"How's your rookie going to learn to follow orders when my #1 homicide detective can't take an assignment without giving me feedback? There's a forensics unit on the way, will beat you by twenty minutes."

"Who's the lead?"

"I ask you questions, you ask the scene questions." And the radio went dead.

"What was that all about?"

Case hunched his shoulders and tightened his grip on the wheel. He made a U-turn at the next light and kept driving without answering. Rodriguez's Latin temper was starting to rise.

"Look, I'm your partner. You don't want to trade recipes, that's okay with me. But something about the job, I should know about it. It affects you, it affects me."

"Don't push it."

But he was pushing it.

"What did you ask the Capt. about? The lead? What lead? The lead of the forensics unit? Somebody you don't like. Somebody that don't like you?"

"I said forget it."

"No man, I want to know what it is, man." Case could see he wasn't going to let up.

"Bob McCulley's the one in charge of the unit."

"So? Who's he? What'd he do, dump your sister?"

Case let go of the wheel with his right hand and grabbed his partner's shirt. Then he let go and they drove a couple blocks in silence. The tension in the car was almost as thick as the smog outside. Case turned on the AC. Rodriguez turned on the radio, a Spanish station.

"Now we gotta listen to that?"

"Man, how come you're such a hard case? Somebody drop you on your head when you were a baby or something?" That brought a smirk to Case's face. "First time I seen you smile, sort of. What's so funny?"

"Actually, I was."

"What, dropped on your head?"

"Sort of." Case thought a minute. "We used to live in a two story house. My mother said she was holding me at the top of the stairs. I guess I twisted around and got loose. She dropped me and I rolled down the stairs. They weren't carpeted. Didn't do me any harm, though."

Rodriguez just looked at him. Then, "That explains a lot. So what's the deal with this McCulley guy?"

"Quit bustin' my chops. This isn't the time or place."

"Then where, when?"

Case thought a minute. "You gotta go right home to Conchita after work?"

"Consuela."

"Whatever."

"No," Rodriguez said "Why?"

"Then meet me at the Sow and I'll fill ya in if that'll get you off my back. Do you know it?"

"The Blue Sow? The cop bar on Wilshire Blvd.?"

"That's it."

"Yeah, I know it. Never been there."

"You'll love it. See you there later," Case said.

Rodriguez just looked at him, not so sure about loving the place, which was probably a dive. "So that's all you got? Your mother dropped you on your head. No other family? At least you weren't raised by wolves, which is the 5 to 3 favorite."

Case knew Rodriguez wasn't the enemy and they were supposed to depend on each other, even though he would rather just watch his own back.

"What the hell. I'll give it to you quick. You're not going to have time for notes so listen fast 'cause I'm only saying it once. No questions. Father took off when I was a kid. Sister died in a cross walk when she was five; drunk driver. Three brothers: one in Downey, wife and four kids, real zoo at his house. I generally stay away. Another up the coast, one of those small towns, San something or other. San Rafael, San Leandro. Maybe Santa Clarita. I can never keep them straight. He lives with his wife. They raise chickens and walnut trees I think. The last one is a mechanic. Got a garage on Crenshaw. Never married. Comes in handy if I need an oil change, whatever. That's it."

"What about you mother?"

"I said no questions." They were five minutes from the address the dispatcher gave them and Case was anxious to start work.

"You can't leave her out. Is she still alive?" Rodriguez realized he was probably venturing beyond his bounds, but he didn't think he'd get such a chance again.

"Yes."

"How old is she?"

"Almost 80."

"Where does she live?" He was going to keep going as long as he got an answer.

"Probably Kansas."

"You don't know?"

"One of those corn states. Look, we're not in touch. All I remember is she loves it there, hates to travel, never goes or been anywhere.   And this interview's over." Case paused. "And Manny."

"You called me Manny."

"Yeah. You bring up any of this personal bio B.S. again and I'll meet Consuela. When I see her at your funeral."

He pulled onto a quiet, tree-lined residential street. "We're here."

Chapter Four

They parked next to the curb behind city vehicles which filled the street directly in front of the small, 50's style, 3 bedroom house. Case led the way past the black and white and ambulance in the driveway, up the steps and opened the screen door. The front door was already standing open. In the small living room was a uniformed officer standing in the middle of the floor and a young woman, mid to late twenties, very distraught, sitting on the couch.

"Detective Case. This is my partner Detective Rodriguez," he said to the officer who motioned with his head to the left down the short hall.

"Forensics is already here; last door on the left."

"Thanks." Case and Rodriguez followed his direction down the hall. The small bedroom was already crowded with the team and another uniformed officer. No one complained about the close quarters, especially not the room's occupant. She'd never complain about anything again.

"Officer," Case read the name tag on the uniform, "Baxter. I'm Detective Case, my partner Rodriguez. What do you have so far?"

"911 call came in at 1:17 this afternoon. Woman in the living room, name of Melissa Ramirez, came home from her afternoon jog, found the body, her roommate, called it in."

"She have anything else to say?"

"Haven't had a chance to interview her yet. We just got here ourselves and secured the scene." Case nodded to his partner who went out to interview the primary.

"Any other witnesses? Anybody see, hear anything?"

"Don't know yet. Like I said, we just got here. My partner and I were waiting for you before canvassing the neighborhood. But it looks awfully quiet."

"Okay, Baxter. Go ahead. Maybe somebody can tell us something."

When the officer left, McCulley glanced in Case's direction. They each gave a curt nod to acknowledge the other's presence and McCulley went back to directing his team while Case surveyed the room. The first thing he noticed in the well ordered, small room was the smell. He could still detect the faint trace of scented freshener in the otherwise overpowering stench of released body fluids, from sweat glands and otherwise. Overlaying the olfactory soup was an aura of fear, a final statement of the young victim's existence.

Case knew better than to ask McCulley's advice, input or impressions. He looked at the body. No blunt force trauma, no blood, but from the deep purple bruising, wrapped completely around her neck from one side to the other from hundreds of broken capillaries, strangulation was obviously the cause of death.

Case looked at the face. He could well imagine that she would have been pretty. Her macabre death mask of mascara, having run then dried, open mouth and bulging eyes definitely was not.

"Finished here?" he asked the man taking pictures

"A couple more."

Case stepped back and squeezed his hands into tight plastic gloves. The photographer moved away and Case leaned in and closed the eyes. Then he gently turned the head from side to side, peering closely at the neck. She was definitely strangled, but he found it interesting there were no signs of violent trauma: no fingernail scratches, broken skin or finger or thumb indentation marks. "She was strangled," he thought, "but the perp did not use his hands."

The guy dusting for prints and McCulley moved to the vanity area and Case edged to the side of the bed near the window. He got down on his hands and knees to snoop around for anything out of the ordinary when he noticed the two neat holes drilled in the wall a foot above the floor. He wondered what they were for. They looked fresh, but there was no sign of wood dust, and the carpet just below the holes was cleaner than the surrounding area. Only that spot had been vacuumed.

Case put his left hand flat on the floor to get up when he heard, rather than felt, a small crunch. His hand had a few crumbs on it. He looked at the carpet and there were more crumbs from the pretzel he had just crushed. He took a small plastic evidence bag out of his pocket then took one of his business cards out of his breast pocket and scooped the remainder of the pretzel and what crumbs he could into the bag.

"Hey, guys." Case held the small bag up in the air. "Anybody know what this is?" Heads turned to look. McCulley had his back to Case and turned his overweight 6' frame around, reluctantly, to look. His close set eyes under a close-cut crop barely glanced at the bag.

"You tell us. You're the detective."

"Anybody know about it, why it's here? Who might have dropped it?"

"You think my guys snack on the job? This is a murder scene! We're not amateurs. You think you're the only professional, *Detective*?"

"No disrespect. It just seems out of place, that's all."

"Why? So she liked to read in bed and eat pretzels. What's the big deal?"

"No book on the night stand. No pretzel bag."

"So she cleaned up before she went to bed. You're the hot-shot detective. You figure it out. C'mon. You guys done in here? We have more work to do."

Case got down and looked at the two little drill holes again. Then he inspected the closet. Not too many articles of clothing on the hangers, nothing fancy. There were no more than a half dozen pair of shoes hanging in a shoe caddy, mostly Earthwalkers and running shoes. He then inspected the dresser drawers. Nothing unusual. Everything folded and put away. The hamper next to it was empty except for a set of workout clothes. That caught his attention and he looked back in the drawers. Two more sets of sweats. When he was satisfied, he nodded to the medic standing by and went out into the living room where his partner was sitting on the couch talking with Ms. Ramirez.

"Need me, Sarge?" Rodriguez asked.

"Give me ten minutes."

Case went into the kitchen at the right side of the living room. He opened cupboards, drawers and looked in the refrigerator. He then went out the side door to the back of the house. There was a small yard surrounded by a chain link fence that backed on an alley. He stopped by the victim's bedroom window looking at the ground and the shrubs. He continued on around the side of the house to where the fence ended at a chain link gate that was latched. He retraced his route, came back in by the kitchen side door and back into the living room.

Rodriguez introduced his partner to Melissa Ramirez. She was also in her late twenties, dark hair and eyes. Petite, no more than 115 lbs. She was wearing a blue running outfit and sneakers. Shock and fear registered on her face. She had been relatively calm after the shock of finding her roommate, but now the fear started to takeover.

"Who would do this? Why? Why did someone do this to her?" As if on cue the attendants wheeled the covered body out, one on either end of the gurney.

"Oh!" And she looked away.

"Who would do this?" she repeated. "Why?" It crossed her mind: What if Shawna was out running and I was home. Would that have been me?

"We're going to find who did this," Case assured her. He had nothing to go on so far, and he knew it, but it was just the beginning. "Right now we need any information you can give us, anything you can think of."

"I already told…" she stopped.

"Manny Rodriguez," Manny offered.

"Yes, .. I'm sorry. Manny. Do I call you that? Or detective? This is so terrible. What's it all about?"

"Please try and relax a little if you can. Would you like a glass of water? Let me get you a glass." Case said.

"I'll get it Sarge," and he went into the kitchen.

"This is very terrible, Miss, and I know it's difficult right now. I'm also sure you have been very helpful with Detective Rodriguez. But going over it again can be very helpful. Sometimes you'll remember something you didn't think of the first time, anything, a small detail. I might ask some things Detective Rodriquez .."

"Thank you" she said as Rodriguez was back with the water.

"… might not have asked. I mean, he is a smart up and comer, but he's still a rookie."

"That's right, Miss. Listen to him. He's a very wise, *old* man."

Case continued. "So I apologize if I ask anything Detective Rodriguez already asked. I believe you will be very helpful to us if you don't mind starting over. Believe me, it's our best way of catching whoever did this. If you prefer, we can go somewhere you'd feel more comfortable."

She looked at Case, at Rodriguez and then back at Case, then took another sip of water.

"Okay. I want to help."

"That's fine. Just take your time, Miss."

"Well, like I told Detective Rodriguez, I was out for my morning run."

"What time was that?"

"I always leave the house at 10 A.M." Rodriguez stepped to the side and discreetly took out his notebook and opened it to take down any information she might not have related with his interview.

"Was ...um.." Case looked to his partner for help. His partner flipped back a few pages in his notebook.

"Shauna Anderson, Sarge."

"Was Shawna your roommate?"

"Yes. Her room is the last one at the back. Mine is across the hall from hers and the third one is empty. We rent from the landlord, an old Chinese guy. He's nice. Leaves us alone."

"And what was Shawna doing when you left?"

"She was getting ready for a job interview."

"Did she seem upset about anything? Do you have any idea who might've done this?"

"No! She was really sweet. This is a total shock. I don't know anyone who was mad at her at all."

"Any recent fight with a boyfriend?"

"She was dating a guy for the last couple of months. I met him a couple times. Seemed really nice. They just went out a few nights ago. When she came home she was in her usual good mood."

"Do you know his name?"

"Foreign.. um .. something. I can't think right now."

"That's alright. She probably has his info on her phone." Case continued. "How long did you know Miss Anderson?"

"We met when I moved in, about 6 months ago. I moved up from Torrance. She had been living here two or three years, I think."

"Did you get along okay? Any problems?"

"We got along fine. We weren't super close, but we liked each other and were friends." She stopped and looked from one detective to the other. She started to get agitated. "Do you think I...?"

"No, no. I'm just wondering how much she would let you into her personal life if she felt in danger."

"I don't know if she would or not, but like I said, she gave no indication that anything was wrong. As long as I knew her she was happy and upbeat. That's why I can't believe this. It seems so random. Do you think it could have been me if I was home and she wasn't? I can't stay here. I have to leave."

"We're getting a little ahead of ourselves. Please, just try to remain calm. When the uniform officers get back I'll have them escort you. That's certainly up to you. But I don't really believe you are in danger, although it's perfectly understandable to want to leave after what's happened."

She took another drink of water and relaxed a little. "Why don't you think it's random?"

"There's no forced entry or signs of a struggle. The bedroom windows are locked and there's been no one outside there recently. Do you always keep the doors locked?"

"Yes."

"Did you lock the door when you left, even if someone is here?"

"Yes. We agreed to. One of us might be in the shower.

This is a safe…," she looked down, thought about the irony of the statement and started sobbing. Case glanced at Rodriguez who said "That's okay, Miss. We're almost finished."

She angrily went on. "*Was* a safe neighborhood, and quiet. But we didn't want just anybody walking in on us, so we always kept the doors locked, even when we were here."

"That's why I don't think it was random. Either she knew here assailant and let him in or she felt no threat when she opened the door. You go jogging the same time everyday?"

"Yes. I always leave at ten."

"And always in the same area, the same routine?"

"Yes." She started getting impatient.

"I'm sorry, Miss, just one or two more questions. Where do you go and do you always return about the same time?"

"I always jog down to the park. It's about two blocks from here. There's a nice mile and a half trail. I always do that twice, then I hang out for about a twenty minute break, do twenty minutes of aerobics, then stop for a salad for lunch another block further on."

"And then you head back?"

"No. After that I like to just walk west through the neighborhood and make a loop around and head back from the other direction."

"What time do you get back?"

"It's always just after one. Then I change and go to work. I'm a fitness instructor at Always Aerobics on Victory Blvd."

"Do you ever vary from that routine? Do you always get home after one?"

"Yes, it's always after one. And no, I don't vary. I look forward to my jog and walk and the timing works perfect for me. What does that have to do with Shawna?"

"For one thing we know it happened between ten and one, broad daylight. Whoever it was didn't expect to be disturbed so he must have learned your routine for at least a couple of weeks which means he had a specific target and it wasn't you."

Melissa thought about that. "Well, I can't stay here anyway. We were looking for a third roommate to share the rent. I can't afford to stay here by myself. But it doesn't matter. You think I could stay after this? I'm calling my sister in Studio City. Can I go now?"

Case nodded. "I think that's all we need for now. When the uniformed officers get back I'll have one of them stay with you and lend any assistance you might need. Please give Detective Rodriguez your sister's address and number in case we need to contact you. And we'll give you our cards in case you think of anything else, anything at all. We really appreciate your help."

He leaned over to his partner and spoke in a half voice. "Stay with her until they get back," and he went back into the empty bedroom to retrieve the victim's wallet and cell phone and laptop. When Case reentered the living room Officer Baxter and his partner Len Paulski were talking quietly with Rodriguez.

Case joined the group and said, "Rodriguez and I are heading in. Give Miss Ramirez any assistance she might need and when you finish up here, you can give us what you found, later at headquarters."

Baxter said, "We can give it to you now. We have nothing." He showed Case his empty notebook. Case looked at Paulski who just shook his head. "Nobody saw or heard anything."

Case and Rodriguez headed back downtown in normal, heavy L.A., four o'clock traffic. They were each considering what they saw, their earlier conversation forgotten. Case's driving reflected his impatience to get on with things, not shy about jumping through yellow lights. Rodriguez tightened his seat belt, wondering what it would be like if they were actually in hot pursuit.

When they got back, Case bounced the cruiser down the ramp into the underground. Five minutes later they were on the third floor, at their own desks, facing each other.

Case finally spoke. "Let's get these prelims written up."

"What do you make of it?" Rodriguez asked. "Not much to go on. Could be any number of motives, but no obvious suspect, not even a potentially obvious one. Regardless of what you told her roommate, I still think it's random."

"It looks that way. Learning the roommate's pattern was just speculation."

"So is that how you're writing it up, random for lack of any evidence?" Rodriguez asked.

Case reached into his jacket pocket and tossed Rodriguez the evidence bag with the 2 ½" length of thin pretzel and second broken pieces with crumbs.

"What's this?"

"I found it partially under the victim's bed."

"So?"

"So what's it doing there?"

"She liked to snack in bed when she read. A lot of

people do that," Rodriguez offered.

"That's what McCulley said."

"You talked to him?"

"I asked about the pretzels, he responded, couldn't be avoided."

Rodriguez was going to pursue it but decided to save it. Instead he tossed back the evidence bag.

"But you doubt it?"

"I don't know. Seems out of place. Doesn't feel right. Just doesn't seem to fit."

"Why not?" Rodriguez asked.

"For one thing there was no book on the night stand, or anywhere else in the room. You saw the treadmill?"

"Sure."

"I checked the kitchen. Looked through all the cupboards and drawers. No cookies, no chips, no candy and no..."

"Pretzels." Rodriguez finished for him.

"No snacks of any kind. At least not of the junk food variety. There were health bars and the fridge had frozen yogurt. It's their lifestyle. The roommates got along. She's an aerobics instructor. They were both into fitness, not munchies."

"So how did they get there? Did the murderer like to snack on the job?"

"I don't know. Maybe we'll get something from the M E. Just doesn't seem to fit," Case repeated.

Fifteen minutes later they were finished with the preliminary reports. The Capt.'s office was busy so they put them in their desk.

"We'll give them to the Captain in the morning. Let's get out of here."

"We still stopping by the Blue Sow?" Rodriguez asked.

"Are you going to forget about McCulley?"

"Nope."

"Then let's go."

Chapter Five

The Blue Sow was a cop bar. It was originally an Olde English style pub complete with a shingle hanging over the door. On the sign was painted an enormous blue sow. When the original owner died, a retired cop bought the place. He hung out there so much after duty, while he was still on the force, that it seemed like a good idea to buy it for his retirement. He changed the interior to a sports theme but the old name stuck; there was a certain irony in it. Joseph Wambaugh, an ex-cop turned writer dubbed them blue knights. Reminiscent of what cops were called in the sixties, along with Wambaugh's term, the old pub's name was perversely appropriate. So he left the blue sow hanging out front where it had always been as far back as anyone could remember, and the name became somewhat of an inside joke. Today's cops liked it and the place became a cop's haven /sports bar.

The inside of the Blue Sow was a little seedy and well worn, not the modern and attractive sports bar. There was sawdust on the floor which rendered spills and peanut shells irrelevant. Cops could be as sloppy as they wanted. There was a long bar to the right of the entrance with a few tables and chairs in the middle of the floor flanked by booths against the opposite two walls. Scattered pictures of past greats and the obligatory beer ads of well-endowed young ladies was the extent of the wall décor. A couple red and white plastic Budweiser blimps hanging from the ceiling completed the owner's idea of interior decorating, or at least his interest in the subject.

A juke box in the corner played continuously, nothing after the '70's. Wooden chairs scraped the wooden floors as the patrons shifted around or got up to go to the can. Rumbling conversations were occasionally broken up by raucous laughter. Not too well lit. The place appealed to no one but the regulars.

A worn out pool table at the back wall, a dart board and a couple of video games was what the Blue Sow offered as entertainment. But the drinks, stories, arguments and occasional face offs were the real entertainment.

Case had arrived first and was in a booth at the back, nursing a beer, when Rodriguez came in. Rodriguez looked around, saw Case and came over.

" 'should have figured you'd be in the back," he said sliding into to the booth opposite Case. "Do you like to drink alone?"

"Love it."

"I thought you liked to watch your waist line. You're having a beer?"

"My one lite for the week."

Rodriguez got up again. "Be right back."

"I'll be here."

Rodriguez came back with a Pacifico. "Didn't have Dos Equis. These are good, too. They don't have any lime, though. What kind of a place is this?"

"I sit with you all day in the car, now here too?"

"Hey, this was your idea. So tell me about McCulley. You're not going to talk too long and I'm only going to have one beer anyway. I gotta work with the guy, too."

"It's no big deal. We don't see eye to eye on some issues so we try and stay out of each other's way."

"So?" Rodriguez emphasized by suddenly sitting up straight. "That's it? We didn't come here for that. What issues? I bet there's some history. What it is? Give."

"Look. I changed my mind. I don't feel like gabbing about it. Finish your beer and let's get out of here."

Rodriguez started to object when one cop who obviously didn't start his drinking at the Blue Sow stumbled by with two of his friends to shoot some pool. He stopped short and beer sloshed out of his mug when he noticed Case.

"Hey, Lou." He said to one of the other cops with him. "It looks like they'll let anyone in here." He looked at Case long and hard, and then in a much more sober voice, "No matter what kind of cop he is."

Case glared back. "I was just telling my partner that very thing." Case didn't take his eyes off the red faced cop with the beer mug. He glanced at the name tag on the uniform blouse, the bottom two buttons open over the paunch, one shirt tail hanging out. The tag said O'Rourke. Officer O'Rourke looked at Rodriguez.

"This your new partner, huh? He don't look too smart to me, but if he was smart, he'd ask for another partner while he was still healthy."

"C'mon Shawn, let's shoot some pool and leave these guys alone. They're not bother'n anybody." He put his hand on Shawn's shoulder but he pushed it off.

"They're bother'n me!" Shawn yelled.

Case stood, almost nose to nose with O'Rourke. "Sorry you feel that way. Why don't we go outside and talk about it?"

O'Rourke shot back, "What's wrong with right here?"

His other friend grabbed his arm. "C'mon, Shawn. I don't need another suspension. Neither do you."

Shawn shrugged him off, too, and just stood, eyeball to eyeball with Case, not moving.

While everyone else was trying to think what to do or

say to defuse the situation Rodriguez finally said,

"Hey Sarge, I'm hungry. How about you? Since you're up, why don't you order us a couple of burgers? I'll have the works, no mayo."

Case kept staring at O'Rourke, probably 2" taller and 40 more pounds. Then he suddenly grinned. Without taking his eyes off the other, he said "Sure. Why not?", and he brushed past. As Case headed towards the bar O'Rourke yelled at his back "And don't forget the cheese on yours. Rats love cheese."

Case spun around and O'Rourke swung at him and missed. The force of his miss, the beer in his gut and stepping in the beer he spilled on the slick floor all caused him to slip. Going down he cracked his chin on the edge of the table and hit his head on the floor, out cold.

Case looked from one of O'Rourke's friends to the other. "We done here or what?" The second one turned to Lou. "Gimme a hand." They stood on either side of O'Rourke, each grabbed an arm, pulling it behind their own neck, and drug O'Rourke out of the bar.

Rodriguez asked Case what he wanted to do now.

"I still want to get that burger. Fighting always gives me an appetite."

Case came back and slid into the booth. "Dick'll send the burgers over with Bonnie. He's getting backed-up." The place was starting to fill up.

"Fries?" Rodriguez asked.

"Of course."

"Curly and seasoned?"

"Don't push it."

"So what was that all about with those guys? Don't people generally like you? I'm getting the feeling you don't make a lot of friends."

"Friends are overrated," Case stated.

"Like everything else?"

The burgers showed up sooner than expected.

"Dick likes me. See that? Excellent service." Case took a big bite.

"Yeah, well, that O'Rourke guy sure doesn't."

"He was drunk." Case took a swig of beer to wash down the burger. "You know how some guys like to pick a fight when they're drunk. Probably claim I sucker punched him."

Rodriguez was enjoying the burger, too. "Probably."

Then he laughed. "But that's the first time I ever saw anyone sucker punch himself."

"He's a clown."

Rodriguez munched a couple fries. "What did he mean by that crack about staying healthy?"

Case put down his burger. "You might as well know who you're partnering with. I guess I should have told you right at the start. I'm surprised no one else came out and told you."

"So what, you moonlight as a security guard, you running something off the books on the side?"

Case gave Rodriguez a hard look. "My partner was killed on duty. Happened down in San Diego two years ago. We were partners for eleven years. Bill Flaugherty. Good cop. We were on separate assignments. I was working narcotics/homicide division; he caught a DEA drug bust, big one they set up at a border crossing. Like now: budget cuts, interdepartmental man power loans."

"Yeah," Manny said. "I hope we don't catch any outside duty here, although the OT would be good."

Case had no response to that and went on. "Somebody tipped the cartel. They don't know who. Somebody on the inside definitely paid off. Had to be pretty high up. The whole operation was a disaster. People were killed."

"I read about that operation. They didn't give too many details."

"Of course not. One of the dead was my partner, Bill. Good cop." Case repeated. "Long story short, the brass transferred me up here. When I came up from San Diego there's always somebody curious, see what they can find out about the new guys. Somebody always does background checking. They found out it was my partner one of the ones killed. Doesn't put me on anyone's Christmas list."

"They blame you for that? You weren't even there. You weren't any part of that assignment."

"He was my partner. That's all anyone knows or cares about. You don't let anything happen to your partner. More superstition than anything else. No one wants to work with a guy loses his partner. Bill was a good cop" he said for the third time. "Had a family." He sat and didn't say anything for a couple of seconds, then suddenly, "You finished? C'mon, let's get out of here."

They got up and Case left money for both burgers.

They were heading out when Rodriguez said, "I still think that goon was way out of line, and that crack about being a rat. Lucky he knocked himself out so you didn't have to do it. Totally uncalled for."

"That wasn't the same thing. Whole different story

which you also need to hear, but some other time."

"We've had enough fun for one night. Tell me later."

They got to the bar at the front, near the door, and were about to leave when Case suddenly stopped. "You know what? I changed my mind. You in a hurry? We're here, let's get it done. Dick, two more of the same."

Dick said, "Uh, that was a Bud lite and Pacifico?"

"Right." Case said. "They're on him."

Case grabbed the beers, and Rodriguez followed him back to the same booth they were sitting in. The table had already been cleared. They sat down, each took a swig of their beer, then Case began.

"I'm nobody's friend around here because I testified in an IA case. Turned out good for the brass, they did a lot of house cleaning, but not so good for the guilty. There were fines, firings, loss of pensions and even jail time. And, naturally, those guys had a lot of friends on the force. Those friends were unhappy about what happened to the guys fined and jailed, never mind they were guilty. Nobody likes a cop taking IA's side. There were Idle threats, but the brass took it serious, had concerns for my safety. That's why I left San Diego. I guess L.A. wasn't far enough."

Case took a long drag on his beer. "The locals are

curious about someone new transferring in, especially someone on the force as long as me. Word gets around; there are always ways to find out things. When a new guy has had a killed partner he becomes an immediate pariah. Then they found out about the Internal Affairs case."

"Oh," Rodriguez said. "Yeah, some guys can get awful hot about testifying against other cops."

"I didn't testify against other cops."

"But you said..."

"They weren't cops."

"But, I don't get it. Then how was there an IA case if they weren't on the force?"

"I didn't say they weren't on the force, I said they weren't cops."

"OK, I'm lost. How were they on the force if they weren't cops?" Case was laying the groundwork.

"That's the point. Let me give you a civics lesson." Case took another swallow, his second beer that week. He'd have to remember to skip next week, and he began his lecture.

"People want to live in a safe, protected civil society where they can raise their kids without fear of leaving their homes.   So the first thing they do is decide how everyone should act for everyone's benefit. The results of that public meeting are public laws designed for the public's safety."

"Like traffic laws," Rodriguez put in, wondering where Case was going with this.

"Exactly. Some people have a 'who's going to make me? 'attitude, 'you and what army?' Well, we're the army. Without enforcement, those laws are just paper dreams. This all gets very expensive for the working, law abiding citizen who could better use his money for his family if, ideally, no one broke those laws."

"And we'd be out of work."

"So would judges, jailors, guards, public prosecutors, public defenders and all the rest. As I said, it gets pretty expensive for the people that have to pay for all that. There's also the cost of our equipment, training, plus court houses, prisons; it goes on and on."

"Yeah, so?"

"So, after paying for all that, how protected is the public? What are they getting for their money? Criminals still break the law everyday, even with a well-armed, around the clock, fully functioning police force. Think how it would be without us."

"But we're here. The public foots the bill; we serve the public as best we can," Rodriguez countered.

"And that's the point of it. That's all the public can and should expect, to get what they're paying for. IA gets involved because not everyone cashing his public provided paycheck, is...is working for the public. Some of them are also taking money *NOT to do their job.* So who are they really working for? When a so called 'dirty cop' takes money to tip off a raid, or lose evidence or in any other way provide aid and information to the criminal element, undermining our work, endangering our lives, while still cashing his public tax dollars pay check, under false pretenses, stealing," and Case was starting to get hot, "money that would go to someone who *would* do the job that money was being paid for, who, I ask you, is he really working for? Someone once said: 'You can't serve two masters'."

"I think that was Jesus."

"Yeah, somebody way up there like that."

"You said a 'so called dirty cop'. I guess you call them something else?"

"Au contraire, mon ami."

Rodriguez raised an eyebrow.

"It means 'to the contrary, my friend' in Italian."

"French."

"Whatever. One of those sissy languages."

"Your mastery of linguistics is exceeded only by your charming wit and sparkling personality."

"I know." Case didn't miss a beat. "Anyway, the point is that's why I said I didn't testify against cops, because I don't call them cops at all. If you're working for the fire department, you're a fireman. If you're working for the crooks, you're a crook. In fact, it's no different than if the organized mob hired guys to go through the Academy and get on the force, just to have their people on the inside, working for the crooks, not us. It would be a good investment for them. Again, who would they be working for? Not the police department, so they're not cops. Undercover crooks. Wolves in sheep's clothing. It's in the Bible. Look it up."

"The Bible?" Rodriguez said, surprised.

"Yeah. You've heard of it. Made all the best seller's lists."

"I see your point. And you take your soap box wherever you go?"

"Why not? 'The truth shall set you free.' Also Jesus?"

"I'm pretty sure." Rodriguez finished half of his Pacifico while he was taking it all in. "So this IA case, it involved dir.., uh, crooks on the force, and you testified against them?"

"That was the size of it. After my partner was killed in the tipped off sting operation there were investigations on the local and Federal level but it never went anywhere. I did some investigating on my own, and I couldn't get anywhere. I think it just went too high up, but I did uncover a pretty wide system of crooks wearing uniforms, on the take, covering for various rackets. I was the star, make that only, witness willing to testify. The results you know. You'd think other cops wouldn't have a problem with that, unless they weren't really cops either."

"Seems like the public is always the one that pays out and loses out," Rodriguez agreed.

"That's what I'm talking about. The public should be outraged that they're paying criminals in police uniforms to work against the public interest. The public has better things to do with their hard-earned money."

Rodriguez downed the rest of his beer. "It doesn't make sense, when you think about it, that cops should have a problem with IA. From the public's point of view, the IA is protecting them by identifying, what you're calling, crooks in police uniform. They give us all a bad name. If a cop takes his oath and job seriously, he shouldn't have a problem with the IA doing theirs."

Case had just finished his beer. "But not all minds work the same way. Some guys don't want people punished because either they are or have done the same thing. Or they might in the future. When that happens, they can point and say: 'Don't punish me, he did it too!'. To them it's a brother officer testifying against another brother officer. They're on the take; they're no brother of mine. I already got enough brothers. C'mon. Let's get out of here for real this time."

"Right behind you." Rodriguez followed Case out of the Blue Sow and into the parking lot.

"Case?"

"Yeah?"

"I don't think you're a rat."

"No? I was born in 1960."

"So?"

"Do you like Chinese?"

"Not too often."

"Next time you're in a Chinese restaurant, look it up."

"What, 1960?" Rodriguez asked, thinking. "Is it…"

"Yeah. The Year of the Rat." Case headed over to his car.

"See you in the morning," Rodriguez called.

"Bright and early," Case said without turning around.

Chapter Six

The next morning, 7:15, the two detectives were facing each other behind their desks.

"I got here about ten minutes ago," Case said. "I already turned in our prelims to the Captain. He'll buzz us when he's ready."

"So where do we start?" Rodriguez asked.

"Officers Baxter and Paulski turned up nothing. Just the names of the people they talked to, the nearest neighbors, who saw and heard nothing."

They spent the next hour going through the victim's personal information from her laptop, compiling a list of sources to get background information when the Capt. called them in.

Case rapped once on Capt. Murdock's glass door, rattling the thin glass.

"Come!" As Case and Rodriguez stepped inside, the Capt. said: "Close the door." He was sitting behind his desk and continued writing without looking up. Captain J. Murdock was retired Marine Corps. He had put in his 20 and was now double dipping, 17 years on the force. It wouldn't be long before he would retire again.

At 5′ 11½″ he still had his military bearing, Semper Fi, but he was starting to show signs of a slight paunch. His muscular frame was starting to lose a little of its rigidity and his sandy brown military cut was going a light steel grey, but his coal dark eyes did not lose their intimidating glare when he meant business. As he always did. His wife of 32 years thought he was a sweet, old bear. That opinion was shared by no one else, except possibly his two grandkids. He put down his pen and looked at the two detectives standing in front of him.

"You don't need to sit down and get comfortable, this won't take long. You're not giving me much on this Hollywood strangling."

Case spoke. "We're looking at her background to see what leads we can develop. We're hoping the M E will have something to go on."

"Local interviews?" Murdock asked.

"Two uniforms canvassed the area. They drew a total blank. It might have been passion or revenge, but it looks like the perp did his homework. Doesn't look like it was hasty or random. Nobody saw or heard anything. It appears he took his time in planning, learning the roommate's and the general household routine." Rodriguez just stood there and nodded his agreement.

"Well," Capt. Murdock said, thinking about it, "there's always a good side and a bad side to everything." He leaned back in his chair contemplating. The two detectives stood there waiting. Rodriguez started to say something but Case shook his head. He knew if the Capt. had more to say, he would. If not, he would dismiss them when he was ready.

"The good thing is," the Capt. said looking at them both, "if it was not an arbitrary, random killing, then we don't have a serial killer on our hands. Another one of those, we could do without. The bad thing is if it was isolated and planned, it's going to be tough to close this case for lack of evidence. The forensic boys aren't holding out any hopes they'll turn up any. I want you to talk to the doc on this one." Now he was only looking at Case who started to object.

"Save it, Case. Find out what you can from the M E then see Dr. Leonard. We need to get into this guy's head and that's what we pay the shrink for, so let him earn his money."

Case couldn't accept what he had to accept without a little feed back. "I think it's a little early... let me work on it some first. Most likely there's a simple, straight forward motive. Find that, we find the killer."

"Work on it with what? I read your report. We have no hard evidence, no leads and no witness statements. In fact all you found at the scene are some pretzels. What the hell good are pretzels? You're not going to get any prints off them. What are you going to do, ask every store in L.A. that sells pretzels who they sold pretzels to in the last 6 months? I want you both to see Dr. Leonard as soon as you get back from the morgue. It shouldn't take long over there. They're expecting you and I'll tell Dr. Leonard to expect you within the hour. That's all."

They started to leave the office. "Case." He stopped and turned when the Capt. called his name.

"I told you yesterday you're our best homicide detective. Don't make me a liar. This doesn't look good, a young girl murdered in cold blood in a neighborhood like that. I want you and your partner to solve it. ASAP. Now. Period."

Outside the office Rodriguez said, "That stuff about being the best. He says that to all the detectives just to get results, right?"

"How many times has he told you?"

"I'm just a rookie."

"And don't forget it."

As they were leaving the building Case said, "Wouldn't have to go back 6 months."

"What?"

"The pretzels were fresh."

At the city morgue on Mission Rd. they donned the proper gear for viewing dead bodies; paper gowns, gloves, etc. There were four bodies on the available six slabs in room M-1B. Shawna Anderson was the near one in the second row.

"It was obviously strangulation," Case was saying to the technician. "Is there anything unusual about it, anything to go on? What can you tell us?"

The technician was a man in his forties who had already seen more than a lifetime of corpses, but still took each case seriously and was very good at his job.

"Hemorrhaging around the eyes indicates slow strangulation, which is consistent with the neck ligature marks. The surprisingly even pattern of bruising indicates the constriction of the esophagus as well as the crushing of the pharynx was accomplished by a very slow, gradual method. By the look of the capillaries and lack of abrasions, a soft lined mechanical devise was employed. We are still looking for fibers. Only something mechanical could apply pressure at such a fixed, steady rate of constriction. She was definitely not strangled manually."

Rodriguez asked, "How long would it take?"

"From the start of bruising to final asphyxiation I would say from eight to ten minutes. The ligature marks at her wrists and feet also indicate she was securely restrained.

You can see the massive bruising. I'd say she struggled right to the end."

"Did you check the contents of her stomach?" Case asked.

"Nothing solid in the last twelve hours. Just liquid, citric; orange juice in the morning I'd guess."

Rodriguez was taking notes but not writing much. "So that's all you can tell us?" he asked.

"Well, with the slow, steady closure of the air passage she was unconscious premortem."

"So..."

"She died in her sleep."

The morning was friendlier than yesterday; the heat hadn't let up, but traffic wasn't too heavy and breathing not quite so painful, as the smog had eased noticeably from the day before. They got back in plenty of time and were getting out of the elevator on the fourth floor in less than 50 minutes of their allotted hour. Case would have preferred to be late, he hated being early.

On their way down the hall of frosted glass doors with stenciled names on them Rodriguez asked, "So this Dr. Leonard's some kind of shrink?"

"Police psychologist."

"What do we need to see him for?"

"Captain thinks we need a refresher perspective into a killer's mind."

"I thought you were the be…"

Case didn't let him finish. "It's for you, Rookie. In case I'm not around. In case you have to take over the lead."

"You goin' somewhere?"

"You never know."

"Does the Captain think you're gonna age out? You're not *that* old. Yet. You may look it, but you're not that old."

"Alright, look. Here's what Murdock's doing. You ever play Texas Hold 'em?"

"Not really, not in a regular poker room, but my brother-in-law has friends over once in a while and we play. What's that got to do with anything?" As an after thought: "By the way, if you…"

"Did you ever play a garbage hand and flop a winner?"

"No, but Jesus', my brother-in-law, must have been on the big blind, he had a 7-3 one time and the flop was 7,7,3. Now he plays 7-3 all the time and never wins with it."

"That's what the Captain's doing. My opinion, and it stays with you and me. There was a case we couldn't get a handle on, about a year ago. First time the Captain got the idea of inviting a shrink in on it, to see if he could come up with an angle. Well, he did. Some off-the-wall idea that actually cracked the case and got us a conviction. So guess what?"

"Now he wants to get the psychologist's viewpoint every time."

"Bingo."

They were at Dr. Leonard's office. Case rapped on the door. They entered at the verbal invitation from inside.

Dr. Leonard, a man in his middle forties, although he looked ten years younger, was sitting behind his desk, smiling pleasantly. The doctor's equanimity and unhurried expression immediately got on Case's wrong side, the only one he ever evidenced. Case did not want to be there and didn't mind showing it.

"Detectives Case and Rodriguez," Dr. Leonard began. "Have a..." Case was stretched out in the chair in front of the desk,"...seat," Dr. Leonard invited. Rodriguez glanced at the diplomas on the wall behind the desk and the medical journals on the shelf and also took a seat.

The doctor closed the thin file. "I've just finished reading the file on this case, such as it is. With so little to go on, the Captain requested this meeting because he thought it would be helpful to approach this case with the added perspective from a psychological rather than purely evidentiary standpoint."

"That's his idea," Case broke in.

"And you don't agree."

"I think we should be out on the street squeezing information than in here studying tea leaves."

"Since we need to get through this I suggest it would be more pleasant if we approach it with an air of mutual respect for each others' fields of expertise." The doctor was slow to bristle but knew he was being baited and did not like it, which is what Case had hoped.

Case shot to his feet. "There's nothing pleasant about a cold-blooded murder. Why don't you sign a form we were here and we'll got back to our jobs."

"I can't do that or I wouldn't be doing *my* job. Please sit down." Case just stood there. Rodriguez squirmed in his seat and finally asked an innocuous question of the doctor, which he ignored, cleared his throat and began his topic.

Larry C. Rothman

"It may seem redundant but I always start a subject from the very beginning, considering all possible options, then eliminating the obvious candidates for elimination to arrive at a single focus. I regard it as the logical approach."

"The 'logical approach'," Case repeated. "Why didn't I think of that?" and sat down heavily.

"Your work," Dr. Leonard began again, "involves means, opportunity, and motive. My work, delving into a killer's mind, involves only motive, stemming, of course, from a variety of basic psychological stimuli. There are many types of death to eliminate before we conclude murder, the only one requiring a motive: accidental, inadvertent or unintentional, as with collateral as a result of another crime. And I think we can eliminate natural causes."

"And I thought we were wasting our time coming here," Case put in. "You've got a stranglehold on the obvious."

The doctor took out a pad of paper from his top, right hand drawer, picked up a pen and started writing while talking out loud. "Plays well with others but has difficulty accepting authority figures."

Case took out a pack of Blackjack gum. Without offering any to anyone he unwrapped a stick, inhaling the ambient odor from the wrapper, then folded the stick into his mouth. The licorice flavored gum improved his mood, slightly.

"So we have a premeditated murder by a guy who did his homework, knowing he wouldn't get caught, giving himself plenty of time so he could use some kind of erector set instead of just strangling her with his hands." Case got all that out in one breath.

"So," the doctor looked from one to the other, "was it a random killing or was the victim known to the killer? Mind if I munch?"

"Munch?" Case asked.

Dr. Leonard reached into another drawer and pulled out a ziploc bag of baby carrots, offered them to both detectives. "No, thanks," Rodriguez said. Case just stared.

"It helps me think, to munch. They're good for you; also supposed to deter the smoking habit."

"Supposed to be good for the eyes, too," Case put in. "But I see you're wearing glasses."

Dr. Leonard, self conscious, put away the carrots.

"Can we get back to the case or are you going to discuss good grooming habits next?" Case's gum was already starting to lose its flavor and he jammed in another piece.

"A random killing gives us no viable lead without the establishment of some kind of pattern. A targeted victim, on the other hand, can provide us with clues as to the motive behind the killing." Dr. Leonard sounded like he was quoting from a text book.

Case responded to Dr. Leonard's statement by saying "...and that leaves us back where we started. Thanks for the perspective." Case once again started to get out of his chair.

"What's your hurry?"

"You got more?"

"What's he telling us?" Dr. Leonard said by way of answer.

"Who, the killer?" Case asked.

"Are we talking about someone else?" Dr. Leonard answered, adding a little sarcasm of his own.

Case didn't have a ready answer, momentarily surprised the doc wasn't a complete pushover.

Rodriguez took the opportunity to jump in. "We're going with a premeditated targeted victim."

"That's right," Case added. "Too much prep time and planning; windows of opportunity and timing. And all we have are two freshly drilled holes near the foot of the bed and near the head, but not even sawdust left behind. So it wasn't momentary rage from a jealous boyfriend, wasn't robbery, nothing missing, nothing to take. Wasn't sloppy. Nothing left behind. No fibers, prints, DNA. Looks like revenge to me. Revenge is a pretty strong motive."

"But talking to her roommate, she doesn't seem the type to have a lot of enemies." Rodriguez offered.

"I agree with the revenge motive," Dr. Leonard said, having just finished munching his second carrot. He had absent mindedly opened the drawer and taken the bag out again. Before Case could make an expected remark, he put them away again. "According to the coroner's report it was not a violent death, but slow and controlled. So, again, what's he telling us?"

"You're the shrink." Case said.

"I wish I was. I'd make more money. I'm just a psychologist."

"So you have an angle?"

"RCA." Dr. Leonard answered with a satisfied flair.

Case looked at Dr. Leonard without saying anything. Rodriguez looked at Case and then at the doctor.

"RCA? What's that?" Rodriguez asked since Case apparently wasn't going to bite.

"It's a very common form of childhood ailment that

manifests itself as aggressive behavior in adults. Repressed Childhood Aggression. Children that can't express their frustration caused by a variety of sources: domineering parents, too restrictive school environment or just not being allowed to express their creativity by a conformist society.

I suggest by the method he chose he's telling us he is in charge. He's the boss. He doesn't have to hurry, can take all the time he wants and in the manner of his choosing. We don't even know exactly how he killed her. Nothing to indicate the murder weapon, but since he wants complete control I'd say that it was something of his own brainchild. Everything from start to finish was his choosing."

Rodriguez asked, "So that's it?"

"I believe so. The victim could have been a dominating girlfriend and RCA caused him to snap."

"Too premeditated," Case said. "Too much pre-planning. I'd say revenge, pure and simple. He's smart enough not to leave any clues, but revenge is never complete unless someone knows the perp made good his revenge. And I think he thinks he's smart enough to make that known without getting caught."

"With the method of constraints and slow methodical strangulation I recommend following up with recorded RCA cases." The doctor advised.

"And I think he wants us to know he made his revenge complete." Case retorted.

"I'm a little confused." Rodriguez broke the deadlock. "If the killer wants whoever out there to know he got even, but has covered his tracks so well we have no clues as to who he is…"

Case interrupted again. "My partner is right. This isn't the whole picture. We don't have enough to go on if he wants to send a message. He has to give us more information, which means there will be more victims. This guy's gonna kill again."

"But what if his revenge is already complete because there was only one intended victim?" The doctor put in. "In that case he let the victim know he got his revenge and he's satisfied."

Case would not agree. "Every revenge case I've ever worked on never involved just one other person. Someone is always taken advantage of, or cheated somehow, and others are either involved or know about it. It could involve public humiliation. There might be one central figure responsible, but there are always others who either assist or participate in some way, or just facilitate through their silence. This guy isn't through. I think he's enjoying himself and just getting started, in which case he's leaving us a bread crumb trail, thinking he's smart enough to give us the whole picture without getting caught."

Case thought about what he had said. "... And that's a dangerous tight rope to walk, revealing his motive without revealing himself, which is why we'll catch him in the end. But we need to get ahead of him soon. If he leads us around, we'll be following corpses."

"All you have at this point is supposition," Dr. Leonard countered, "with no evidence to base it on. With an RCA evaluation we have a much clearer picture of..."

"There's more than supposition." Case interrupted. "We found some..."

"You think the pretzels are the 'bread crumbs' he's leaving us?" Rodriguez asked.

"They're something. They don't fit."

Dr. Leonard scoffed. "I read that in your report. Maybe she liked to snack while she read in bed. Maybe she's not a good housekeeper."

"We ruled all that out." Case replied. "They weren't hers."

"Are you suggesting the killer brought snacks to a murder? Why would anyone do that?" The doctor, who was supposed to be a guide through the psyche of the murderer, was not being much help, no surprise to Case.

"Maybe that's what he wants us to figure out. All I know is he made no mistakes; left absolutely nothing to go on. Nothing out of place. No obvious motive to connect to anyone. No forensics evidence. Nothing except…"

This time Rodriguez finished for Case…the pretzels."

"That's ridiculous." The doctor started getting heated. "He sat there and munched while he watched her die? And if you're right, then that makes no sense: no forensics, no incriminating evidence, even vacuumed up shavings dust from beneath new drilled holes. Why would he be sloppy enough to leave something like that behind? It doesn't fit his meticulous profile."

"Exactly." Case smiled. "Thank you Doctor, you made my point."

With nowhere to go, the doctor gave in. He pushed back his chair, opened his drawer and pulled out the bag of carrots again. "Well," he took out a carrot and started to munch, "if that's all you have, and the papers get ahold of it, they're going to give the guy the sobriquet: The Snacking Strangler."

Chapter Seven

It had been three full working days since the murder of the young woman in the quiet North Hollywood neighborhood and Case and Rodriguez had little to show for it. The grieving family could provide no directly useful information, but gave background leads to check. Most were dead ends with nothing promising or even potentially promising. However, everything had to be followed up and everyone she knew interviewed. There was no telling what would lead to something that would connect to something that would put them on the trail of the killer. One thing was certain, there had to be *something*.

There was a thread somewhere. All they had to do was find it. Pull the right thread and the whole thing should unravel. But time was not on their side. A strong sense of urgency was the elephant in the room no one wanted to talk about and it kept getting bigger every day. The next victim, Case felt sure, would be the next phone call, or the one after that. He had no idea when that would happen or how much time they had before it did; his gut just told him it wouldn't be enough.

Pay stubs took them to employment records that lead them to her two previous jobs. They offered no one of interest with anything remotely like a motive. Like the jobs, those leads were dead ends. They interviewed her current boyfriend, a man from the near East named Achmad who worked as a night cook at the local Denny's. Thursday was his day off and they woke him up at his second floor apartment.

"I have no idea why someone should do this. No idea."

"How were you two getting along?" Case asked. Rodriguez stood by with his notepad.

"Fine. No problems. We like each other very much."

"How often did you see her?'

"At least three or four times a week. I work nights as you know. She was temporarily out of work. We saw each other, two, sometimes three weekdays and always weekends. Please, sit down. I will make some coffee." His black hair hadn't been combed and he was barefoot, in sweats he wore as pajamas, having just gotten up.

"Don't bother. We won't be here very long."

"But I need some. Do you mind? I will answer your questions while I make it."

All three went into the small kitchen. Case continued, "Since you saw her so often was she upset lately? Was anything bothering her? Could you tell if she acted unusual?"

"Unusual in what way?" Case pressed.

"In any way, worried about something. Scared?"

"No. I noticed nothing at all."

"Anything you can think of? Anything or anyone in her past that she might be concerned about?"

"I'm sorry, I can tell you nothing of what you ask." Achmad hesitated. "Perhaps, but, no..."

"What?"

"Well, I just remembered, it was about two weeks ago, I had a night off. We went to a club on Sunset Blvd. We were there about twenty minutes and someone came in that she knew and she wanted to leave."

"Did he threaten her?" Case asked.

"No. I don't even think he saw us."

"Did she say who he was, why she wanted to leave?"

"She just said that he was someone she used to know, I thought probably an old boyfriend she did not want to see. When I asked who he was she told me his name was Dwight something, or Dirk. No, wait! Derek. Yes. That was it. Derek. I can't remember his last name if she told me."

"Do you remember what he looked like?"

"Yes. He was tall, not heavy, blonde."

"Did she tell you anything else about him?"

"Only that he lived in Venice Beach. I don't think you should have trouble to find him."

"We'll check him out. Thanks for your time." Rodriguez clicked his pen and put it and his pad away. Achmad stood there with a frown on his face.

"Something else?" Case asked.

"Well, according to Shawna's parents, I've visited them, tried to give comfort, they're very distraught. According to her parents, the police have nothing to go on. Whoever did this did much careful planning, left nothing incriminating. The police don't even know exactly according to what method."

Case glanced at Rodriguez.

"I want very much for you to find who did this, but according to Shawna, I do not think Derek is capable of such a thing."

"Why not?" Case asked.

"He is a surfer."

Case and Rodriguez jumped on the 405 for the short

drive to Venice, short as the crow flies, but they weren't crows. Patience was still a virtue, and an important one, anywhere in that area, on any roads at any time. They could have taken Santa Monica Blvd. straight out to the pier and then south on Pacific Ave. to Venice, no difference in traffic; 405 had about a dozen fewer lights.

"So, Case..." Rodriguez settled back. "Lawrence, do I know you well enough to call you Larry?"

"You'll never know me that well."

"Why not man, aren't we tight yet? I mean I want to have you home for dinner, even though you never come."

"Not the point. You can't get that tight because nobody ever calls me Larry... and lives."

"You don't like Larry?"

Case lifted his right arm off the rest, made a fist and stuck it under his partner's nose. "See that scar?"

"OK."

"A kid in school, two years older and 20 pounds heavier called me 'Larry'. I gashed my knuckles on his front teeth. I don't know which bled more, my hand or his lip. I hate 'Larry'."

"Thanks for the tip. Note to self: hates 'Larry'."

"First of all, it isn't my name. Second, it's a stupid name. Names tell you everything about a person and Larry is just plain dumb."

Rodriguez had the feeling he was onto something. This could be an interesting ride, at least better than the usual all business or all silence. "Really? I didn't know that, Sarge."

"That's why they teamed you with me, so you can learn, Rookie."

"Funny, and I thought I learned at Stanford."

"How does it feel to find out different?"

"OK, professor, so what's wrong with Larry?"

"Have you ever heard of anyone named Larry who ever did anything important, or was ever good at anything?"

"Sure. What about Larry Byrd, Larry Czonka?"

"Who?"

"Oh yeah, not into sports."

"Look, way before Letterman seemingly pulls 'Larry' off the top of his head, every time he wants to come up with a name for a dumb guy, dumb guys for years have always been named Larry. Maybe that's why he uses it."

"But Lawrence is different?" Rodriguez was happy to

play.

"Are you kidding? Lawrence Olivier. Greatest actor that ever lived. 'Course he gets fifty free points out of 100 just for being English. He was even knighted. Then he went from being a knight to being a lord; from Sir Lawrence Olivier to Lord Lawrence Olivier. The worst English actor is better than the best we got over here. Gotta be their breeding." Case was getting on a roll. "And Lawrence Harvey. Real classy actor. Played Col. Travis in *The Alamo*. Although he did seem out of place. Too Oxford for those Texicans."

Case moved one lane to the right as their exit got closer. "So: actors. What do we have for a Larry to compete with Lord Lawrence Olivier? Let's see, um…, an actor named Larry?" He pretended to just think of one. "Oh! I know, Larry Fine, of Larry, Moe and Curly Joe."

"My kids like The Three Stooges."

"My point. So let's look at another *Larry* in show business, Larry Storch. An overacting, B grade, second banana whose career peaked in an imbecilic TV sitcom."

"Now, wait a second. I've been watching an old TV–shows station Frank in the property room told me about. All that old stuff, only black and white, from the early days of TV, no color: Gunsmoke, Have Gun - Will Travel, The Donna Reed Show, Father Knows Best, The Twilight Zone, Dragnet, Leave It To Beaver, Ozzie & Harriet,

Sergeant Bilko, Naked City, The Untouchables, The Rifleman, The Lone Ranger."

"So?"

"Well, they might have been good for their time, 50 years ago, but I can't watch them for more than five minutes, except two, which I watch whenever I can: The Honeymooners and F Troop, and F Troop is just as dumb as all the rest except for Larry Storch. He's the only reason I never miss the show. That's a funny guy!"

"You're nuts. And F Troop was in color."

"Not its first season. That was black and white. It was a transitional show in the middle sixties, went from B&W to color."

Case, never to concede a point, ignored the exuberance of youth and went on. "Whenever they need a dumb guy, it's always Larry. Style, sophistication, quality, class – then it's Lawrence." Case paused. "Bob Newhart."

"What about him?"

"The token dumb guy on his show? Larry, along with his two brothers named Darryl."

"You gotta get out more, Sarge."

Case was not to be deterred. "Science? The Lawrence Livermore Laboratories. Adventure? Lawrence of

Arabia. Great movie"

"Who was in it?"

"Peter O'Toole, amongst others."

"Not Lawrence?"

"Lawrence of Arabia, a real person."

"That's it?" Rodriguez asked after a hesitation.

"That's not enough? Anybody named Larry to go up against all that?"

"Don't know."

"And what about the greatest detective on the L.A. police force? Lawrence."

"There's another homicide detective named Lawrence in the department?"

"You'll never make 1st Grade being a wise guy." Case put on his blinker and got in the right hand lane. "Here's our exit." They got off on Venice Blvd. Case turned west, crossed Centinela and Lincoln Blvds., and stopped at Pacific. Ave. Nothing between them and the ocean now but the beach and the Venice boardwalk.

"Wow!" Rodriguez said looking out his window.

"Yeah. We'll park here and walk back a couple blocks, see what we can find. Hopefully we won't have to get into that zoo on the boardwalk."

They walked back past a small restaurant, beach apparel shop and corner drugstore on Washington Blvd. Case indicated an Italian restaurant on their left.

"If you ever get tired of tacos and refried beans, bring Chaquita..."

"Consuela."

"... to this place. J&R Trattoria. You can eat outside, they play nothing but Frank and Dino on the speakers in the trees and they have the best Italian food you've ever had or will ever have. I've been through the whole menu and even their plain old spaghetti and meat balls can't be beat. If you don't admit it's the best you've ever had I'll do your paperwork for a month, and I'm almost a month behind on mine. They know me here. You can use my name."

"You mean if we admit we know you they'd serve us anyway? And what do I owe you if you're right?"

"Nothing. It's my gift to you."

They turned up the first semi-residential street. There weren't many pedestrians but they got lucky on the third try. A kid knew of a Derek who lived on the next block, he thought, nodding in the direction away from the ocean. They walked around the corner. The houses had seen better days. They all had a lived-in, very informal look, expected that near the beach, in what was not an upscale neighborhood. The houses almost gave the feel of beach bungalows, even though they were standard, 1,100 sq. ft. 3 bedroom homes.

They started knocking on doors without any success. At the fourth house Case and Rodriguez approached was an elderly lady in a large sun hat pulling weeds in her yard. She directed them to the end of the block where three or four guys shared the place. "I bet they could tell you," she said grumpily, and went back to her digging. "Can't miss it," she said over her shoulder. "End of the street. Can't miss it."

The "home" at the end of the street, the woman obviously meant, looked like a hangout for castaways. It had an all sand lawn. Even though it wasn't in keeping with the look of all the other houses on the block, it seemed to add to, rather than detract from, the local atmosphere.

Case's third knock woke up and brought to the door a barefoot twenty-year-old in cutoffs and a ratty undershirt. His black mop looked more like a mop than a real one did.

"Sorry if we woke you." Rodriguez said.

Trying to get his eyes fully open the ex-teenager said, "What time is it?"

"Little after three," Rodriguez replied.

" 's alright. Should be getting up pr' soon anyway."

"Got to get ready for work?" Case asked.

"Huh? Work? No, but gotta get up sometime, ya know? Any way, who're you guys?" as if noticing two men in suits for the first time.

Case simultaneously showed his badge, introduced them and asked his question.

"Derek? Yeah, he's...," Ralph looked behind him, not seeing Derek, turned back, "he's probably working the rings."

"The rings?" Case asked.

"Yeah, 'til the moon surf gets up. Me and Stoner, uh, Jase, ..Jason, we will too, when we get up. Except I'm already up."

"Right, you are. We're looking for Derek. Where is he? Is he here?" Case pressed.

"Naw, man. I told you. He's probably on the rings." Ralph stepped back as if to the close the door.

"Why don't we come in and look for ourselves?" Case

suggested, taking a step forward.

"Hey! You got a warrant?"

Case went into aggression mode. "We can get one and turn this place upside down, but I doubt anybody'd notice."

"Chill, man, I'm tellin' ya, Derek ain't here! He's down on the rings."

"What rings?"

"Down on the beach, ya know? Haven't you been to the beach?" Then he focused and looked closer. "No, I guess not. Just go to the beach, head up that way on the walk, 'bout four blocks. Derek will be on the rings. If he's not, ask some of the other guys there. Somebody'll know."

"If he's not, we'll be back and..."

"Yeah, yeah, upside down," and Ralph closed the door.

Case and Rodriguez walked back towards the beach. "He's hiding something."

"Sarge, I don't think he could hide a taco in Tijuana."

Venice Beach, as usual, was very crowded in Southern California's perpetual Summer. The pedestrians gave the narrow boardwalk a kaleidoscopic look as it was squeezed between the broad sand beach and the jammed together small shops, offering anything they might want. The participants in the kaleidoscopic parade were of every description from casual strollers, skaters, bikers, old hippies, young surfers and middle-aged Rastafarians, many liberally tattooed, tanned or both, wearing little to a little more. There was no standard, but if there was one, it was tie-dyed bandanas, shades, bare to the waist (or halters), calf-length cargo shorts and flip flops, the Rastafarians additionally with dreadlocks and chicken feet necklaces.

The shops themselves appeared to be in no particular order, as if put there by a child playing with giant blocks. The most frequently appearing, a sign of the times, was the medical marijuana shop, with their large green three-leafed plant signs prominently displayed and proprietors in their white lab coats, pretending to be doctors. Case and Rodriguez passed exactly seven of them in two short blocks. They also passed a camera crew shooting an outdoor lunch scene at a café with a recognizable TV actor. The semi-interested crowd clogged the walk around the camera crew who probably didn't have a city permit but would be gone before anyone got too excited. All part of the atmosphere. Where no one got too excited.

The shops were only on the east side of the boardwalk, facing the ocean. None of them seemed to have front doors, or indeed, even front walls as the passersby could wander in for a Jamba juice, crazy tea or a toke without breaking stride. No clouds in the clear blue beach sky protected the people below from the sun's strong rays. A salty breeze tinkled the chimes, spun the pin wheels and fluttered the bright rainbow plastic streamers in front of some shops. Rodriguez idly looked at the displays as he and Case weaved through the crowds. They managed to do the impossible in that menagerie, to stand out like raw steaks in a vegan convention. Nowhere else in the Golden State were two suits more out of place.

As there was no rule of the road for foot traffic, they dodged in and out, ignoring stares, until they came to a large area of the beach where exercise equipment was erected right on the sand. They both knew it when they saw it: large metal rings suspended from chains that hung from metal cross beams. The rings were about 7' above the sand. A muscular guy in his early twenties wearing only cargo shorts and a full body tan swung from ring to ring, his legs hunched up beneath him, giving the not so vague appearance of a chimpanzee at the zoo. Swinging from one ring to the next he went all the way down the line of about a dozen rings and then back. It was a lot harder than it looked and took a lot of strength and coordination.

The two detectives stood on the walk and watched. "Could you do that, Sarge?"

"I'm not twenty anymore."

"Si. Mucho." Rodriguez suppressed a grin. "But could you, when you were twenty?"

"You mean like that? He's doing it the easy way."

"What easy way?"

"He's using both hands. Try using one hand. It's a lot harder with only one hand," Case said satisfied.

"You could swing from ring to ring with only one hand?!"

"It's all in the timing."

"Ai carumba! Ees all in thee beans!"

When he got back to the first ring the lanky, muscled blonde dropped to the sand.

"Pretty impressive," Rodriguez said. "But my partner here used to work the rings with one hand tied behind his back."

"Thanks. The rings with one hand? Never seen anyone do that, man."

"I don't think anyone has." Rodriguez replied.

"Are you Derek?" Case asked.

"Yeah. Who're you guys?"

They showed their badges. "Detective Case, and my partner, Detective Rodriguez."

"Detectives. Cops? What's this about?" I didn't do anything."

"We understand you knew a Shawna Anderson."

"Shawna who?"

"Anderson. Did you know her?" Case pressed.

"No, I don't think so. Who is she?"

"Was. She was murdered last week; in North Hollywood. Strangled, we think." Case realized too late he shouldn't have let the last two words out. Getting sloppy in his old age or maybe just this heat, and he loosened his tie. Or maybe the whole general atmosphere around here.

"You think she was strangled? You don't know?"

"We'll ask the questions. So you didn't know her?"

"Maybe. I don't know. I know a lot of people. If I did I guess I don't remember."

"We have e-mails from her laptop says you knew her enough to threaten her if she tried leaving you." Case showed him Shawna's picture.

"Oh, yeah. Right. Right. I remember her now. I heard about that. Bad Karma," Derek frowned.

"Yeah, real bad. When did you last see her?"

"Uh…let's see." He tried to think. "What is this… May, June?"

"May." Rodriguez helped.

"Oh, yeah. Right. Right. So the last time musta been last year. Uh, about, let's see. Yeah! I know now. Had to be at Thanksgiving. Ralph and Stoner picked up this big bird, a turkey. They said we had to have it because it was Thanksgiving, but we couldn't cook it. So we figured we needed somebody to cook it, so I asked Shawna but she bailed on us. We never hooked up again after that so that's been, let's see, this is…"

"Still May." Case put in.

"Oh, yeah. Right. Right. So Thanksgiving woulda been…"

"November." Rodriguez offered.

"Oh, yeah. Right. Right. So must be 3 or 4 months. You do the math."

Case said, "OK, since you seem to be having trouble with it. It's not 3 or 4 months, it's 3 *and* 4 months, November was 7 months ago."

"Oh, yeah. Right. Right."

"Do you know of anyone who would want to hurt her?"

"Uh……………….." He almost went comatose. "I'm drawing a blank."

"I can see that." Case pressed harder. "So you were pretty mad about her wanting to split. That gives a pretty good motive for the "bad Karma."

"No way, man. I wasn't mad. I didn't even remember her until you showed me her picture." The surfer looked from one to the other. "Wait. You think I know anything about what happened to her?"

"You tell us. Where were you last Wednesday?"

"Right here, in Venice."

"Anyone verify that?" Rodriguez asked.

"Sure, Ra…."

"Anyone besides Ralph and Stoner?"

"Sure, everybody in Venice, practically. It was annual nets week." He motioned with his head north, up the beach. There were several volley ball nets set up on the sand. "All week we play volley ball most of the day, break for some siesta time, then cook chicken, burgers, heat up jojo's on the firewood pits, you know, whatever, suds, then go moonie surfin'. Nuthin' like shootin' the curls hangin' ten with the only light comin' from Big

Daddy Moonglow. What a rush! The ocean goes all sparkly diamonds. Outta sight!"

Rodriguez glanced at Case and wondered if he was thinking the same thing: what a rough life the poor guy lives.

"And this goes on for a whole week?" Case went on.

"Seven straight: Sunday morn 'til Saturday night."

"And you were here the whole week?"

"All seven. Wouldn't miss it. Ask anyone. I was here. Even almost won the nets tourney. Came in tied for fifth," Derek answered proudly.

"So why the threatening e-mails?" Case asked.

"I didn't threaten her," Derek objected.

"You told her you'd never let her go."

"So? That was a year ago. I tell 'em that. So what? Don't mean nuthin'. Then they want to split, or I want to split, we split. Come and go. Like the surf, man. I'll never let it go either, but it comes and goes."

"We've come, and now we're going to go, but if we have anymore questions, we'll be back." Case nodded to Rodriguez. "We know where to find you."

"Sure man, for now. But it's a long coastline. Sometimes

I come and go, up North, down South."

Case gave him his card. "Be sure you let us know before you do."

The surfer just shrugged, stuck the card in his jean pocket and turned for another run at the rings. Rodriguez stopped him. "By the way, did you ever find someone to cook the bird?"

"What bird?"

"The turkey. Last Thanksgiving."

"That bird. Oh yeah. Right. Right."

"Did it ever get cooked?"

"Sure."

"When Shawna bailed out on you, you found someone else to cook it?"

"Naw. No chicks around here know how to cook a turkey."

"So, one of the other guys, then?"

"Ralph or Stoner? No way."

"So, who cooked it?"

"I don't know. We traded it for a case of beer."

Back in the car Case asked, "So, what do you think? Does Derek the Dim look good for it?"

"Not to me. I think whatever actually happened is way beyond his focus." Then Rodriguez added, "He's a surfer."

"Oh yeah," said Case. "Right. Right."

Chapter Eight

Traffic wasn't looking too bad and not wanting to get back on the 405, Case decided to drive up the coast on Pacific Ave. He made a right on Santa Monica Blvd. in front of the famous pier with its Ferris wheel, shops and other attractions. Few people noticed the plaque embedded in the wooden planks that marked the official end of an historic journey. It confirmed what The Manhattan Transfer sang, "..winding from Chicago to L.A., 2,000 miles all the way." The plaque marked the Western terminus of old Route 66.

Rodriguez was enjoying the drive, remembered Consuela was having a home party for her girlfriends tonight and said he didn't even have to watch the kids, so he asked Case, "Hey, I've got a few free hours tonight. Wanta stop afterwards at the Sow for a quick brew?"

Case glanced over at him, a little surprised. "On a Thursday? You tellin' me you like the place?"

"It's alright."

"You feel comfortable there? I go there when I want to remind them they don't intimidate me, but you don't have to."

"They don't intimidate me either, and I don't want them

to think they do."

"You're starting pretty young to be making enemies."

"You're my partner and I've got just as much right to be there as anyone else, right?"

"Right." Case agreed.

Rodriguez laughed.

"What's so funny?"

"Now we're starting to sound like Derek."

Back at their desks they were just finishing up their DR's when Rodriguez said," C'mon Sarge, let's go to the Sow. I'll buy you a beer."

"Next time. I've got some work to finish and then I'm going home to turn in early."

"You don't have anymore to put on your daily report then I do and I've been done for ten minutes. Don't make me go home. Consuela has all her girlfriends over for some kind of make-up party or something."

Joe Cappeli, a cop who had no problem with Case overheard their conversation as he was putting on his jacket and leaving. "You guys going to the Sow?"

Rodriguez answered, "If I can talk him into it. You going?"

"No, going home. This is meatloaf night, but Stinky Pinkie'll be there. My partner Bill says Stinky Pinkie is always there, at his regular booth, for Thursday Sports Central, Celtics and 'Sixers tonight. Should be a good one. But I'd catch it somewhere else. Why go looking for trouble? Good night guys."

"Stinky Pinkie? Is that what he said?"

"You heard him right," Case confirmed.

"Who's that?"

"I don't think you met him. Tough–guy cop. Guy named Hugh Strong."

"And they call him Stinky Pinkie?"

"Not to his face, or within earshot," Case warned.

"What's that all about?"

"You really don't want to go home?"

"Really."

"O.K. Let's go. I could use a bowl of chili. We'll take your car." Case grabbed his jacket. Rodriguez called home to tell Consuela his plans which didn't surprise her.

On the way to the elevators Rodriguez said, "So what trouble is Joe talking about; like last time?"

"No, that was nothing. Most guys mind their own business. O'Rourke was just drunk and feeling ornery. Doesn't happen too often. Joe meant McCulley will be there. Practically lives there. He's the one guy that really has it in for me over the IA case. I think one of the guys went to jail was his brother, or brother-in-law or something. Too bad for him."

"Maybe Joe is right. We don't have to go to the Blue Sow. Why go looking for trouble? We can go somewhere else if you want."

"If *I* want? What happened to not letting them intimidate you? If McCulley has a problem with me, that's his problem."

"So it's the Blue Sow."

"Where else?" Case asked.

On the short elevator ride to the parking level Rodriguez said, "Stinky Pinkie, huh? What's up with that?"

The elevator doors opened on the underground parking.

"Where's you car?" Case wondered.

"This way." Rodriguez led them a dozen spaces to the rear and unlocked the doors to his Lexus.

"This your car?" Case was impressed.

"Of course."

"What, are you on the take?"

"It's not so expensive. Consuela runs a tight ship at home. She's frugal. We can afford it. She helps pay for it with her home parties. What do you drive?"

Case got in the passenger side, put on his seat belt and changed the subject.

"How long you figure on being out?"

Rodriguez pulled out into heavy evening traffic. "Couple hours or so."

"Your wife's fine with that?"

"Sure."

"You didn't draw any flak?"

"No, man. She's cool. So what's Stinky Pinkie? I'm listening."

"It's just a nickname..."

"I figured that." Rodriguez interrupted.

Case gave him a scowl. "I thought you're listening."

"Zip." And Rodriguez made the motion across his lips.

"Short, simple story." The light turned red and they stopped four cars from the intersection. "Patrolman Strong and his partner were making a drunk, disorderly arrest. The guy resisted, there was a scuffle, not exactly sure how it happened. Things got pretty hairy in a hurry. Strong was probably trying to apply a choke hold and with all the struggling and twisting his hand slipped across the guys face. Somehow he either got some fingers in the guy's mouth or the guy tried to bite his hand and he wasn't able to free his little finger. The guy bit it clean off."

"Ouch!"

"Yep." Case agreed.

"Did Strong get his finger back?"

"Eventually."

"What happened to it?"

"The guy swallowed it."

"He *swallowed* it?" Case nodded towards the windshield. The light had turned green; traffic was moving but Rodriguez wasn't. He let the car roll ahead. They were approaching the turn for the Blue Sow.

"Yep. His partner was able to apply the choke hold. Apparently the guy took a gasp for breath and swallowed the pinky. Strong and the disorderly both went to the hospital. They were unable to get the guy to bring it up. They gave him a sedative, an enema and got it out the other end. Then they reattached the pinky to Strong. The whole incident was no secret. Somebody thought it was funny, because how they got the pinky back and hung the nickname on him. End of story. Stinky Pinkie."

They pulled into the side parking lot of the Blue Sow and got out of the car.

"That's some story. Did it really happen?"

"It happened. Or you can ask Hugh Strong, but I wouldn't advise it," Case cautioned.

They entered the bar. It was crowded and noisy. Case led the way to a still empty booth.

"Here comes Shirley. Only works here a couple nights a week. Has another gig at a fancier place." Case glanced up.

"Hi, Toots. Chili, Tabasco, crackers and a Miller Lite. See what the new guy's having. One tab; give it to him. My rich partner here drives a Lexus."

Rodriguez smiled. "Manny. Nice to meet you, Shirley."

Shirley was in her 50's; dark hair, lightly graying; blue eyes, twice divorced cops. She waitressed at the Sow nine years but managed to keep her weight and figure in a respectable range so her slacks and white blouse complimented her.

"Welcome aboard," she smiled. "Ready to order?"

"Sure." Rodriguez replied. "I'll have a cheeseburger, well done, with the works. No mayo. I'm a mustard guy."

"Fries?" She asked.

"Great."

"Be back in about ten." She checked at another booth on the way to put in the order.

"So Case, what do you make of the murder?"

"I think we have a long way to go. But do want to talk about it now?"

"I don't know. What do you want to talk about?"

"I don't. I want to eat."

Rodriguez was silent a minute. "Was that just a story for a rookie? Is Strong here?"

"I don't se..." Just then the door banged open.

Case looked over his shoulder towards the door then back to Rodriguez. "You must be psychic. That's him just come in. Hugh Strong. Remember Howie Long?"

"Of the Raiders?"

"Yup."

"Tough, mean player," Rodriguez remembered.

"That was his rep. You can see Hugh is built like Long, kind of looks like him. Same haircut. Name even sounds the same. People started calling him Howie and being a big Raiders fan he liked it. That was before he got his new nickname. His buddies call him that when they want a reaction, but nobody else does. Here comes the chow."

Case hadn't noticed that they were sitting diagonally across from a booth where O'Rourke was sitting with Lou, Ike and a fourth cop. But O'Rourke noticed Case and Rodriguez ever since they had come in and was in the mood to get even for the other night. He got their attention from across the aisle.

Case looked up, then back at his chili. "What do you want?"

"Not you. But you're not going to be around forever and I figure your partner here is going to want friends on the force after you're gone. He shouldn't appear unfriendly. Why doesn't he meet some of the guys? Start with Officer Strong who just came in. Walk right up to him, stick out your hand with a big smile and say 'Hi, Stinky Pinkie. Pleased to meet you.' He would like that. Why don't you introduce yourself?"

Case put down his spoon full of chili and said, "Why don't I introduce my foot to your ass?"

O'Rourke got red and started to push himself out of the booth. His partner grabbed his arm. "Let it go. Everybody's just foolin' around here. Besides, I'd hate to see you make Case uglier than he already is."

That calmed O'Rouke a little. "That guy's gonna get his."

Rodriguez said, "You guys are on a collision course. You're gonna get into it one of these days."

"I'm not worried."

"I am."

"You think I'm too old to take care of myself?"

"It's not you I'm worried about. Two or three of his friends will have to help and then I'll have to jump in to bail you out. It won't look good in my PF so soon on the job, let alone explaining to Consuela how I can't get along on the playground."

"O'Rourke keeps looking for trouble, he's going to find it." Case said.

"Finish your chili and let's split."

"We just got here," Case objected.

"So what?"

Case swallowed a mouthful of chili and tore open a cracker packet. "I thought you didn't want to go home."

"We can leave anytime," Rodriguez said.

"Not 'til they do."

"What is this, the 5th grade?"

They spent another hour plus and then Rodriguez dropped Case back at the underground garage. "See you in the morning," Case said as he got out of the car.

"Oh, Case. Can you swing by and pick me up in the morning? I forgot, I won't have my car. Consuela convinced me to let her brother borrow it for a couple of weeks. He finally landed a job. It's inconvenient but worth it to finally get him off the couch and drawing a paycheck. I can find another way if it's a problem."

"Give me your address. I'll be out front at 7:15."

Chapter Nine

It was going to be a hot day in L.A. Case pulled up in front of the small, typical 3 bedroom light blue, stucco house on Heathwood. Unlike some of the neighbors it was very neat. Case could see rose bushes, snapdragons in beds on either side of the small porch and a well tended lawn through the chain link fence. He was three minutes late and Rodriguez was already out front. Closing the gate behind him he frowned as the battered Caprice pulled to the curb. "What's this?" he asked still frowning and looking the car over.

"What's what?" Case answered.

"This…..car."

"It's your ride to work, Gonzalez Gonzalez Gonzalez, get in." Rodriguez opened the passenger door, got in and got the door to latch on the third try. Case pulled away from the curb, glad he didn't have to shut off the engine.

Rodriguez looked around. "Where are the seat belts?"

"You won't fall out."

"So what is this, Henry Ford's prototype? What year is it?"

"I don't know. Nineteen something. Does it matter?"

"How do you keep it on the road?"

"I told you I got a brother with a garage on Crenshaw. Mechanical wizard."

"He must be. Too bad you don't have a brother with a body and detail shop, too."

"Why?"

"It's your ride, man, but it looks like you could be an undercover narc in wheels you hot wired from a salvage yard. How does it feel driving around in some homeless guy's home? Is it legal?" Rodriguez asked.

Case didn't respond. He drove for a couple blocks, then: "Not much traffic."

Rodriguez was trying to look through the windshield around the bugs, not having much luck.

"I guess."

"Not many people out this morning, either. Sidewalk's pretty empty."

Rodriguez looked out the side window, puzzled, looking for a point. "Yeah."

"You know what else looks like it belongs in a salvage yard?"

"What?"

"You, after walking 5 miles downtown in this heat."

"OK. I take it back. The car is beautiful. I wish I had one just like it."

Case glanced at Rodriguez's feet. "Those shoes don't look so comfortable either."

"Hey, you ought to win the Car & Driver award for style and glamour, OK?"

"Buckle up. Belt's under the seat somewhere, I think."

The heat was starting to mount under a bright, cloudless sky as they made their way downtown through increasing morning traffic. There was an inverse proportion to the level of carbon monoxide in the air and the depth of breathing of the citizenry. As the killer gas in the atmosphere increased, breathing became more and more shallow. Not yet 8 AM and already a faint but growing tinge of poison weaved its insidious tendrils through the breathable air and into 5 million sets of lungs.

Pulling into the underground garage at Parker Center, LAPD Headquarters, Case parked as near as he could to the front of the building and reluctantly shut off his engine, crossing his mental fingers that she'd start again at first try. Once on the third floor at their desks

Rodriguez asked Case how he wanted to start this Friday.

"There's lots of leg work to do right here at our desks. Let's see how many leads we can pick up through background checks. Maybe we'll get lucky and not have to chase bad guys out there today. The air conditioning in here won't even keep up by this afternoon. We'll do face-to-face interviews once we gather and organize all the data, if we don't catch another 911 homicide in the mean time. But I can already smell weekend OT."

It would not be too many hours that day before Case and Rodriguez did get called away from their desks. Deaths occurred daily in big cities like L.A., many involving vehicles of every description, either directly through collisions or just as deadly, though indirectly, through asphyxiation. The second kind was reserved primarily, if not exclusively, for seniors. The smog was worst for them. Though violent and tragic, these deaths were outside the purview of the homicide detectives. Case and Rodriguez, at around 4PM that afternoon, responded to a death that was premeditated, well-planned and precisely executed. It was completely within their purview. It was murder.

Happy with how the Shawna Anderson episode went, he mentally checked her off and was anxious to eliminate #2. Each episode he knew would have its own distinctive style and flavor. He parked his car around the corner and two blocks east of the second victim's house.

From the laundry room she wasn't sure she heard the knock on the front door, but definitely did hear something, after what sounded like another knock. She glanced at the clock on the wall over the dryer.

"10:30. Right time, wrong day. I'll bet she thinks its Saturday again. Doesn't do any good to get her a calendar if she doesn't use it."

Her neighbor, Mrs. Jenson, 85 and widowed, liked to stop by for a morning cup of tea and gossip for 30 minutes before her pre-lunch weekly bridge game. Today was Friday.

"It could be she knows its Friday, but is just lonely. Her husband's only been gone 6 months," Stephanie thought as she opened the door.

"Hi Mrs. Jenson..."

It wasn't Mrs. Jenson.

"Oh! I'm sorry. I thought you were the lady next door. Can I help you?" she asked, startled.

"Stephanie? Stephanie Disher?"

"Yes, well, I was. I'm married now. It's Dodson now. Can I help you?" There was something vaguely familiar about the man standing on her porch.

"I know. I thought I'd use your high school name just for fun. We both went to Simi Valley High. I work for an on-line publication and I'm doing a human interest story about local area alumni, you know, "Where Are They 10 Years Later?" I do my interviews all week long and then submit on the weekend for the following week. I have you and two others before I put it together. Would it be alright if I came in and asked you some questions if you're not too busy?"

He handed her his phony business card, shifting the black briefcase he held from his right hand to his left to retrieve the card from his inside jacket pocket. It read:

WILLIAM RICHTER, *Freelance*

www.alumthen&now.com

She didn't remember the name at all but he still seemed vaguely familiar. She had no reason to remember the name. It was as phony as the card.

"I do this for High Schools all over Southern California, from San Diego to Santa Barbara."

"It must be interesting."

"It is. Especially this time when I get to do my own Alma Mater. Most people like to catch-up and reminisce. Of course there are lots of Web sites where people can do that on their own, but the media still likes to keep in it. The way it works is a lot of people don't have time for daily postings so we try to do a big 10 year splash that brings as many people together as we can. Alot of the local print media like to run these stories."

"Did we have classes together? I don't quite remember..."

"I'm sorry. That was quite a while ago. I know we had at least one class together, but I wasn't in any clubs like I know you were. And my appearance has changed quite a bit since then. But I have to say, you haven't changed a bit. Not even one year older. How did you manage it?" He could see his flattery was having the intended effect. "What about that interview? It would help alot."

She straightened her collar and ran her hand over her short, brown hair. "My husband won't be home until five."

Actually he knew it would be closer to six, but he wasn't going to contradict her. "We can go to the coffee shop around the corner if you'd feel more comfortable."

He gambled and won. She felt too frumpy for that. "I'm actually right in the middle of a load of laundry."

"I guess I caught you at a bad time. I apologize. I do a special section called "The Mostly Likely To...". I was hoping to get you in, but I guess I'll just go with what I have. Again, sorry to disturb you. It was nice seeing you after all these years." He started to turn to look convincing. He already knew he was not leaving the porch. One way or another...he was not walking away.

She opened the door a little wider. "What's the special section about?" And she was landed, proving once again, curiosity...

"From the yearbook section of the kids voted most likely to do this or that. You were one of them." And flattery...

"I suppose it will be alright."

...will open any door, he thought as he stepped through hers into the living room.

The living room was typical for an older, 3 bedroom house: couch against the far wall, new in the last 3 or 4 years, kitchen off to the right, hallway off to the left leading to the bedrooms. He noticed the converter box on the TV. "Haven't even gone digital yet," he thought. "She may have been popular in school, based mostly on looks," he guessed, which she still has, he admitted, "but it hasn't translated into success. I wish she were rich, so when I show her who has the real power and control, that superior, snotty look will turn into fear and respect for someone who is really a success at what they do." He tightened the grip on his briefcase to control his emotions. He didn't want his excitement to cause him to need his inhaler.

"Will this take long? I have to pick up my daughter at preschool before noon." She looked at the dining room clock. Not an actual dining room, just a table and chairs to the right of the kitchen near the entrance. The clock read 10:40.

"I should be out of here in twenty minutes, and you should be dead in fifteen." He didn't verbalize the second half of his response. He knew it would take a little longer than that as he snapped open his briefcase and had the chloroform out and over her mouth and nose before she could turn around.

The 28 year old victim came to on top of her still made but ruffled bed. Her clothes and hair were slightly more askew than when she had answered the door, having been dragged down the hall by her armpits, and then dumped unceremoniously on the covers before being hauled into her present seated position. She blinked a couple times, then sat there for a moment trying to remember what had happened. Something was wrong. She felt uncomfortable and somehow awkward. She suddenly wanted to jump up but found she could not. Something was restraining her. Confusion turned to worry, then to the threshold of panic. She struggled to move but could not. Her arms and legs were secure. And then finally she realized that she could not even turn her head. Full blown panic set in and she broke out in a clammy seat.

"What... what's happening? Why can't I move?" The words came difficult, through a fear constricted throat.

"Look around."

Unable to turn her head made that difficult. Down at her feet she could see there were cords around her ankles. She could also see a cord that secured her right arm to the bed frame. She pulled hard to free it, but there was no slack at all. Her effort merely resulted in a sharp pain. Again she tried to look around, but turning her head more than half an inch was impossible, held in place by the brace screwed into the wall behind, that and the curious metal finger at her right temple. Real fear began to set in.

"What *is* that? What do you want...who are you? I haven't done anything!"

"So many questions. I know one shouldn't answer a question with a question, but I'm in charge now. I'll make the rules. I'll ask the questions. How do you feel now? Still so high and mighty? Where's that 'I'm better than you ' look? All you look is pathetic."

She frowned, confused, a complete loss as to why this was happening.

"Before we get started I think a certain amount of privacy would be in order." He tied a dish cloth tightly across her mouth. "We wouldn't want you to attract any attention from the neighbors if you start getting hysterical, which I suggest you do not, so as to better control your breathing. Premature death is in no one's interest. Asphyxiation is not on today's menu. This way I'm sure we won't be disturbed. We have a nice little window of opportunity. The mailman is already gone, your daughter's school won't miss you until 12:15 or 20, and your husband won't be home until six, not five like your little white lie. I know. I've watched. But no matter. Either way our little game will be over and I'll be long gone before that.

Now, before we begin I'll need to explain the rules, but before I do that I notice you haven't finished looking around, and that's the most important part. Direct your attention to your left."

She could twist her head slightly more to the left with no round metal object against her head below the brace on that side. Her peripheral vision could just make out that her left arm was sticking out from her body at a 90° angle. It was supported in the air by a vertical brace, underneath her arm, holding it straight out from her body. She tried struggling against it.

"Oh, I wouldn't do that. At least not yet, until I've explained your particular challenge in this game. But first you need to see the whole picture. You can see part of it if you follow the line above your left wrist to the ceiling, and then over and down as far as you can."

Larry C. Rothman

She saw a blurry thin line tied to her wrist extending up to the ceiling. She squeezed her eyes closed and blinked a couple of times to clear the sweat and tears, then looked again. The line ran straight up to the ceiling, through an eye screw, across the ceiling through another eye screw, and then straight down until it disappeared from her sight.

"Here, this will help. You'll see the whole picture." Standing by the bed to her right the intruder held a mirror in which she could see herself, and the line, as far as before. He then tilted it slowly down and down and down. Watching the mirror as it slowly tilted down, she followed the line down until it finally angled around the grip, inside the trigger guard and ended, tied to the trigger of the gun mounted in a bracket next to her head, the barrel with homemade silencer pressed against her right temple. He could tell by the look on her face and her bulging eyes that she now saw the whole picture.

"As you can see, you don't want to lower your left arm, even two inches, for if you do, since there is no slack whatsoever in that line, you'd be blowing your own brains out."

She tried to speak, plead, cry out but could not make a sound.

"I'm sure you have questions, but that gag is staying in place. You'll only know what I want you to know so you need not speak. It's obvious what you want to know anyway: Who, What, Why? The who? Well, let's just say I'm Dr. Kevorkian. I'm not killing you; I'm just assisting your suicide. The death is by your own hand, well, in this case, arm, if you move it. The 'what' we'll get to when I explain the rules, and the why, well, I think I'll let you figure that at on your own. I will tell you, though, I actually do like bananas."

There was something familiar about him, but she was sure she had never seen him before. Bananas? What...?

He went back to the foot of the bed and started to pace. "So here's what we're going to do." He paced back and forth as he warmed to his subject and went into lecture mode.

"I will remove the support from your left arm while you continue to hold it up in the air. Even a one inch drop will result in right side cranial entrance, left side cranial exit, accompanied by grey matter splatter on the left wall. For how long do you have to hold it? Well, that's the game. I actually tried it. At two minutes your shoulder starts to feel the strain. At three minutes your arm starts to tire and becomes very heavy, and at three and a half minutes your muscles tighten and neck gets real sore, picking up the strain.

I could not make it to four minutes. But I wasn't under the same incentive you are not to lower my arm. That's where the real test of endurance comes in. A person is always able to go beyond what they think their endurance will allow, especially in a life or death situation. The problem is at a point it is beyond your control. Your muscles will tighten and seize up and keeping your arm in the air so as not to blow your brains out will not be up to you."

He suddenly stopped pacing and looked directly at her. "The good news is I won't let that happen. At precisely 4 minutes and 15 seconds I will replace the support. The added ingredient of hope should give you that extra little push. OK, ready? And now to begin."

Out of her field of vision he had set up a small travel alarm clock. There was a loop of the same thin cord around the plug, between the prongs in the socket and tied to her wrist. She was placed at the edge of the bed so that the moment her arm fell to the floor it would pull the clock's plug from the wall socket.

"It is,..." he looked at his watch, following the second hand to the twelve, and then removed the arm support. "...exactly 11:15." Her arm quivered slightly when the support was removed. "I will be back at 11:19 and 15 seconds. I don't want to distract your concentration," and he left the room, closing the door behind him.

Back in the living room he turned on the TV, not to watch, but for cover noise. He took the vacuum cleaner out of the closet, plugged it in and left it running. More cover noise. That and the homemade silencer on the .32 caliber handgun would make it so not even he would hear the shot. He had no intention of reentering the room in less than 15 minutes.

The visitor left the curtains partially opened, as they were when he got there, and sat on the couch. Out of view from the outside, he started to patiently wait. The TV was tuned to a soap opera but he didn't bother to change the channel. It wouldn't be long. He glanced at his watch: 11:17 and 10 seconds. A little over two minutes had gone by. He took a magazine out of his briefcase to catch up on an article he had been reading.

He read a couple pages then glanced again at his watch. Almost 11:19. Not quite four minutes had elapsed; he still had over eleven to wait. He might even finish the article, he thought, as he turned another page. It was an interesting article, about experiments with mood altering drugs that blocked neurotransmitter receptors in the synaptic membrane of specific areas of the brain.

A few more minutes went by; he turned a few more pages. When he looked at his watch again the second hand had just passed the 12. It was 11:29. He had two paragraphs left on the page he was reading. He turned the page and saw the article ended with one more column. There was time to finish it and so he did.

With 10 seconds to go he noticed the next article looked interesting, about the influence of tides on equatorial nocturnal quadrupeds. He marked that to read later. He put the magazine back in the briefcase and snapped it shut after removing the screw driver and small hand vac to disassemble his work. "A Louie, Louie. I gotta go."

With screw driver and vac in one hand, he opened the bedroom door with the other, quietly, gently, as if not to disturb a sleeping person. Then he smiled to himself. "She's sleeping, alright. Sleeping for good."

He looked at the body on the bed. It didn't look so bad. He walked around to the other side. An entrance wound you couldn't see and an exit wound leaking some. He glanced to his left, with some wall splatter, just as he had described. He retrieved the small clock. It had stopped at 11:21 and 19 seconds. "Wow. 6 minutes and 19 seconds. I never would have thought that possible."

He calmly started to disassemble the simple setup. First a couple screws in the head brace. He lifted the head forward to clear the brace and then let it fall back. He was in no hurry. Just a few more minutes to remove the gun mount and eye screws in the ceiling and he would be done.

With the TV and vacuum cleaner still on he didn't hear the car come up the driveway. The killer was almost finished, just had to remove the restraints when he froze. Was that a car door he could just make out over the noise coming from the living room? He thought fast. He definitely heard a dull thud and over the noise it had to be close, from this driveway. His sixth sense told him that it was, which meant he couldn't go out the front. Although this was totally unexpected, he didn't panic. His self-assuredness never called for a plan B, but there was no feeling of being trapped. The bedroom window opened onto the side yard. He would calmly go out the ba... The briefcase! It was still in the living room!

Without hesitating he dashed back down the hall, reached the corner of the living room and heard the screen door rattle and swing open. He looked. There was the briefcase, standing between the coffee table and couch. The door knob was turning as he made three long strides across the floor, banged his shin on the table, pulled it away a couple inches by one corner, reached out and grabbed his briefcase. Turning to escape back to the safety of the hall, he knew he would not make it before the door opened.

He quickly glanced and saw the door did not open but move slightly back and forth in the frame. The knob had not turned as he imagined, of course, because it was locked. He locked it. He chastised himself for his momentary panic. There was no room for that. He knew her husband, if that's who it was, it must be, since there was no knock but an attempt at entrance, expected to walk right in. Having to fumble for his keys, find the right one, insert it into the lock, turn it, open the door... That bought him the extra few seconds to disappear around the hall just as the door opened.

"Honey, surprise inspection today. We got sent home early. Steph! Why'd you lock the door?" Probably in the laundry room, Luke thought. He headed to his right for the kitchen while the killer was heading to the left down the hall. Luke did not find his wife in the kitchen and went on into the small laundry room. Not finding her there he retraced his steps.

In the bedroom the killer quickly loaded his gear into the small briefcase, no time to remove the restraints. He was just sliding the bedroom window open as Luke returned to the living room. The killer realized the noise from the TV and vacuum were now working in his favor as it masked any scraping sound lifting the window made. Stepping through into the side yard he took the time to close the window, not wanting to draw attention to his escape route. He didn't know how much time he had before the husband was in the bedroom, and he still had to get out of the yard. The window did not slide easily and made a creak and pop when it closed.

Back in the living room Luke stepped on the pedal to shut off the vacuum cleaner just as the bedroom window closed. He thought he heard a noise coming from down the hall, but wasn't sure with the TV on.

"Honey? Are you in the bedroom?" If she laid down for a rest it was odd to leave the vacuum running. He walked down the hall and pushed their bedroom door open. "Steph. Are you in he..."

Luke's eyes still functioned and his brain still functioned, but independently, not together. There was a disconnect. A short. The brain could not interpret, could not understand, could not process the messages the eyes were sending it. He didn't see what he saw. Instead there was a clarion in his head. A shrill cacophony of discordant cymbals, and rapid striking of steel hammers on firehouse bells exploded in his skull. This caused pinpoints of sharp lights to swim in his field of vision. He had vertigo and nausea. He tried to move; he tried to speak. Nothing functioned: vision, muscles, thought.

Outside, in the back yard, the author of the tragedy Luke was struggling with made it unobserved to the chain link fence separating the yard from the back alley. It was easy enough to drop his briefcase on the other side and make it over the top, landing lightly on his feet in the gravel and weeds. He headed to his right, calmly walking to where the alley met the street, six houses away. Three or four pre-teens rode their bikes past him while he was still in the alley. He didn't turn his head and they paid no attention to him as they pedaled past, talking boisterously with one another.

The man with the briefcase made a left out of the alley,

walked to the corner, crossed the street, and walked one more block in the same direction, heading away from the house where he left his latest victim. At the end of that block he turned right to where he had left his car on the side street. His remote entry unlocked the door. Opening and getting in the driver side, he put the briefcase on the passenger seat, the key in the ignition, the car in gear, drove half a block to the main street, turned left into light traffic for two blocks, got on the 110 and was gone.

Case and Rodriguez got the call from the 911 dispatcher and were given an address in Glendale where they were to proceed. They arrived at the house a few minutes after noon. Parked in front were two black and white cruisers, an EMT vehicle, a plain, late model government sedan and the usual crowd standing behind the yellow crime scene tape. Case pulled up behind one of the B&W's parked at an angle. He and Rodriguez got out, showed their ID's to a uniformed officer who allowed them through.

They quickly surveyed the scene in the living room and were directed down the hall to the bedroom on the right by another uniformed officer. The bedroom now contained a forensics team, someone dusting for prints, a photographer and the detectives, who had to step around people to see the actual crime. Straps to both ankles and right arm kept the body in a seated position. They made their way around the other side of the bed to view the mess made by the bullet's exit. It had already been dug out of the wall.

"Looks like a .32." the forensics lead said.

"Weapon?" Case asked.

"Hasn't been found."

Rodriguez looked at the scene. "Her right arm is strapped down, her left arm is hanging loose, and she was shot on the right side."

"She had help." Case replied.

Case noticed the wedding band on her left hand. He recognized the man with the victim in the picture on the dresser as the civilian in the living room. "Did the husband say anything?"

"The EMT guys are with him. He's in pretty bad shape."

Case motioned Rodriguez back to the living room. The print guy and photographer finished in the bedroom and left the room. Case then began to scrutinize for any detail that didn't belong. As he narrowed his field of attention, he fine tuned it, then narrowed it some more, like turning the focus wheel on a microscope, so as not to miss any data that might reveal useful information.

Case noticed the tiny holes in the wall to the right of the victim's head. He immediately decided they must have some significance and searched for more but did not find any anywhere else on the wall. On his hands and knees, he looked all the way down to the baseboard first on the left side of the bed facing the wall, away from the body and the right, but did not find any more. He did, however, find a couple of small, round objects on the right side, on the carpet. Using a small pair of tweezers he kept in his jacket pocket, he carefully picked them up, turned them over, and then dropped them into a small plastic evidence bag that sealed at the top.

Case stood up, stretched and leaned his head back to get the kinks out of his neck. That's when he noticed the single small hole in the ceiling directly over his head. He stared at it for a couple seconds. "Two in the wall near her head. One in the ceiling?" Case said to himself. He stood there staring up, his eyes roving up and down and then back and forth across the ceiling. And then he saw another hole directly across from the first one. Standing on his tip toes he could see they were fresh, like the ones in the wall. Case made a mental note to ask the husband about the holes, but he didn't expect him to be of any help. Case was convinced they tied this murder to the Shawna Anderson killing.

Case continued exploring the room for any other seeming incongruities. After satisfied there was nothing else in the way of evidence to help solve the crime, he made another complete circuit of the room. That's when he noticed the scuff marks on the window sill. They, too, looked fresh. He hadn't as yet touched anything with his hands. Now he put on thin plastic gloves and opened the window. The lawn had been recently mowed. Case went back to the living room and told Rodriguez he was going out back.

"OK, Sarge."

Case found a single, fresh, partial footprint in the flower bed. He looked to both sides of the yard, houses on either side, and saw that the back chain link fence separated the yard from the alley. That was the obvious escape route if the killer left by the window. Case walked across the yard to the fence and looked out, up and down the alley. It was empty. He started back to the house when he noticed a little soil smudge on one of the links about waist high.

Back in the living room Case was about to talk to his partner when the phone rang. Luke Dodson grabbed the cordless phone sitting in the charger stand at his elbow on the end table, fumbled and dropped it. An officer picked it up and handed it to him.

"Hello...Yes." He covered the phone. "Oh, no!" he said to no one in particular. "It's the school. My daughter! I forgot. She should have been picked up 15 minutes ago."

"I'm Detective Case. Is there anyone, a close relative, that can get her and keep her at their house for awhile?"

"Uh… yeah…uh, my sister. She lives not far, over on 8th, on the way to the school."

"OK, give me the phone. What's your daughter's name, and your sister's?"

"Julie. My sister is Anne."

"This is Los Angeles police Detective Case," he spoke into the phone and handed Luke his cell. "The Dodson's will be unable to pick up their daughter, Julie. Julie's father, Luke, is calling his sister right now," he nodded to Luke who started to dial. "Mr. Dodson's sister, Anne will be picking up Julie today. Please hold on while we confirm."

Luke reached his sister and without going into detail confirmed she would be able to pick Julie up and nodded to Case.

"Okay," Case spoke again to the school. "Anne," …to Luke, "What's her last name?"

"Burnam."

"…Mr. Dodson's sister, Anne Burnam will be there in 5 minutes to pick Julie up. Here's Mr. Dodson again."

Case informed Julie's father, after he hung up, that a

uniformed officer would meet his sister at the school and accompany them back to her house.

"An officer will take you over there. I assume you can stay at your sister's place with your daughter for a little while?"

The husband sat there deflated, his head hanging down.

"Mr. Dodson. Are you feeling alright? I think you need to meet your daughter. Do you want one of the EMT to check you out? Mr. Dodson?"

"I can't understand who would do this. What reason...Who would want to hurt her?"

"We're going to find out." Case repeated his question about the EMT.

"No...I'm fine, it's just..."

"I think then, if you are up to it you should go see Julie. She'll want you to be there. We're gathering all the information we can and we will talk to you very soon."

While the teams inside finished up and the coroner removed the body, Case and Rodriguez canvassed the neighborhood. The crowd outside had dispersed, after an hour had elapsed, and there was nothing to see. The next two hours and fifteen homes turned up no reports of any suspicious vehicles near the Dodson house or any unusual noises. The pair of detectives finally left the scene and headed back downtown. On the way they shared what little information each had and were frustrated by the overall lack of anything to work with.

Chapter Ten

Case and Rodriguez were both sitting in the Captain's office; Case somewhat slouched, in an indolent manner, lost in thought, Rodriguez looking more attentive. Capt. Murdock got right to the point. "What have you got for me?"

Rodriguez was waiting for Case to answer, but when it was evident he wasn't going to, Rodriguez, glancing at Case one more time, began.

"Twenty-eight year old victim, Stephanie Dodson, shot once at extremely close range in the right temple. Obviously not sui…"

"It's the same guy." Case sat straight up. "We're dealing with the same killer."

"The same as who?" Capt. Murdock didn't hide the irritation in his voice. He didn't like change of direction in direct reports. He wanted to follow one idea at a time.

"The same as 'whom'," Rodriguez thought, but didn't say it.

"The same as the killer of Shawna Anderson." Case replied.

"What tells you that? And don't tell me your gut."

"My gut tells me."

"I just said…" Capt. Murdock gave up. "I want your reports on my desk in one hour, but after you tell me now what they're going to say. You first Rodriguez."

"Yes sir. While Sergeant Case investigated the scene, first inside the bedroom where the husband states he found his wife, shot, and then out behind the house, I interviewed the husband. He couldn't tell us much, he was pretty distraught. We will question him more, later.

It appears he was unexpectedly let off from work a half day early and came home to find his wife dead in the bedroom. Shot, as I said, once in the right temple. It appears it was planned in a space of time when she would be alone. Mr. Dodson got there before their daughter was due to be picked up from preschool."

"Okay, Case. What ties this in with the Anderson murder? And I'm not asking your gut. Convince me we're looking for one suspect here, because that's the last thing we need. I don't want the press running with a serial killer."

"It's the same MO," Case stated.

"What do mean? Wasn't Ms. Anderson strangled, while this was a shooting?"

"That's just the means. I'm talking about the overall

method. The style. The planning and timing. The guy is definitely smart and he wants us to know it. I think he's going to keep killing until he gets his point across or until he's finished. So we better figure out what that point is, and real soon."

Capt. Murdock wasn't satisfied. "You haven't convinced me. I think if the guy is trying to tell us something, as you say, we'd have to know it's the same guy. And if we have to know it's the same guy, he'd have to do it the same way. The Anderson killing was controlled, slow strangulation and this one was a quick gun shot."

"I don't think it was necessarily a quick gunshot," Case objected. "From the pronounced indentation at the entry wound from a round object, it appears the gun barrel, or maybe a silencer, since no one heard anything, pressed against her head for an extended period of time. Her right arm was tied to the bed so she didn't pull the trigger. And I can't see someone else standing there for a long period of time just pressing the gun to her head. Then there are the little, freshly drilled holes."

"What holes?" Murdock wasn't happy.

"Remember there were small, freshly drilled holes in the wall by Shawna Anderson's bed, but no residue from the holes on the floor? There were the same holes in the wall next to Stephanie Dodson's head, plus on the ceiling above her bed. Again, no residue. For my money it's the same guy."

"So what is the idea of the holes?" Capt. Murdock asked.

"Starting with the strangulation, we know it was slow and controlled, not done manually, therefore by some mechanical devise, which would have been mounted in place. We know the Dodson woman didn't shoot herself, it's unlikely someone else did it himself, she was secured in the same way, although this time the bindings weren't removed, …"

"Yeah, because the husband came home early. The guy was lucky he wasn't interrupted and possibly caught. I'll admit the first guy was probably smart but not this guy. I'd call that sloppy," Capt. Murdock observed.

"I'm coming to that. I believe the bindings were used so that he could perform his murder scene according to his plan. It certainly seems that way in the first instance and I think it accomplished the same performance in the second. Stephanie Dodson's left arm was not secured. It was loose, hanging off the bed. And it's not that she managed to get it free; it was never secured. No ligature marks from a struggle like the other three limbs. I don't think that was by accident. The murder was completed without ever binding her left arm. Little holes in the ceiling. All part of the same picture. I'm telling you it's the same guy."

Case went on. "And you said it was sloppy? I don't think

so. The husband himself didn't know that morning that he was coming home early. That was something the killer had no control over. But he didn't panic. He got out. And in an unanticipated situation, he did it without making a mistake.

He left none of his work behind the first time, so I think he was interrupted by the husband coming home, since he didn't remove the bindings like he did before. He had no time, had to get out. That's where he was smart. When I saw the scuff mark on the window sill I was going to order a cast made of the print in the soil of the flower bed outside. But he knew enough, even in a hasty exit, not to leave one. He stepped with the point of his foot until he got his other foot on the grass. Then I saw where he went over the in the backyard fence into the alley. He would have had no trouble getting to his car, probably parked not far away, but out of sight of the Dodson house."

Capt. Murdock thought it over then turned to Rodriguez. "Do you have anything else?"

"We canvassed the immediate neighborhood but turned up nothing. No one saw or heard anything suspicious. I'm thinking we almost caught a break. If the husband came home even five minutes earlier it would be a whole different story, but right now, we have nothing but backgrounds to check. At least with two of them, there might be a tie in to put this together."

"Well, that's why you guys get the big bucks. So get to it and drop those reports before you leave."

Capt. Murdock turned back to Case. "What about you, anything to add?"

"Nothing and everything. I was saving the best for last. The icing on the cake of why I know it's the same guy. We don't know the 'who' or the 'how'. I don't think he ever intends to let us know that. But the why, I'm convinced he wants us to know. Just like the Anderson killing: nothing to find, nothing to go on, just the elephant he left in the room. The same is true in the Dodson killing. He left an elephant in the room." Case pulled an evidence bag out of his pocket and held it up for the Captain to see.

"What's that?" Murdock asked

"I don't know what they are, but I know he left them behind."

"Let me see those," Rodriguez said and took the bag from Case. "Candy pebbles. My kids love these. They look like real rocks. My kids like to play with them, try to fool their friends like they're eating rocks. Dr. Leonard's nick name for the killer won't fit now. He didn't strangle this one."

"And you know that was left by the killer, because…" said Capt. Murdock.

"Because there was no blood on top of the rocks. Only on the bottom. They were put there after she was murdered."

Case and Rodriguez left Capt. Murdock's office. Murdock had directed Case to the 5th floor Personnel to update some of his records already months over due. They took the stairs.

"You didn't have to come," Case said to Rodriguez.

"I figured it couldn't hurt. I'm still learning my way around." A suit and a gold braided uniform passed them in the hall going in the opposite direction. Neither little group paid attention to the other.

"Besides, the more I'm around you the more chance great detective work will rub off on me." Case turned his head, "Sure," and almost walked into a woman coming out of an administration office.

The woman abruptly stopped and took half a step back. "Excuse me," she said. She was 4 or 5 inches shorter than Case and spoke before even looking up.

Case was about to respond in kind but stopped himself with recognition. "Excuse m… oh,...Lucy."

"Lawrence! I didn't expect running, literally, into you up here."

"Just going to Personnel." They looked at each other for a beat.

She spoke. "So, ...how are you?"

"I'm fine." Another pause. Rodriguez looked from one to the other, they were still pausing, then Rodriguez cleared his throat.

"Oh, have you met my new partner? This green rookie is Manny Rodriguez."

Lucy and Rodriguez shook hands. "Very nice to meet you," she said. "How were you lucky enough to be teamed with the department's #1 detective?"

"Clean living."

"Well, watch and copy everything he does. You'll be promoted in no time."

"That's the plan. I can't believe how much I've learned already."

"Like what?"

"Well, before you told me, I had already learned he's the #1 detective on the force."

"How did you learn that?"

"He tells me himself every day."

"Alright, alright. Are you two through? C'mon Manny. We have a couple homicides to solve."

Lucy turned her attention back to Case. "It was nice seeing you again..."

"Uh, yeah," He looked at Rodriguez who just stood there looking at him with a quizzical look on his face.

"Yeah, it is... or was, I mean,... I'll see ya."

"OK, bye."

"Bye."

"Bye, Manny. It was nice meeting Detective Case's new partner."

"Nice meeting you, too; very nice."

Case and Rodriguez continued down the hall while Lucy headed toward the stairs they had just come up. Rodriguez glanced back at Lucy twice before she disappeared down the stairwell.

"Aye, carumba, Case! She's a nice looking lady. It's obvious you already know each other, right? And I can tell she likes you; I can't tell why, but I can tell she does."

"Let's just stick to police work."

"I am. I'm a detective. I'm detecting."

"Very funny."

"So what gives? Have you two gone out? I think you should ask her out. She looks like a very nice lady and I'm detecting she likes you; I'm just not a good enough detective to detect why."

"You're repeating yourself."

"So ask her out. Later you can bring her to our house for dinner and Consuela will stop bugging me."

"Back to that again?" But Case was well past that.

Case was definitely attracted to Lucy Pennyhill the first time he saw her coming out of records archives in Parker Center. Must have been her shoulder length jet black hair. He had a weakness for jet black hair. If he ever thought about it, it must have something to do with his weakness for black licorice. Her frame wasn't bad either. She was of English descent but there was definitely some Greek blood which gave her a Mediterranean complexion. That and her greenish blue eyes put Case in a momentary trance. Maybe five surplus pounds, but when it came to that, flesh and bones, he preferred flesh over bones. He didn't know anything about her except she was too young for him. He preferred people his own age and she couldn't be over 32 or so. Turns out he was better at solving crimes, as she definitely was in his age group at 43.

At that juncture Case wasn't opposed to making an attempt at overcoming his inertia towards life. He stopped, said hello, she had a nice smile, responded with a hello of her own, brief mutual intros, chit chat/small talk and before he knew it he was surprised when he realized he had just asked her out. What was even more surprising was she accepted.

That weekend they met at a bistro in a more upscale part of town than Case normally frequented, but he felt at home with her right away. Conversation flowed easily and natural curiosity always gets around to age. Case played his cards right telling her he didn't want to ruin his own good fortune, but she was a little young to go out with an old guy like him. When she admitted she was 43 he was genuinely surprised. He stayed on track by not dominating the conversation, mostly because he wanted to find out more about her and reveal less about his own less than stellar background.

Case found out she had been divorced ten years, to an ex-cop no less, lived in Ventura in the house she had grown up in, then purchased from her mother who lived with her until she passed away 2 years ago. She jogged when she could for fitness, had a total weakness for hot fudge sundaes with walnuts and loved movies. Her favorite hobby was cooking; she loved to cook which was why she jogged when she could. Case couldn't believe what he was hearing. So far, he could see no faults. If he didn't know better he'd think he was being set up, but he wasn't an international spy, and he didn't have any sensitive defense secrets or plans to a new generation of weapons. He was just an ageing out L.A. homicide detective who read too many Tom Clancy novels.

Over the next few months they went to several movies, the kind he liked: intense action, international intrigue, murder mysteries and crime dramas that often ended tragically on a down beat. It didn't occur to him she might like something different. To Case, those were what movies were supposed to be, not a therapy session to find your inner child.

After one Lethal Weapon fest they went strolling on the Santa Monica pier. "I'm not complaining," she told him, "but don't you get enough of that at work? Wouldn't you like a fun, upbeat movie?"

"If you try to drag me to a chick flick, this merry-go-round can stop right now."

It was a warm, tropical night with a light breeze. The sky was so clear and the stars so close, you could reach up and prick your finger on the sharp edges. On the pier were mostly other couples enjoying the idyllic evening, none aware of the presence of anyone else. Lucy hugged his arm.

"It's so beautiful tonight. I've lived here all my life and

still love it. I don't know why… I'm divorced, practically middle-aged, not much future at work, live alone and here I am scraping the bottom of the barrel and look what I found: Dirty Harry." She squeezed his arm again.

"Sounds like a match made in Heaven."

There was an odd tone in his voice. She looked at him puzzled. Was she getting ahead of herself? She knew she was really starting to like him and thought he liked her, but now she sensed a subtle change. She knew he had been divorced and at first seemed open to and wanted a new relationship, but maybe he was changing his mind. She looked up at him. He didn't look back; he seemed lost in thought, as he just walked, looking ahead.

Lucy thought back over their few months together, wondering if she had messed up somehow. She didn't think so. They never found anything to disagree about, well, so they had a different taste in movies, but that wasn't Earth shattering. She was probably going to get a 'It's not you, it's me' line. Well, it probably *was* just him. She could already hear him. He's convinced his life is such a social failure, who's he kidding? He's more comfortable in his own world than to try to reach out and share someone else's and bring them into his. She had no way of knowing a couple months ago that he was plagued with a defeatist attitude. It made her think of what her father had told her long ago, what Henry Ford said, "Some people think they can't do it and some people think they can do it and they're both right."

Lucy remembered the one and only time she had cooked for him. Ventura meets the ocean at an elevated point where 101 offers a broad, sweeping panoramic view of the curving shoreline before heading into L.A. That's coming from the north. The view was not quite as breathtaking from the south, the route Case drove when accepting an invitation for a home cooked meal at Lucy's house. But Case accepted Lucy's offer of a home cooked meal as much to sample it as an excuse to tool up the highway, away from the city.

The house Lucy purchased from her mother was small, but the view said it all. That's why she would never move. Although well away from the beach, it had an open, beach house feel to it and high enough for a great view of the Pacific. Case thought it was great.

"It reminds me of my Grandmother's house."

"Your *Grandmother's* house?! It's old, but I don't think it looks like a Grandmother's house."

"I don't mean like lace and doilies. I guess it's just the comfortable, kind of cozy feel I get from it. The only other time I felt that way about a house was at my Grandmother's. When I was about eight, my Mother took my brothers and me on a train to visit her Mother in Wichita. I don't remember much about the train but what I never forgot was my Grandmother's house.

Mostly I think it was the smells, of family cooking. It just felt comfortable and homey. I guess your house just kind of reminds me of that feeling."

During dinner Case told her she should quit her job at the department and get a high paying job as a professional chef in a restaurant. "You're just used to fast food and microwave," she told him.

"No, this is really, really good!"

She knew she had talent in the kitchen. Others had told her the same thing. After dinner she put on a jazz station they both listened to which surprised both of them. Suddenly Case felt like opening up and didn't see any harm in telling her more about him. Two hours went by in twenty minutes. Case didn't want to overstay his welcome and it was fine with her when he called it an early night, kissed her on the cheek and left around 10:30. Heading back down the highway he was feeling pretty good.

Then she thought of their last date before this one. They were leaving a theater after seeing *Lethal Impact,* on their way for a late night taco, he thought. After his choice of movie, she was getting a hot fudge sundae or nothing.

"What's the matter?" she asked.

"What do you mean?"

"You're not your usual jolly, jovial self. Didn't you like the movie? Not enough mayhem? Blood Lust III is coming out next week. I heard they had to order another 50 dozen squibs, and has Heinz on speed dial, to finish the shoot."

"Very funny." But he wasn't smiling.

"Okay, we don't have to get a sundae."

He thought about coming up with a lame non-answer but then said, "I got a call from my ex last night".

"I'm surprised you gave her your number."

"I didn't. A determined woman will find a way."

"Uh huh. So, what did she want, if you want to tell me? Was it a money thing?"

" No. That would be easy: I don't have any."

"Don't tell me she wants to get back together. Should I be worried?"

"No. That would be even easier."

"Listen, we could change the subject. It's none of my business but you went there, and curious minds..."

"My daughter got married six months ago," he

interrupted. "The invitation must have got lost. They're going to have a baby."

"Oh, that's…"

"Yes, it is."

She remembered he never shook the melancholy, first blaming the job, then himself: he wasn't the stuff of happy-ever-after.

"Okay, I get it. As for relationships you're the kiss of death." To salvage the situation, she started lying, a little. "Fortunately, I'm not looking for anything serious. Remember what Rocky said about gaps? So we spend free time together. I mean, you're slightly more fun than crosswords."

As they strolled to the end of the Santa Monica pier, a couple of squabbling gulls brought Lucy out of her reverie. Still morose, Case hadn't changed his attitude from their last date when he told her about his daughter. It seemed a real distraction to him, a game changer. Lucy wondered if he was losing interest. Maybe this merry-go-round *was* coming to an end.

A week later it did. She wasn't surprised when he gave her a version of the '…it's me' routine. Case felt like he had ruined enough lives and had wanted to spare Lucy. At least that's what he told himself. He even felt gallant, chivalrous, sacrificing himself for the fair damsel. She didn't see it that way.

"I'm grown up and can watch out for myself."

"Trust me, you can't trust me. It's for the best."

"For who?" And then these semi-arguments spiral downhill where they wind up not making any sense at all. "So, are you afraid I want a commitment, or are you tired of me already?"

"No, definitely not." Some more of the 'it's not you' stuff. He threw some bits and pieces about case load, distractions and other detritus into the pot.

"At least I distract you." Lucy groused.

"Without a doubt. You're great. You don't even have a cat."

Case, at the time, was hoping she would call him a lousy, whatever, or a big dumb something or other as her proof they didn't really belong together, show her 'true colors', and then he could feel he was doing the right thing after all, but it didn't end that way. It took a completely different turn and somehow, unexpectedly, ended on a positive note. Case was ultimately happy it did.

Lucy wasn't happy with this turn of events, thought it

probably had a lot to do with timing, and did not want to burn bridges. The back and forth went something like:

"You deserve a nice, decent guy."

"I don't want a nice, decent guy. I want you."

"You got grit, gal."

"Okay."

"Okay, what?" Case had asked.

"Okay, not seeing each other anymore if that's what you want." Lucy replied.

"That's it? Just like that?"

"Just like that."

"Still friends?"

"Sure, why not?" She admitted.

"Well, this must be the least acrimonious break up on record."

"Someone owns a dictionary."

"I try to learn a new big word every month."

And that was that. They ran into each other occasionally in the course of the job and true to her words, there were no recriminations, still friends. Case felt pretty much like a jerk, not unique for him, but told her he was happy they remained friends and he appreciated her attitude.

Not given to emotional outbursts, Lucy took the pragmatic approach. "I'm no worse off than I was before. I always look for the silver lining."

"Which is?"

"At least I don't have to watch anymore of Dirty Harry Meets Godzilla."

"Yeah, I guess if you're looking for a real sensitive guy, there's no one home at Detective Case's house."

"Lighten up. I'm just kidding. I had fun. Uh oh, I'm going to be late getting these down to records." Up on tip toes she kissed his cheek and walked away. He watched her go when she suddenly said over her shoulder, "Don't lose my number. I think you owe me a hot fudge sundae." Not only pragmatic, Lucy was patient. "Pressure is counterproductive," she thought to herself. That was two years ago. Lucy was patient.

With Rodriguez chirping at Case all the way they made it back to their desks to work on the Dodson killing.

"Let's get these prelims done so we can find a connection to the Anderson murder."

"That's the way you want to work this?" Rodriguez asked. "There are so many other shootings: husbands and wives, wives and husbands, besides the straight up suicides. I have to agree with the Captain. There's just nothing to connect them. In both of these we have no motive or witnesses."

"That's a similarity itself. That's my gut talking. Suicide? Have you ever seen anyone shoot themselves in the right temple with their right armed tied at their side? That's self evident talking."

"What?"

"And the red flags the guy keeps leaving to play with our heads. That's the obvious tie-in talking that tells me that not only are these two connected, but that somebody is on some kind of a campaign." Case was convinced.

"I admit, that seems odd, but even if it is the same guy, we can't trace that bread crumb trail. Where do we go from here, how do we proceed?"

"Ah, my friend, that's what we get paid for: police work, research. Find the needle in the haystack that ties these two together, because as weak as it is, that bread crumb trail does tie them together. Follow Anderson's and Dodson's trail backwards and see where they converge."

They spent the next couple of hours at their desks in near silence. They researched Dodson just as they had researched Anderson but found no similarities in their job histories, family backgrounds or activities regarding club affiliations or memberships.

Rodriguez took a break where he was sitting and leaned back in his chair, stretching his arms behind his back. He looked over at Case who had not let up.

"You come up with anything, Case?"

He rubbed his eyes and leaned back as Rodriguez had done. "Not yet, you?"

"Not really. Just one thing. While Stephanie Dodson attended Riverside, Shawna Anderson didn't go to college, but they both went to the same High School, Simi Valley High."

"Yeah, I saw that, too. Ten year old alumni. We need something more solid than a vague coincidence."

"Do you think we should check it out, two victims going to the same High School, still living nearby after ten years?" Rodriguez suggested.

"It's not that unusual. A lot of people grow up, go through school, get married and live in the same place, even buying the home they grew up in from their parents and living in the same house."

"Yeah, it's just all we have so far."

"We can check it out later, after we have something stronger to go on, but if that's all we have, well…, we're just going to need more."

"Do these guys ever get in your head?" Rodriguez wondered out loud.

Case thought about past unsolved murders. "It's never happened to me. Not that I'll admit. There are many drawn out serials, some solved, some not that have caused some detectives real mental anguish: Green River up in Seattle, Zodiac; lots of others. I want to stop this guy first, put him away before there's a #3, whether he's planning one or not."

The guy was planning a #3. That was the bad news. The worse news for Case and Rodriguez, and especially the third target was, Case didn't get his wish. He didn't stop him first.

Chapter Eleven

" Valley Realty." Pause. "I'm sorry, Shirley Turlock is out of the office showing a property. I can give you her cell." Which she did. This was 10 A.M. The caller reached the real estate agent on her cell and she agreed to meet him at one of Valley Realty's new exclusive listings in Baldwin Park at 11:15. She would never make it if she were not just about finished showing the property in Arcadia. As it was, there would be no time to hurry to her Pasadena home, which was in the opposite direction, to freshen up first. She pressed the key fob door lock button, her tight skirt hiking up as she slid behind the wheel of her BMW with the cobalt blue paint job and the delinquent lease payment. She checked herself in the mirror. "That'll have to do," she thought. Her deceptively youthful looks that enabled her to snare a much younger man were starting to give way. No time to worry about it now as she put the car in gear, pulled away from the curb and made a right at the end of the block to jump on the 210 heading east. At the next freeway interchange she took the 605 south to Baldwin Park.

This was all according to plan. The killer could tell she was excited to have an unexpected back-to-back appointment. An appointment he had no intention of keeping.

The doorbell rang at a Pasadena home at 10:45 AM. Shirley Turlock was just leaving Arcadia to keep her phone appointment in Baldwin Park as her annoyed husband got up to answer the door. The only calls he gets at the front door are one of the delivery services, none of which he was expecting. Too early for the mailman, unless it was an Express, again, not expecting. Shirley always lets him know when she's expecting something. She never forgets to warn him. That wasn't it.

These thoughts went through Jim Turlock's mind as he left the little room in which he had set up his Apple to try his hand at day trading, after he was downsized at Radio Shack. He was really going to be annoyed, and was working himself up if it was two guys in cheap black suits with white shirts and ties, wearing backpacks full of tracts wanting to convert him. He squinted through the peep hole at an ordinary looking guy, no suit, just jeans and a T-shirt. Looked pretty harmless. He heard something about a Volksmarch going through the neighborhood. Was that today? Maybe this guy was lost.

Jim Turlock opened his front door for the last time of his life.

"Can I hel-" The Taser hit him like a thunderbolt.

It was relatively easy for the intruder to drag the

unconscious victim, 5'8" weighing only 155 lbs., into the room at the back of the house where the treadmill was. The victim woke up lying face down on the rough treadmill belt, his arms extended above his head, almost straight up, painfully pulling at his shoulder sockets as his wrists were duct taped to the treadmill's guard rails. The killer had little other prep work to do with plenty of time to finish by the time the victim managed to struggle to his feet.

"What's...?" He was still dazed with a sharp tingling throughout his body. He saw his bound wrists.

"What's going on?" He looked in both directions and saw the intruder standing just behind him on his right. "What's this about? What do you want? There's no money in the house. I have a little cash and credit cards in my wallet. They're in the computer room."

"Thank you. That's very generous of you, but that's not why I'm here."

"Who are you? What do you want?" He struggled now with the binding; twisting and pulling.

"Who am I? Maybe later. What do I want? Same as everybody else: entertainment. You remember what it's like to have someone entertain you, a comedian or a clown. It's very funny, right? Well, this entertainment is in the form of a game, kind of like a TV game show, Beat the Clock. See that small electric clock I set up? You can watch that to see how well you're doing."

"How well I'm doing what? What's this all about? Who are you?" He didn't notice the twine tied around the clock's wall plug, the other end tied to his belt with only two inches slack.

"I told you, "who?", maybe later. But your first question goes to the crux of the matter, which I'm about to explain, so pay careful attention. I know you're a little disoriented but this is very important."

"Look. I don't know what this is, but trespassing and illegal detainment is also very serious. My wife will be home any minute and she has the police on speed dial."

"Your wife right now is hurrying on her way to show a property. When she gets there, she'll wait for her tardy "client" to show up. After 15 more minutes she'll receive a call from the office telling her the "client" is stuck in traffic and will be there soon. By the time she finally gives up, with hope for a sale keeping her there even longer than she feels reasonable, she still won't leave right away, even after an obvious no-show. Then she has to drive all the way back through traffic. We have more than sufficient time, by a wide margin."

The victim on the treadmill, by now, had moved beyond his initial disbelief, shock, frustration and anger. These feelings were slowly being replaced with worry and helplessness and he could start to feel a tinge of panic.

"Here's what we're going to do." The killer switched on the treadmill, but nothing happened. The victim glanced at the wall socket and saw that the treadmill's cord was plugged in.

"Yes, the treadmill is plugged in, but the motor no longer operates the belt. That's what you do. You see, you're a hamster on a wheel. As long as you keep the belt moving, it will generate power to the electromagnetic switch on the trapdoor of the container you see to your right. That container will soon hold cyanide capsules. Stop the belt, the power is cut, the door at the bottom falls open, and the cyanide capsules fall into the container of acid below, releasing the poison gas."

The victim turned his head and stared at the container mounted on a collapsible metal stand. A wire from the treadmill was connected to the container. There was a glass bowl a few inches below the container. The bowl was full of a clear liquid, presumably acid. The trapdoor at the bottom of the container was hanging open. Then the victim stared incredulously at the intruder.

"I'm sure you are full of questions, but all of an irrelevant nature: who, why etc. The only thing that needs concern you is to keep that belt moving once I drop the capsules in and let go of the trapdoor. If you stop, this room becomes a good, old-fashioned California gas chamber. You'd be killing yourself."

"But…I… don't understand."

"I thought I explained it clearly enough. Stop the treadmill…die in a gas chamber. But moving on, that's the simple logistics. Any game has to have an element of fun, which is derived from a challenge. You may not have thought about it, and I won't bore you with the math and physics that I've worked out in exact detail, which I'm sure you wouldn't understand anyway, but this room has quite a bit more cubic feet than your typical gas chamber, meaning the prescribed amount of cyanide gas would dissipate much more rapidly in a larger room, diluting the parts per thousand to a non-lethal dose. The obvious solution is to increase the dosage. However, a condemned man, well, you're a condemned man, let's say with a slim chance; but one serviced by the state, controls his breathing to the shallowest degree possible, while you, on the other hand, are faced with an ironic conflict of interest. The energy you will be expending, keeping that belt moving at the minimum threshold level to keep the trapdoor shut, means, if and when it does fall open, you will be literally gulping air, calculated to offset the rate of dissipation due to the greater cubic footage of the room. So that's the game. Have I confused you? Your challenge, whether you want to accept it or not, is to keep your eye on the trapdoor. If it starts to open, you'll need to increase your speed while trying to control your breathing, keeping it to a minimum.

Just two more points and we're ready to begin. One:

time. Obviously, you would eventually tire and have to stop at some point. Of course, I've tested everything. At the rpm's the belt must maintain, to keep the power up and the door closed, for someone not carrying extra weight like you, the first twenty minutes should give you no problem. After that, within the next five minutes the electromagnet will start to lose power as the rpm's drop and the trapdoor will start to budge, but not open enough to let the capsules fall. You will then go down hill rapidly as muscle energy loss, therefore endurance, is not a straight line decline, but is the square of the previous minute's loss. Of course, the obvious incentive factor will add to your endurance. That's why I've allowed 30 minutes. You'll have a chance, but it won't be too easy. At exactly thirty minutes after you get the belt to close the door and I drop in the capsules, I will be back to see how you did. Still running, I disconnect and you made it. If you're lying face down on the belt, well, you just didn't want it bad enough."

The intruder could see the victim not concentrating on the instructions, but starting to look defiant.

"No, you can't just refuse to run the belt. In that case, I drop the capsules in anyway, but eight, not two, and they fall directly into the acid. I'm only a few seconds from the door and can get out before any danger.

Now, point two: Shouting for help won't do you any good either. For several reasons. You're at the back of the house out of earshot and your neighbors are used to your rock'n roll station drowning out any calls for help. Being just outside the door, I would hear the first call anyway, in which case I will gag you and then you'd have a real problem. Getting enough air through your nose to maintain the exertion required to run that belt at sufficient speed, with a gag, would be impossible.

 Okay, now, ready to start the game?"

Now the victim was going into a full panic. "Wait! What do you want? Just tell me! What's this all about?" Sweat beads were showing on his forehead under his short-cropped sandy hair.

"I already told you all you need to know. And never was 'Save your breath' more appropriate. You definitely are going to need it. So let's get started. We won't be interrupted, but we don't have all day, either. Let the games begin! Or, maybe, more appropriately: Start your engine!"

With that the intruder held the capsules over the container ready to drop them down the unobstructed path to the acid below.

"I'm going to count to ten and then drop the capsules, but before I get there, I suggest you start that belt because it will take at least four seconds to get up to speed."

The man on the treadmill could not afford to call his bluff and started walking. At the count of six the intruder, with his other hand, lifted the hinged trapdoor shut. At the count of eight he tilted his open hand with the capsules. At the count of nine he removed his hand below the trapdoor. It remained closed. At the count of ten his hand tilted the rest of the way and the capsules fell into the top of the container.

"Now it's up to you. I'll be back in exactly thirty minutes." Jim Turlock noticed the stranger did not look at his watch but turned around and walked out, closing the door behind him. The treadmill faced the door so he noticed the faint dimming of light where the bottom of the door almost met the floor. The stranger had stuffed the opening with towels on the other side.

The man on the treadmill sweated profusely as he kept the belt turning, more sweat than there would normally be from his exertion alone. The man in the next room waited patiently, casually glancing through a magazine. The man duct taped to the metal guard rails glanced again at the small electric clock. 16 minutes. The man in the next room glanced for the first time at his wrist watch. 23 minutes.

The hands on the small electric clock were frozen in place. It took 5 minutes for a single revolution of the minute hand and the second never moved, or so it seemed to Jim Turlock. At last, 17 minutes. Still an eternity before he would be set free.

The hands on the wrist watch were impatient. Another glance showed the 30 minutes were already up. Finishing the article, the man with the magazine turned pages looking for something else interesting to read. He found an article on changing approaches to public school test scores. Sounded boring, but he still had time to kill.

Towels were removed from the base of the door. The door opened. An unpleasant odor. The man walked in leaving the door wide open. His presence in the exercise room raised the living population from zero to one. The dead man on the treadmill was suspended by his bound wrists, head nearly touching the belt. The living man quickly opened the window and plugged in a portable, rotating electric fan.

He was right. It wasn't necessary to fill the room with gas. By the time [he glanced at the clock, unplugged at the moment of death, 33 minutes, 22 seconds, impressive] the gas was released, he was gulping so much air in such close proximity that turning his head either way, trying to avoid the gas, did no good.

As the fan did its job, the intruder retrieved the clock, collapsible stand and container with its trapdoor hanging open. He disconnected the electromagnet, and then carefully poured the residual acid into a glass vial for later disposal. He tied up the fan's chord and packed everything into a canvas bag. From the canvas bag he then retrieved a pair of scissors, cut the duct tape from the victim's wrists and let the body fall. He peeled the tape from both wrists and stashed it in the bag, along with the scissors and everything else. Satisfied that there was nothing to indicate anyone but the victim had ever been in the room, he carefully placed on the floor one small bit of incongruity that said otherwise.

At the same moment a canvas bag with an odd assortment of paraphernalia was leaving a home in Pasadena an angry real estate agent in Baldwin Park was crushing out a cigarette. She folded her arms, rapidly tapped her foot, unfolded her arms, glanced at her watch for the last time, bumped her head getting into the leased, cobalt blue BMW and headed for the 605, the 210 and her home in Pasadena.

Chapter Twelve

At 12:32 PM a frantic 911 call was relayed by the operator to an ERT. No, she didn't think her husband was breathing. She had just arrived home to find him collapsed on the treadmill. The Emergency Response Team of the Fire Dept. arrived on scene ahead of an ambulance and the police, also directed to the Pasadena residence.

The police were called after the distraught woman insisted her husband could not have had a heart attack. He was in perfect health, did not smoke and had no family history of heart problems. She informed the police she had just got home from a client no-show in Baldwin Park to find her husband. She was not having a good day.

To mollify her, even though there were no signs of foul play, which the coroner undoubtedly would confirm, one of the officers called the L.A. Detectives Division, Homicide Bureau, planning to leave a message. He was surprised to have his call picked up on the first ring.

"Detective Case, homicide."

"Oh, this is Officer Banyon." He gave his location and explained the situation.

"Let me talk to Mrs. Turlock." The officer put her on.

"This is Detective Sergeant Case. I understand you came home and found your husband collapsed on the treadmill?"

"Yes. That's right. The people here think he had a heart attack, but that's impossible."

"What makes you sure?"

"For one thing, he was in perfect health. He doesn't smoke, like I do, but never around him. He jogs and makes sure he eats right."

"I can't give a medical opinion, of course, but it does happen. Maybe a heart problem he wasn't aware of."

"He just had his annual check-up. They always check his heart. Perfect. No high blood pressure. He always gets his annual right before his birthday which was last week."

"How old was he?"

"29. And something else doesn't seem right."

"What's that?"

"Well, he lost his job recently, about three months ago. The company he worked for, Radio Shack, he managed a store for them, suddenly closed his store, you know, downsized. He used to day trade a little when he worked there so he was trying it on a full time basis for the last three months.

He had his job at Radio Shack for two years. He loved jogging but he couldn't with all the hours he was putting in so he bought a treadmill to use before work. But for the last three months, since he's been home, he went back to jogging everyday after the markets close. He hasn't used the treadmill in three months."

Something told Case something. He had an itch. "Put Officer Banyon back on," he said.

"Are you going to investigate?"

"Yes, ma'am, we are. But I need to speak to Officer Banyon first."

When Officer Banyon came back Case told him to keep everyone out of the room where the body was found, stay in the room and not to let anyone touch anything. He and his partner were leaving Parker Center now on their way to the scene.

When Case and Rodriguez arrived at the Pasadena address they saw a thirty's something, more on the 'something' side than the thirty side, woman pacing back and forth in front of the house, nervously smoking a cigarette. She threw it on the lawn when she saw them pull up.

"Are you the detectives?" Case and Rodriguez showed their ID. She led them into the house.

"You're the wife of the deceased?" Case asked.

"That's right. Shirley Turlock. My husband Jim is lying in the exercise room. He was murdered."

Case nodded to Rodriguez to make sure the room was secure. "Let me ask you just a couple of questions and then my partner will get more basic information."

"Ask all you want."

"You said on the phone that your husband did not use the treadmill, where you found him, as much lately as he had before."

"No. I said he hasn't been using it at all ever since he lost his job. He hasn't touched it. He goes out jogging everyday. That's how I know it was a setup. So you can't just write it off as a heart attack or some other whitewash excuse. You have to find out what killed him and who."

"That's the first thing we are going to find out, how he died. You've already raised a suspicion. I believe there is foundation for your doubts. I'm in charge of an ongoing investigation and I'm probably, when we get the results back, going to make this part of it."

"What ongoing investigation?"

Rodriguez came back into the living room.

"It's too early to release any details, but that's what I want you to talk to my partner, Detective Rodriguez, about. Starting with anyone you suspect might have wanted to do your husband harm."

"No one would want to do anything bad to Jim. That's what makes no sense."

"Well, we're going to want some basic information. Detective Rodriguez can take you downtown or wherever else you'd feel more comfortable."

"I want to stay here. What can I tell you?"

"Are you sure you want to do this here? We will be releasing your husband to the ambulance out front soon."

"Yes. Just let me help however I can."

"Okay, then. Just try and give Detective Rodriguez as complete a list as you can of you and your husband's acquaintances, both current and former. Include people you work with. We'll check with his former employer. We'll also need to borrow his trading information. We're trying to cross reference all the material we can. If this turns out to be from other than natural causes we'll need all the information we can get. Later we can get both of your daily routines and schedules, right up until you got home today, if all that's not too much for you right now."

"No. I want to help all I can right away."

"Fine. Why don't you both sit over there? Just take your time. We'll both give you our cards if you think of anything later and want to contact either one of us."

Case entered the room where the body was. Nothing seemed out of the ordinary. Had he not known about the deceased's recently giving up use of the treadmill, first appearances did suggest a heart attack while exercising. However, the condition of the body would not lead to that conclusion. The man lying on the belt was young, looked fit, not overweight. And his widow said he had no family history of heart problems. Well, cause of death would be known soon enough.

He looked around the room before coming back to the body. Nothing seemed out of place. But he was patient and methodical. He knew the smallest incongruity could reveal much. Small keys unlock large doors. He travelled slowly around the room. Everything seemed pretty normal. Nothing silently communicated "Look at me!"

Case, having circumnavigated the room, was back where he started, at the body on the treadmill. This is where he would find his leads, if he found anything. Still, nothing looked out of place. The deceased was wearing jogging clothes and running shoes. But he probably got up and dressed that way, even to do his day trading. When he was finished, he would then be ready to go out jogging. So why did he suddenly change his mind and use the treadmill, if this was an innocent death?

Case surveyed the scene again. That's when it struck him something wasn't right. The treadmill was plugged in, okay. The switch was still in the on position, okay. The belt was not moving, okay, the body was laying on it. But the motor was not running. The motor was making no noise at all. Why was that? That would have to be checked out.

Case examined the body. There should be a gash or a bump or at least a red mark where he hit his head if he suddenly fell while leaning forward in a running position. But there was none. Did something break his fall? Was he able to reach out and catch himself before landing hard? His palms should be scraped. They weren't. But he noticed an area around his wrists. They had definitely been taped. There were bare patches where hair had been torn out and the skin was red. Case stood up and examined the tread mill rails. They were smooth until he got near the top and found what he had expected. There was a sticky area on both rails, about two inches wide, just on the sides and underneath, confirming to Case the victim's wrists had been taped there.

On a hunch, Case looked closely at the ceiling. He then examined the wall next to the treadmill. No small, freshly drilled holes. But then he saw it; what he was afraid, but not surprised to see. What he hoped would not be there to convince him they were in fact dealing with a possible unending string of murders by one person. But it was there. The killer's calling card. He knew it was the same killer, small, freshly drilled holes or not. He took a plastic evidence bag out of his pocket and scooped the broken, crumbly pieces into the bag and sealed it. He called in a forensics team. This was a murder investigation.

Case was about to leave the room when Rodriguez came in. He took a few minutes to look around and get an overall impression of the room and the body on the treadmill. He didn't see anything unusual, but he just got there.

"He's wearing workout clothes. Overdid it. I can see what she's talking about, doesn't seem like a candidate for a heart attack, but it happens. Seems pretty legit to me." He looked at his partner's face and saw he wasn't buying it. "You don't think it was a heart attack, do you?"

"The Captain's not going to like it. Anderson, Dodson and now this one. They're all tied together. We don't know how long this guy is going to keep killing," Case raised his voice, "and we have nothing!" He looked to the door and caught himself, hoping no one heard him. "We haven't moved off the dime. Our asses are still nailed to square one, and now the Captain is going to have to admit there's a serial psycho out there and we're still chasing out tails."

"What's got you so convinced?"

"Besides the fact this guy's wrists were taped to the treadmill," Case held up the evidence bag.

"What's that?"

"It was on the floor right there." Case showed him where he found it near the treadmill. Rodriguez was trying to figure out what he was looking at.

"Some kind of munchy. Candy? I've never seen it before, but I believe you're right. If that's what it is, it's planted. Doesn't fit with the victim, just like the others; so that would certainly seem to tie them together. What do you think that stuff is?"

The bag contained several pieces of what was about an inch long, tan colored, crunchy candy with a rough, cocoanut dusted surface. The pieces were all broken in half. Case managed to scoop most of the dry, powdery crumbs into the bag with the larger pieces.

"I haven't seen these in years. I used love them when I was a kid. I forget what they were called. I think…I think they were called Zagnuts. I might be wrong. We used to call them something else…I'll remember. Anyway, we'll check it out, but I got a feeling what they're called is not important, but why they're here, what they mean, has to be because, so far…" He didn't finish his sentence. Instead he told Rodriguez that the victim's wrists taped to the treadmill only supported the wife's claim she thought it was supposed to look like a heart attack.

"Let's go. You can fill me in on whatever Mrs. Turlock had to say on the way downtown."

Back in the living room Rodriguez spoke to Mrs. Turlock. "We're very sorry for your loss. My partner and I will be doing a thorough investigation. An evidence team is on their way. The officer here will take care of you and see to whatever you need right now."

"What can you tell me?" she insisted.

"We need to go back and start our work. You've been very helpful and we're going to find out everything we can and let you know just as soon as we have something to tell you." Rodriguez followed Case outside.

Inside the car Case asked, "So how helpful was she?"

"Not at all that I can see linking this to the other two. Nothing sounded familiar with the other two as far as schedules and routines that I remember. And there were no familial names. But I'll look for any tie-ins when we get back."

They left the scene on the way back downtown. "Well, like the Captain said, 'that's why we get the big bucks'. We gotta find something."

"I think we should talk to Dr. Leonard again. Maybe he can give us a whole different insight, something we're missing. There might be something right under our noses that we don't see," Rodriguez suggested.

"Trying to score pints with the Captain? Voodoo! That's all that is. We need to catch this guy with motive, means and opportunity, not read chicken bones." Case stopped. "Hey! Grab me the evidence bag with the broken pieces." Rodriguez retrieved it from the back seat and handed it to Case. "That's what we used to call these things, chicken bones!"

"See? Maybe there's an element of Voodoo here after all. You still think the Doc can't help us?"

"Don't be ridiculous. Chicken bones, Voodoo. Just a coincidence. The killer's telling us something. We have to find a common link, someone that knew all three, then the motive and all the rest will fall into place. Sherlock Holmes, that's who we need to consult, not Dr. Looney, I mean Leonard."

"I don't know. If we're bringing in an outside consultant, I think I'd rather go with Jane."

"Jane, who's Jane?" Case asked.

"Jane Goodall."

"The one who studied apes?"

"So, your circle extends beyond Dick Tracy."

"What's the ape lady got to do with it? You think we're chasing an escaped gorilla from the zoo?"

"Behavioral scientist. I'd rather consult her than Dick Tracy."

"Let's compromise with Columbo," Case offered.

"Who?"

"Lord, save us."

Chapter Thirteen

Back downtown they had already reported to the Captain, and Case and Rodriguez were sitting across from each other at their desks. The Captain had been none too pleased.

"There's nothing special in this for the media because they are *isolated* homicide investigations. I'm not going to tell the public that someone, we don't know who, is running around killing total strangers, we don't know why, and we don't know how. People are just turning up dead. I'm not going to scare the public and at the same time make us look like we don't know what…, and so far, we don't…, we're doing!"

"Except we know they're not isolated." Case said and put the evidence bag on the Captain's desk.

"What's this?" Captain Murdock picked up the bag and turned it around a couple times in front of his eyes.

"The killer's latest calling card," Case answered. "He left it at the Turlock scene, near the body, like the others."

"So what's it mean?"

"We don't know, yet. He's playing with us, some kind of game."

"Case, you too, Rodriguez," Captain Murdock fought to control his rising temper, "we don't have time for games. We have to have something solid. We need hard evidence. Where's the hard evidence?" Murdock insisted.

"That's the bad news, there isn't any," Case continued. "So far the guy hasn't made any mistakes. The good news is that these little mysteries he keeps planting tell us a lot. If it weren't for them, it appears he could go on as long as he wants and never get caught. With them, we know it is one person, there is a single reason behind it and I think he wants to let us know what that is, without getting caught. And because of that, he will make a mistake, they all do."

"But how many more killings?"

"No more. It stops here. He might be a genius in his planning, execution and get away, but the motive is there somewhere, and when we find it, his brilliant planning will be a house of cards that crashes down on his head."

"I have some bad news of my own," the Captain said. "DEA was here this morning. They're getting ready to set up a sting and they want to borrow man hours I don't have to spare."

Back at their desks, Case was feeling squeezed. He knew what that meant and he didn't like the sound of it.

"The Captain's going to loan us to DEA?" Rodriguez asked.

"Maybe not. Murdock will have to do some juggling. It depends on priorities, which detectives are backed up and which are getting clear. Believe me, I don't want any part of a DEA sting, but it better not even look like we're dragging our feet to avoid it. We gotta find something soon. There's a tie in somewhere, Rodriguez. I know there is and I think this guy knows we'll find it, because I think he wants us to. Like I told the Captain, he's not worried about getting caught. He just wants to tell us something with these stupid clues he keeps leaving."

"I just hope no more people have to die before we get it, amigo."

Three days later Case and Rodriguez were at their desks trying to find a connection that Case insisted was there. They went home each night and came back each morning. In between, they had worked the information they had, with nothing to show for it. Case felt like he was a hamster on a wheel, running but never moving. He had even dreamed one night that he was at the last crime scene, alone, on the victim's tread mill, in his work clothes and street shoes, trying hard to keep running, but the treadmill belt wouldn't move. He struggled, sweated, trying to force his feet to move the belt, but it wouldn't budge. And he couldn't get off. He was stuck to it. He couldn't move, trapped on the machine. And he was alone, all alone in the house. He looked around the room. It swayed slightly, the walls more wobbly than rigid, like heat waves on a desert. He looked towards the open door. He could feel he was all alone, the whole house empty. He called his partner. No answer. Where was Manny?

Three days and nothing to show for it. Case thought about his dream, then shook it off. He wasn't worried the guy was getting into his head; he wouldn't let him. He was determined this would not turn into one of those kind of cases. But it already had.

If one person was responsible for all three murders, as Case felt sure, what was the common link? What put them all into one group? That had to be the root of the motive. They cross checked everything and then started over and crossed checked everything again.

"We need to think outside the box, Sarge."

"I'll think anywhere you want."

"Maybe they were part of a bank heist. Maybe they haven't split the money yet and one of them is killing all the others to keep it for himself. I just checked. There have been 45 bank robberies in the L.A. area alone already this year. That could tie them all together."

"If that's it, why would the killer have any message for us at all? And why not just a quick, clean hit? From the bits and pieces that don't add up: Dodson's right hand secured but not her left, and she was shot in the right temple, the 'heart attack' on a treadmill that was not functional because the motor was tampered with, the first slow strangulation. Why go to all that trouble? He could have done it a lot easier."

"To throw us off?" Rodriguez offered.

"I don't make that group as a bank heist crew. Seems too far fe…"

Case's phone rang just then. It was the coroner's office. They had the results on the Turlock killing. Case was tempted to throw in something of it being 'about time' but he didn't want his frustration to get the better of him, and by extension, this particular case. And he knew he wasn't the only one with a workload.

Yes, his wrists had been duct taped to the tread mill rails. There were enough adhesive residues on both to definitely settle that particular point.

"But how did he die?" Case wanted to know. "There was obviously foul play; no way it was a heart attack."

"No, it wasn't. That's the strange part," the technician replied. "He died from asphyxiation as a result of cyanide gas."

"He was gassed?! How is that possible?"

"That's all I can tell you, detective."

Case got the implication. He knew it was a dumb thing to ask as soon as it came out of his mouth. Case asked a couple more questions then thanked the tech for calling ahead. "We'll look for the full report whenever you can send it over." And he disconnected. Case looked like he just found out a UFO abducted the President.

"Turlock died of cyanide gas?"

"They said his lungs were full of it."

"How is that possible?" Rodriguez mimicked Case.

Case looked at him without answering. Finally he said, "This case might look like it's getting crazier and crazier, but the answer's in here somewhere. We need to find the common thread, pull on it, and see what unravels."

"Let's use the easel," Rodriguez suggested.

"Why?"

"If we lay it all out, side by side, it might help. I'm a visual person."

"Not me. Facts and figures arrange themselves in here." He tapped his head. "I never use it."

Rodriguez looked at him. "Oh, you mean the easel. Mind

if I do? Just to possibly come at it from a different angle."

"Knock yourself out." Then Case suddenly stopped what he was doing. "Wait a second," he said. "You might be right. OK, let's set it up. Change the routine. Change directions." He got up and went to the statistics board. "I'll do it, might see something that's right under our noses."

"Are you getting hungry, Sarge? It's almost lunch."

"Let's work through lunch. I don't want to stop now. If you want to get sandwiches at the cafeteria it's on me while I set this up."

"How can I refuse an offer like that?"

Rodriguez was back fifteen minutes later and Case was leaning back in his chair with his hands laced behind his head, smiling at him.

"Rodriguez, you're a genius!"

"I knew it was only a matter of time before you admitted it."

"Maybe that's overstating it."

"Go with your first impression, Sarge."

"You mean when we first met?"

Rodriguez said a mental 'touché'. "So what did you find?"

"It's so obvious I don't know how we overlooked it. We were sloppy in not seeing it before. But your easel idea worked. It jumped right out at me."

"What?'

"You actually came up with the connection in the first place and I thought it was nothing. Remember when you noticed Shawna Anderson and Stephanie Dodson went to the same High School?"

"Yeah. What was it, Simi Valley?"

"Right. Go look at the High School Jim Turlock went to."

Rodriguez did. Then he turned around and looked at Case. "Simi Valley High School."

"That's the connection, Rodriguez. It can't be a coincidence anymore. A thread to a string, a string to a rope, then we hang the guy. Let's go. Grab your coat. Bring the sandwiches. We'll eat on the way."

Rodriguez followed Case out. "We're going to...?"

"Where else? Simi Valley High School."

Chapter Fourteen

Case and Rodriguez left Parker Center in downtown L.A. They picked up the 101 heading north under a bright sun, the early afternoon temp climbing rapidly as the San Fernando Valley prepared to double as a frying pan. They merged onto 5, The Golden State Freeway, and then, just past Pacoima, they picked up 118 heading west towards Simi Valley. Rodriguez had tried to engage Case in a little personal conversation again, since they would be in the car awhile. Case would have none of it, his upbeat mood from finally getting something to go on suddenly vanished as he retreated into his typical somber outlook. Rodriguez shrugged and turned on the radio, finding a Spanish station.

"Sure, I got lotsa family," Case said, turning off the radio.

Rodriguez was thrown off guard and did a double take. "Yeah, everybody's got cousins living someplace. I mean a close family, or you just don't want to talk about them?"

"What's to talk? You must be the nagger in your family."

"You know how to get a nagger off your back?"

"Yeah, give in. I don't give in." Case insisted.

They cruised through traffic. Outside – noise: traffic, car horns, an occasional siren, inside – silence. Rodriguez turned on the radio.

"How about a wife?" Case said, turning it off. "That close enough?"

"You got a wife?! I don't believe it."

"Yeah, the same kind most people have."

"What kind is that?"

"An ex-wife."

"Very funny. You two have any kids before she dumped you?"

"What makes you think she dumped me?"

Rodriguez didn't think that required an answer and just rolled his eyes at him.

Case conceded the point. "Yeah, we did. One of each."

"You mean a boy and a girl?"

"Are there any other kind?"

"So, where are they? Either one of them live around here?"

"Uh, make that three," Case corrected himself.

"Three what, kids? You forgot one?"

"Yeah, I guess. The quiet one. Never said much, just played video games."

"Just never was much of a family man, huh?"

Case looked over at Rodriguez. "You know, or will know, how it is. The job."

Cruising by Granada Hills, the temperature was still rising as it approached 1:30 PM. They were far enough inland that mountains blocked any possible relief from the ocean air.

"If the job ever came between me and my family, I'd quit. I love kids. You know we have two and we're just getting started. You didn't tell me where yours are."

"Why don't we drop it?"

"Suit yourself," and Rodriguez reached for the radio.

"The older boy wants to be an actor."

"I'm sorry. So I guess he's close by, in L.A. somewhere?"

"Not a film actor. He says he wants to be a 'legitimate actor', on the stage. He moved to New York 7 or 8 years ago. He's on the verge of breaking in, anyway, that's what he told me."

"When was that?"

"I don't know, awhile ago. But I believe him, stubborn kid. Would never quit 'til he got what he wants."

"What's his name?"

"Ron. He was pretty good in high school. I told him he ought to try college sports, but he didn't want to. I told him the military wasn't a bad life. He looked at me like I said he should take up 14th French literature. He graduated high school and the next day left for New York and I haven't seen him since. Stubborn kid."

Rodriguez looked over at Case, thought about it, then asked, "What about your daughter?"

"Lives somewhere up in Oregon."

"Where in Oregon?"

"Wenatchee, I think."

"I'm pretty sure Wenatchee's in Washington. Consuela and I took the kids on a road trip one summer up to Leavenworth, a little Bavarian style Christmas village in the mountains near Wenatchee. Really nice trip. Had a great time."

"Leavenworth? That's a Federal pen."

"Yeah, same name, totally different place. They get a lot of kidding about that. So, your daughter, you're not sure where she lives?"

Case shifted in his seat. "I told you, Oregon."

Rodriguez just looked at him.

"The town slips my mind. A little place near the mountain."

Rodriguez lifted his eyebrow.

"Uh, Mt. Rainier. Near Mt. Rainier." Case knew he should know this.

"That's in Washington, too."

"Mt. Adams?"

"Still Washington," Rodriguez said.

"Mt. Hood? Dammit! She's busy, doesn't have time to write with the kid and all."

"Oh! You're a grandfather. What kind?" to mimic Case. "A boy or a girl?"

Case looked in his rear view mirror and suddenly changed lanes.

"What's its name?"

Case turned on the radio.

They arrived in Simi Valley, surrounded by pretty much

nothing, just the Santa Susana Mountains to the north and east and the Simi Hills to the south. It took them a little over an hour. The temperature was in the upper 80's when they arrived at the high school on Cochrane Street. Rodriguez had done some research and filled Case in. Simi Valley High was an old school dating back to 1920. As the first high school in Simi Valley, it eventually grew to over 50 acres with an offering of an impressive curriculum which included special features such as forensics teams, a mock trial team, medical field entry, Thespian and other societies, also an award winning music program and three business computer labs, digital photo labs, and science and language labs, all housed in three instructional quads each with administration areas. The sports department matriculated many Major League Baseball players, just a part of their athletics curriculum. SVHS was a California Distinguished school three times in a row. With all that could it also have produced a murderer? Case wondered. It came in only at the middle of the pack in *MSNBC's Top 1,000 High Schools* at #555.

Like Dickens's *Tale of Two Cities,* the best of times and the worst of times. That's how high school was for some students. Then there was high school for Paul Underwood Kirby. Compared to that experience, those in the 'worst of times' group should have felt lucky they had it so good. If Fate, or Nature, or the Muses love a practical joke, they had centuries to practice before finally perfecting it in the person of Paul Underwood Kirby.

Paul Underwood Kirby, he was a total wreck. A mess. A walking, breathing, social disaster. Although below average height, one hardly noticed when compared to his more striking physical features. He actually looked like he had just stepped off an easel in an art studio where the students were given the assignment of drawing the most outlandish caricature they could come up with. A cross between Mortimer Snerd, Howdy Doody and Sponge Bob is a good place to begin in describing Paul Underwood Kirby. Actually, that pretty much sums it up. Throw in a terrible complexion, very thick glasses, and large ears to go with the afore referenced buck teeth and overbite. His speech pattern included not only a stutter, but a pronounced lisp. He wasn't a disaster waiting to happen, it happened. And to top it off, literally, his hair was bright orange, not red. A total walking, breathing, social disaster.

None of this, however, would be permanent. In not too many years, every one of the physical characteristics, that made this unfortunate individual the flame attracting the moths of torment and abuse, would be gone. There was, however, one ironic statistic, that of course would never change: his birthday. Paul Underwood Kirby was born on February 29, 1984. It wasn't important, didn't really mean anything, just an odd fact about a seemingly odd individual. But as to his physical traits, he would either grow out of, overcome by force of will or alter them all. The metamorphosis would one day be complete. But that was still years in the future. For grades 9, 10, 11 and 12, that was a million years away. High school for Paul Underwood Kirby would seem like an eternity.

Unfortunately, he was completely unprepared for what to expect in high school. He had gone to a grade school, K-8, where he experienced none of what high school had in store for him. For one thing, his appearance had not yet 'peaked'. For another, it was a much diversified grade school. The students grew together and were more accepting of each other. When abusive teasing did occasionally occur, the teachers were much less tolerant.

So Paul Underwood Kirby walked into a buzz saw. He was initially wide-eyed and eager to start high school. The school portrayed itself as clean cut with well mannered and friendly, smiling students carrying books to their next exciting class. For the most part that was actually pretty close to the truth and Paul Underwood Kirby was looking forward to being a part of it. But it only took a few harassers to turn an eager young student into something far, far different. His change didn't happen all at once. He tried to cope for years. But when it finally became clear that the cruelty would never stop, and it pushed him across an invisible line of no return, he was changed; changed forever.

The bullies and practical jokers in school were merciless. He was their favorite target. In fact, all other potential targets got a complete reprieve. With Paul Underwood Kirby available, there was no need to pick on anyone else. He was just too much fun. He was the flavor of the month, and it was always his month. They were way beyond slapping a "Kick Me" sign on his back. That was the Wright Bros. and this was the age of supersonic transport. The challenge, for that part of the student body so inclined, was to become more and more creative; to outdo one another, always striving for a higher level of sophistication and humiliation. It made their task almost too easy because of the innocence and gullibility of their target.

First we must name our creature. They went through many nicknames. As the old ones wore out, new ones were introduced. He got his first nickname when one clever student did a little investigating and found out his middle name. Now with his set of three initials, it was an easy step to add an 'E' and as a freshman he was known as 'PUKE'. That's what got everything started. Pretty soon someone crazy glued some practical joke rubber puke to his desktop in math class. Then someone crazy glued some practical joke rubber puke to the top of his head. He had to cut his hair to get it off. Of course, no one saw who did these things which encouraged more and more 'practical jokes'.

In his sophomore year, he gained a new nickname that

gave rise to so many pranks, it stuck for awhile. Paul Underwood Kirby's 3rd period class was a language lab. The subject was nonstandard forms of communication. Often the students were given impromptu homework assignments and were then to present their work the next morning, individually, before class, which was supposed to improve spontaneous creativity. This gave one student the idea of creating a fake assignment, and switching it with the real one in Paul Underwood Kirby's notebook. It was easy for a compatriot to knock his books off the desk, distract him and for the other to make the switch.

His name came up fourth the next morning. He was a little confused at the first three reports because his assignment was far different. The assignment heading was Non-Verbal Communication. Well, that was *his* particular assignment. He was to demonstrate how South American spider monkeys, known to be very high strung and excitable, communicated in a dispute over food distribution.

At first the class sat in stunned silence, most of them gaping with wide eyes, the teacher included, as Paul Underwood Kirby jumped and cavorted around the room, throwing papers and shrieking, like,... like a South American spider monkey arguing over a banana, which he unfortunately brought for a prop. The perpetrators of the plot couldn't believe how well it worked, even to the added touch of an actual banana, and unable to hold it in, broke out laughing which broke the spell of shock. Within two seconds the whole class was laughing uncontrollably.

At first Paul Underwood Kirby thought he must be doing pretty well, but when he saw how hard the class was laughing, some holding their sides, some falling out of their chairs and almost all pointing at him, he stopped. It ended with no one fessing up as the author of the counterfeit assignment when the teacher asked to see it.

That's how Paul Underwood Kirby acquired a new nickname which stuck with him for a long time. The nickname was Bobo. This came about when a circus came to town with, among other featured attractions, Bobo, a gorilla that was trained to do various stunts. Bobo was very popular. The distinction between a gorilla and a South American spider monkey was lost on whoever tagged Paul Underwood Kirby with his latest nickname, as it was with the rest of the students that put it to use. It soon caught on and spread like the latest teenage fad.

Wherever Paul Underwood Kirby went on campus, to and from classes, in the halls, and in the cafeteria, the shout could be heard, "Oh no, it's Bobo!" It became a mantra around the school. Students even greeted each other with the call. There was danger of it becoming even more popular than Hermie, or Herman the Pioneer, the actual school mascot.

From there the next stage was to put the appellation to use in practical ways. Once again, the inner circle competed amongst themselves for originality and creativity. It didn't matter if it was a whole new theme, or variations within the same theme; they congratulated each other on their cleverness. One student filled the upper portion of Paul Underwood Kirby's locker with bananas. When he opened it in the hallway during the busy time between classes, the bananas came falling down on his head.

At one school assembly, a student rigged the loudspeakers in the auditorium to play, *"Yes, We Have No Bananas."* It took 15 minutes to get it shut off and the student body back under control, but laughing and snickering kept breaking out throughout most of the assembly. As everyone knew, it was futile to even attempt to find out who did it; warnings and threats weren't even offered.

There seemed to be no end to monkey and banana pranks. On one occasion someone bought 'a barrel of monkeys', the colorful plastic monkeys, all of the same mold, that attach and hang from one another in an endless chain. The student, with a few cohorts, draped them all around the walls near the ceiling, like bunting, of the 3rd period language class. They timed it during the interval between classes having arranged for the teacher to receive an urgent call to the admin building.

On another occasion one of the first students to file in the room as class began had a yellow, plastic object under his jacket. It was a 6' banana that inflated like a life raft. He put it on Paul Underwood Kirby's seat as he passed by his desk. The desk was the type that students slid in from the left side with an arm rest on the right. The prankster pulled the plug on the canister and the banana inflated in 3 seconds, wedging itself between the seat and the desk. It was near the front of the classroom, and as the rest of the students filed in, they reacted in the predictable way.

Within a few minutes each student had found and was sitting in his or her seat. All but one. That was a subtle side effect of the prank. Not only was there the obvious monkey reference, but the object of the joke, Paul Underwood Kirby, was forced to remain standing, since his seat was occupied by a 6' inflated, plastic banana.

Everyone watched him, wondering what he would do. Would he cry? Would he run out of the room? Would he go berserk and start throwing things? Would he throw a tantrum? Because, that was part of the intrigue. Everyone knew that Paul Underwood Kirby never did any of those things. He always just sort of took it, apparently not knowing how to react. But they believed he would break sometime. Everyone had their limit. Even a dam would crack if enough pressure were applied. It's not that anyone had anything against Paul Underwood Kirby personally, they didn't even know him. It was just part of the game. The one that came up with the prank that finally caused Paul Underwood Kirby to explode would be some kind of a hero. That person would have bragging rights. He'd be famous.

Teenagers quickly tire of things and move on to new distractions. That would normally be good news for Paul Underwood Kirby. But in his case it didn't work out that way. It just meant when an old nickname and reference for torment no longer had the same punch, it was discarded, giving rise to a whole new subject 'for fun'. 'Puke' and 'Bobo' were retired and replaced by Porky, for Porky Pig, in reference to the stutter both had in common. The stutter kept him from reacting, knowing that would only make things worse. 'Porky' brought on innumerable situations of embarrassment. As time went on, almost all his other traits were highlighted in one way or another. Practical jokes, teasing and all forms of harassment, some of it vicious, continued to make Paul Underwood Kirby's life in high school something no one envied. He lived, always on the edge of a precipice, in constant fear of what was coming next.

Eventually, most students did tire of the whole topic of Paul Underwood Kirby. It had run its course, like an infectious disease that, in time, will play itself out. But not completely. There is always a dormant strain somewhere. The remnant few who were determined to see him crack began to take it personally, as if he beat them at their own game. The longer he went without breaking down, the more determined they were to break him. And then a couple things happened, unintended consequences of the whole Paul Underwood Kirby episode at Simi Valley High School.

The first was Paul Underwood Kirby's change. The few remaining students still committed to making that happen accomplished just that. But the change was not apparent. It only happened on the inside. When it finally did happen, there was nothing left of the old Paul Underwood Kirby; no remnant, not a single firing neuron in his brain that was the same as it was before. Also gone, of course, was the innocence, the eagerness to learn and grow and fit in at school, but gone also was any capacity or inclination towards compassion, pity or mercy.

Years later, the recipients of his revenge would suffer, paying a high price, because of the lack of these emotions. At no time would remorse ever find a place on the stage of Paul Underwood Kirby's consciousness. Revenge was all that would matter. It was his sole purpose in life. Revenge was his alpha and his omega, leaving him without friends and relationships. And he had no problem with that. He didn't miss anything because nothing could or did distract him. In all that he was happy, the contentment people have when they find their purpose in life. Without purpose life is a desert, with purpose life is a garden. Soon, Paul Underwood Kirby's garden would be in full bloom.

The other unforeseen outcome of the tormenters' persistence was that Paul Underwood Kirby's perception of the source of his distress gradually shifted from the student body in general, to certain individuals in particular. This was partly because they took less care to conceal themselves and partly because they didn't care. School would be ending soon and they would be moving on. They just wanted to get a reaction out of Paul Underwood Kirby.

There was no single incident that made a graduated Paul Underwood Kirby entirely different from the freshman Paul Underwood Kirby, but one incident was at least as responsible as any other.

As graduation time grew near, so did the last major school dance before the Senior Prom. It was the Sadie Hawkins or backwards dance, where the girls asked the boys. Of course Paul Underwood Kirby knew he would not be asked. He had never been asked. Obviously, no girl liked him, well, it was always statistically *possible*, in a relativity sense, that *someone* did, but if they did, they would be too afraid to ask him and set themselves up as a target. Why was he even thinking about it? Why? It was that one chance in a million. That chance to buy the winning lottery ticket. As Ernest L. Thayer pointed out, "…hope…springs eternal in the human breast." And that's what the PUKE squad, as they now called themselves, was counting on.

The PUKE squad consisted of two boys and two girls. They were only 'C' students, barely. So, in the classroom, by comparison, smart kids only made them look bad. Outside the classroom, they shined in their own right, each excelling in a different sport or other activity. But they were not prone to thinking philosophically, so they put their heads together and came up with a plan.

One of them noticed that there indeed was a girl, plain to be sure, but she would have to be to make this plan plausible. She never seemed to join in the laughter at their victim's expense, maybe felt sorry for him, maybe even liked him a little. It was worth a try and knowing Mortimer [current nickname] like they did, he was just gullible enough for it to work.

They arranged for Susie Gilroy to 'ask' Paul Underwood Kirby to the backwards dance. It was a simple job to slip an invitation from her into his locker about a week before the dance. One of the girls wrote it to make it look convincing. They calculated the best time for him to pick her up. Then all they had to do was sit back and watch the fun.

For a week leading up to the dance the PUKE squad noticed a definite change in Paul Underwood Kirby. He actually seemed happy. They never saw him like that before. He seemed oblivious to all the teasing. He must have noticed Susie, too, but thought it was a waste of time to try and talk to her. He passed her a couple of times in the hall during the week leading up to the dance and had a class with her. He understood why she didn't speak to him. It didn't matter. All that mattered was that they were going to the dance together!

After a week of excitation and anticipation, the night of the dance was finally here. Paul Underwood Kirby showed up at precisely the indicated time on the invitation, and he was holding it, when he knocked on the door of Susie Gilroy's house. Susie's mother answered the door.

"Hello M..m..m..m.. mith ith Gilroy," Paul Underwood Kirby lisped and stuttered. "I'm h..h..h..here t..t..t..to p..p..p..pick up Thuthie for the d..d..d..dance."

"The dance?" Mrs. Gilroy was confused. "Susie's not here. She already left with her date."

Paul Underwood Kirby was confused, too. "B..b..but," and he started to hold up the invitation.

"What's that?"

He sensed, and then he knew. He had been had. Again...again...again. Embarrassment, humiliation, anger. All too familiar. He wished there was a hole in the porch under his feet. A deep, dark hole to fall into and disappear; vanish forever. But he was still standing there. He didn't know what to do or how to get out of there.

"I..i..it's n..n..noth..." He lowered his hand with the invitation.

Mrs. Gilroy said "I'm sorry." Somehow, that made it worse. Mr. Invisible. He wished he could just vanish into thin air, not have to turn around and walk back down the path to the sidewalk. He closed his eyes and stood there for another few seconds. He opened his eyes to find that nothing had changed. He would still have to turn around and walk. He felt tears start to form, but fought them back. That would only make a hopeless situation worse. With no choice, he turned and started towards the sidewalk. Halfway there he heard laughter and then saw a car zoom by, the windows down, the horn honking and four people inside, two girls and two boys, laughing, loud enough to hear over the sound of the car.

Chapter Fifteen

The two detectives from L.A. found the main Admin building, parked and got out into the dry heat of the afternoon. They entered the building and approached a busy looking woman in her mid-fifties, sitting behind the main counter that ran the width of the room. She was talking on the phone and did not look up as Case and Rodriguez stopped in front of her. She wore a grey pants suit; her hair was cut short, not unattractive. The name on the 6" rectangular plaque slid into the gold metal holder read Ms. Johnson. Waiting patiently, both detectives looked around the large room, each thinking how little high schools have changed since they went. It was all so familiar: the posters and notices on the walls, reminders of upcoming events, the card files, the few students seated, looking bored, waiting to see someone for some reason.

Finally, the woman finished her call and hung up. "May I help you?" she asked, neutrally.

"Good day, Ms. Johnson," Case answered. Showing his ID he said, "I'm Detective Case. This is my partner Detective Rodriguez. We're conducting an investigation," he avoided using the word 'murder', "and would like to talk to the school principal. We don't have an appointment, but hoped it would be possible for a quick interview. It won't take long."

"I'm not Ms. Johnson," said the harried woman, who so far hadn't smiled. "I'm filling in for her this week. I'll see if Ms. Gaynor, she's the school principal, is busy." She picked up the phone, punched four numbers, waited, and then said, "Ms. Gaynor, there are two police detectives here that would like to see you." "I think they said Los Angeles." She looked up at Case who nodded his head. "Yes," she said into the phone, "Los Angeles." "Okay, I'll send them in." The substitute for Ms. Johnson hung up and said to no one in particular, "She has a few minutes before a 3:15 appointment. You can go in. It's through that door," she said, pointing over her left shoulder. "Second door on the right."

"Thank you," Rodriguez said and both detectives went to see the principal.

Case knocked once on the principal's door and entered without waiting for a response, Rodriguez following. Case made the same introduction as a few minutes before, once again, both showing their ID. When they entered, Ms. Gaynor was seated behind her desk, which was neat and uncluttered. Behind it were her college diploma and other certificates. She was in her middle thirties, conservatively but attractively dressed in a Navy blue administrative suit. She stood up and smiled, shaking hands with both men.

She introduced herself and asked, "How can I help you gentlemen?"

Case answered. "We're following a lead in an investigation we're working on. A murder investigation."

"Murder…investigation?"

"Yes, we're homicide detectives."

"Oh! I'll be what help I can. My secretary mentioned I have a 3:15 appointment. Will this take long? I suppose I could cancel if necessary."

"It shouldn't. We just have a few questions."

"You think this might involve any of my students?" She went back and sat behind her desk. There were already two chairs facing the desk and Case sat in the right one, Rodriguez in the left.

"Not any current students," Case answered. "We're conducting three separate murder investigations and we think they may all be linked to one person, responsible for all three."

Ms. Gaynor looked very concerned as she shifted her attention between both detectives.

Rodriguez took over. "As my partner said, we don't

believe it involves any current students. The reason we're here is because the victims were all alumni of this school, and at the same time. All three were in the same graduating class of 2002."

"That was ten years ago! What do you expect to find now?"

"We're not sure what we will find," Case replied. "We don't even know what we're looking for, but there's a pretty strong reason to be looking here. We're hoping to find someone who can shed some light on it, someone who might have known all three and might know a reason why someone would want to kill them. What we're looking for is a motive."

"But I'm sure after that long there would not be anyone here that remembers them. Obviously, our current students, the oldest, were barely in elementary school. And, quite frankly, I doubt a single member of our faculty was here then. Normal turnover accounts for about 10% per year and we recently went through some major faculty relocations. There were general reassignments. I haven't been here quite three years myself."

Case said, "If you could point us in any direction you might think would be helpful, we would appreciate it." Then Case started to rise. "Well, I guess we can nose around on our own. Thanks for your time."

"Wait! Uh, before you go, let me think. I really don't

want you bringing this up with the students and upsetting them. As I said, there is no way they could possibly be familiar with circumstances connected to students of so many years ago. Why don't I have Miss Caruthers, you met her when you came in, call Personnel for you and see if there is any current faculty who were here at that time, and also any staff personnel, you know, maintenance or security or any other staff? Or if you would like, you can drop in at Personnel yourselves. I'll call them right now to expect you and ask them to help in any way they can. It's just across the hall, the second door to the right."

"Thank you," Rodriguez answered. "If you make that call we'll go to Personnel right now." He gave a side glance to Case who made a small nod.

Ms. Gaynor made the call to Personnel informing them the two detectives would be there momentarily and to render any assistance possible. She hung up. "They're expecting you. You'll let me know what you find? I would like to know so as to be aware of what impact this may have on the school."

"We don't want to make any waves, either," Case said. "And we'll stop back before leaving campus."

Out in the hall Rodriguez asked, "What do you think?"

"She doesn't want to get involved, wants us to go away."

"She seemed helpful enough. Just didn't have anything to offer. You think she's holding back?"

"No. Like I said, she just wants us to go away from her quiet school and not upset the equilibrium."

"Why do you think so?"

"She didn't even ask the names of the students that were murdered."

In the Personnel office Case and Rodriguez found out that the principal was right in her assessment that no current teachers taught at SVHS in 2002. They were a little surprised to find out no one else on the school payroll was working here then. They were told that the school had gone through some cut backs and early retirements just in the last year. They settled for second best: a list of names.

It wasn't long before Case and Rodriguez were back in Ms. Gaynor's office. She was relieved, but had the good grace not to make it evident, that the two detectives were leaving, as they had no one to interview on the school premises. The list they acquired of faculty and personnel, present at the time their three murder victims attended SVHS, could be run down from last known addresses.

"One more thing," Case said. "The class of 2002, they would be having their 10 year reunion this year. Isn't that true?"

"Well...yes, they are, this fall."

"And that means all the people who knew the victims best, the students in their class, that saw them everyday, that went to school with them, that were in their classes, that spent hours with them everyday, will conveniently all be together at one time in one place."

Ms. Gaynor didn't like this turn of the conversation. "Of course, not everyone goes to the reunion..." She looked at Rodriguez, then back at Case. "But I would really protest your showing up at their first big reunion, a happy time for memories, meeting old friends again after years, to conduct a murder investigation! I'm sure that would ruin it."

Rodriguez put in "It shouldn't have to come to that. Our job is to prevent another tragic death. If we could get a year book of the graduating class of 2002, look at their activities, interests, maybe it'll point us in the right direction, to people that were close to them. Progress from those interviews should hopefully make going to the reunion unnecessary."

The principal looked relieved. "Of course. I'll call the person in charge of archives. We have year books dating back to the late '30's. Later years have many leftover books. I'm sure you can take one with you."

"This is a four year school, isn't it?" Case asked.

"That's right."

"We'll need the books for the next three years. If there was one person responsible for all three deaths, and if that person was a student here, then that student would have attended at the same time as the three victims, but not necessarily in the same class, so we'll need those books if he was in a class behind them."

Ms. Gaynor said, "That's a lot of 'ifs'."

"Until we get answers, that's all we have. What about those books?"

Case and Rodriguez were back on 118 heading east, retracing their route back to downtown L.A. They still had better than an hour on their shift and both were anxious to work, probably even some OT. Rodriguez put the printout from Personnel in the back seat and was looking through one of the four books Ms. Gaynor had graciously acquired for them.

 "When we get back," Case was saying, "you start with the year books, they were your idea." He wanted to add 'and a good one' but there'll be plenty of credit to spread around when they crack the case. "I'll start on the printout."

They did not get too far with their investigation before Capt. Murdock called them into his office.

"What's up, Capt.?" Case asked.

"Have a seat, both of you."

Case and Rodriguez looked at each other as they followed the instruction.

"I'll get right to the point. The word has come down. You guys are on TDY; DEA surveillance." The Capt. immediately held up his hand, palm out, in anticipation of their reactions, more to the point, Case's reaction. "I know all the arguments; I know what you're going to say. I can let you blow it out just to let the steam off but it won't make any difference. It's out of my control, orders from above. The Feds say this is *super* important, yeah, what isn't? Everybody's working on something important. They've got over two years into this one, untold man hours and they say on the verge of the biggest bust of the decade. And I've heard it all before."

Case still couldn't sit still. "We're trying to stop a serial killer. We finally got some kind of a break."

"There's a break in the case you haven't told me about?"

"Well, not really a break, just a lead, but something to work with. We have something that connects all three victims. Now we need to find someone who can point us to a motive."

"Look, I told you this isn't a serial killer, not outside this office yet. And I want it solved before this guy makes it four and the press gets ahold of it. So you're preaching to the choir. But there's nothing I can do. Interagency cooperation counts for a lot these days and we're supposed to get some real benefit down the road."

Case knew it was pointless arguing. The Capt. was right, just blowing off steam. "How long is this TDY supposed to last?"

"That's the good news. They think whatever happens is going to happen sometime this weekend. You guys are on for 6 to 2AM starting Friday, tomorrow. Yeah, an eight hour. If we had the manpower we'd run 4-6's, but we have to do 3-8's. If it goes all weekend, which it probably will, Sam is picking up the tab for the OT. Hopefully you'll be back at your desks bright and early Monday morning. So go home now and report back tomorrow ready for the 6 PM shift. You'll need to be here for a 5:00 briefing. Everybody knows it stinks so there's no point in going over it. Just be ready tomorrow and hopefully it'll be over sooner than later."

Outside the Captain's office Case said to Rodriguez

"Let's get here nine tomorrow morning. We can put in a day before the surveillance."

"You're getting gung ho in your old age."

"I don't want to wait until Monday now that we finally have something. You can catch up on your sleep later if that's what you're worried about. If you need 40 winks tomorrow night, I can cover for you."

"Just trying to ride you a little, Sarge. Actually, I'm way ahead of you. I was thinking about taking the year books home tonight and start looking through them to see if anything jumps out. But I might take you up on your offer."

The two detectives left the building heading for their cars without a backward glance, one of them with several books under his arm.

Chapter Sixteen

Case arrived at Parker Center at 8:50 Friday morning and rode the elevator up. When he got to his desk Rodriguez was already there. Case hung up his coat and sat down.

"Who's gung ho now?" Case asked.

"I've only been here five minutes. I wanted to get another look at the murder books after going through the school annuals. I spent two hours on them last night and looking at the brief bios on the victims, something seemed odd. I wanted to check it out."

"What's that?"

"Grab the book on Shawna Anderson. She was the one that died of some kind of strangulation, right?"

"That's right, here's her file. What did you find?"

Rodriguez flipped through the file until he found the coroner's report. "It might just be a coincidence, but you and coincidences are like nature and vacuums, you both abhor the other."

"OK, so give."

"So Anderson died from strangulation and her bio under her class picture reads 'solo vocalist in choir class'.

Apparently she was a good singer and the way she died...closing off her windpipe. She had good pipes. The killer stopped her pipes."

Case leaned forward. "What about Stephanie Dodson, what does it say about her?"

Rodriguez had the page marked with a slip of paper and turned to it. " 'Expert marksman'."

Case looked at Rodriguez. "She was shot in the head."

Rodriguez nodded. "Two for two." He turned to the marked page for Turlock. " 'Track star'."

"Died on a treadmill," Case said.

Rodriguez flipped through the Turlock file. "But it doesn't say he died of a heart attack on the treadmill like we thought at first. He was gassed, remember?"

"How was he gassed? The treadmill's motor didn't work; it was tampered with. The Dodson murder indicates this guy set up some kind of elaborate murder devices, killing them without exactly doing it himself. Maybe the treadmill somehow was rigged to release the gas. His death was still connected to running. The guy is just playing with everyone, us included. He's leaving bits of things that must have some kind of meaning, and killing in ways to amuse himself. This should save us a lot of time." And then it just slipped out. "Good work."

"Either one of us would have found it."

"But you did. And time is everything. The sooner we connect the dots this guy seems intent on leaving us, the sooner this guy goes away for good. 'Time is of the essence' I always say."

"I've never heard you say that."

"So I'll start." Case put away the printout from the school personnel office. "You have a lead. We might as well both work on that. Any ideas to point us to a suspect?"

"If they died by way of things they excelled at, maybe it involves jealousy, someone they beat out for a first place slot getting back at them. Or maybe they cheated somehow."

"Maybe. But then it seems unlikely there's only one killer. They seem like unrelated talents for one person to have, and then taking revenge because of them. This looks like the work of one person."

Rodriguez sat back and thought about it. "It could be a cover, a smoke screen. Two of the victims aren't the killer's real target. It's like the bomblets a plane tosses out so a heat seeking missile doesn't know which one to chase."

"Then why give clues for us to follow? It we take all the trails, it'll take longer, but we would still be on the right one eventually. No, I don't think the methods indicate the motive. Following them will lead to blind alleys. The true motive to point us to the killer is something else."

"So what do you think these three death/bio connections mean, because whatever they mean, they're obviously not coincidences."

"Right. That's obvious. I think he wants us to follow them so he can lead us around by the nose."

"To throw us off?"

"Maybe.'

"So, what are we going to do?" Rodriguez asked.

"We're going to follow them."

"But..."

"I could have spent the whole afternoon on the printout of past employees and staff, turning up nothing but 'moved from area' 'current whereabouts unknown' 'deceased'. We could spend weeks narrowing the search down to someone who even remembers the victims, let alone remembers details that could help. Staff and faculty just don't get that involved with their students' personal lives. Friends they hung out with have what we need. But our helpful principal doesn't want us upsetting the alumni. And she thought we wouldn't go to the obvious, alumni Web sites?

"She gave us the annuals, which show everyone in school at that time."

"After you suggested them. And they give us no help with locating anyone."

"Alright, so let's pull up Web sites for locating alumni. And you still want to follow the misdirection the killer laid down?"

"Why not? Even starting from scratch just with the students, it's a big field. We have to start someplace. We don't have a motive yet, so starting with students in the victim's same areas of interest is as good as any. If we stay in this house of mirrors long enough, eventually we'll find the way out."

Rodriguez thought about the irony. "We're more inclined to follow info from the killer, who shouldn't be helping us, than we are from the school principal, who should be."

"Funny how that works. Like Art Linkletter used to say: 'People Are Funny'."

"Art who?"

Rodriguez checked the SVHS annual for people, starting with the graduating class, with any connection to Glee, choir, even drama, that might have known Shawna

Anderson. Case did the same thing with sports and athletics, starting with the previous year book. After compiling his list, Rodriguez turned to the computer Web site to find anyone on his list with whom he could make personal contact. While Rodriguez used the computer, Case continued his list with the seniors. After more than two hours Rodriguez was able to speak with just two women and one man who were in Shawna's class, also in a school production with her and remembered her well enough to talk about her. None, however, had stayed in contact with her after school. Only one was aware of her murder, all were shocked by it and none could give any reason why anyone would want to do it.

Case's luck wasn't much better. He started with the members of the track team as the most obvious starting point. The third name on his list was a man living in Downey. He worked for a law firm there. Case called the firm and asked for a Mr. Langsford. Case identified himself and the secretary came back on the line, having checked with the attorney, and advised Case he was available and she would connect him right now.

"I have a few minutes, Detective. I have a luncheon engagement, but I have a few minutes yet before I need to leave."

"Thank you. This shouldn't take long. I'm a homicide detective with the LAPD."

"Yes, my secretary mentioned that, but I'm afraid I'm not that kind of lawyer. I only handle torts."

"I'm not calling about your legal expertise. We are investigating possible connections to multiple homicides. I believe you might have known all three victims and most probably at least one of them."

"You think *I'm* somehow connected?"

"Sir, let me give you their names and see if any of them mean anything to do."

"OK."

Case reeled them off. "Shawna Anderson, Stephanie Dodson and James Turlock. Do any of them mean anything to you?"

"Not at all. You think one of them should? Which one?"

"We're looking into possible motives."

"Why do you think I could be of any help?"

"Did you graduate Simi Valley High in 2002?"

"Yes, that's right."

"So did all three of the people I just mentioned. They were in your graduating class."

"As I remember, that was a pretty big class. Must have

been four or five hundred."

"516."

"OK, so I couldn't possibly know all those people."

"That's right, but I'm only interested in these three."

"It sounds like you have a pretty big job ahead of you Detective. To call 513 people to see who knew the other three."

"What I'm looking for is a thread, to find someone to shed light on at least one of the murder victims and see where that leads us. And like I said, I think you're a good prospect for someone that knew at least one of them."

"Yes, you did. And I asked which one am I supposed to have known?"

"None of the names sounds even vaguely familiar?"

"Should one?"

"James Turlock should."

"And why is that?"

"Because you were on the track team with him." There was a silence on the other end of the line. "Mr. Langsford?"

"James Turlock... Yes, of course. Jim. Jim Turkey. That's

what we called him. It didn't really mean anything, but everybody had to have a nickname on the team. I completely forgot about him. He joined the team late in the year. Maybe that's how he got his nickname. Must have joined the team sometime in November, and the similarity to his name."

"They're not that similar."

"*High school*," Langsford responded suggestively.

"Can you think of any reason someone would have wanted to kill him?"

"Jim? I had completely forgotten about him. But it has been ten years. A different world, high school. For all that, all we had were classes, school sport rivalries, buddies and chasing girls. And we think we'll be buddies forever. Then we get out into the real world, our careers and interests take us in completely different directions and we hardly even think about each other anymore. Let alone stay in touch."

"I guess that's what reunions are for."

"I guess. Come to think of it I think something came in recently about that. Sure. Our tenth will be this fall."

"Are you planning to attend?"

"Me? No. Too big a caseload right now. Maybe next time."

"So I was asking about a murder motive. Any serious grudges, serious enough to get even?"

"After all this time? Would anyone angry enough to kill wait this long? You'd think whatever it was, he would have gotten over it long before now."

"Maybe. Because the murderer left so little behind, it looks meticulously planned, researched to learn habits and routines, and executed, in all three cases." Case kept talking to keep the lawyer thinking and speculating. He might still offer something. "There are other indications he could have spent a long time in preparation, details I can't go into."

"I'm sorry I can't be of any assistance. Why do you even think it was anyone from school?"

"Right now that's the only thing that ties the three together. That's something we're not accepting as a coincidence. There are other aspects that point us to the school, which is why I called you."

"Because we were both on the track team? I don't se…"

"I know you're busy Mr. Langsford. Let me just ask you one more thing. You said Jim Turlock joined the team late in the year. We know he was not a late transferee to the school. He had attended it since 9th grade. Did he suddenly develop an interest in track?"

"I don't kn...wait. I do remember. There was some controversy. You're right. He didn't transfer in late and he didn't just develop an interest. I remember, he had tried out several times but never made the team. Sometimes only a fraction of a second too slow eliminates you from a slot. There were only so many slots and he was off by whatever it was. Once he was on the team, I believe it was relays, he was pretty good.

 "So what was the controversy?""

 "Well, the reason he got on the team, was not because he got any faster, but someone else had to drop out. That was the controversy. It wasn't even an actual controversy, just rumors. The member who dropped out, boy, I'll have to really think to come up with his name; he got in an accident, well, a fight. Yes, that's,... now I remember it... what happened. Just one of those incidents that happen and then are long gone and forgotten. And I remember his name, Bill Richardson."

"Councilman Richardson?"

"As a matter of fact that's right. We actually were in touch for awhile after high school because we were both going to study for the bar. Then he suddenly goes back East to an Ivy League school and goes into politics. I was surprised when I found out he was back here and was running for councilman."

"You were talking about rumors with Counc-- Bill

Richards."

"They were about the reason he had to drop off the track team. Pretty basic. He apparently got into an argument with a couple of guys. It turned into an altercation resulting in a fracture, or break, of a leg. I remember it wasn't serious. But he was in a cast for a couple of months, and of course was off the team."

"And some people thought Turlock put these guys up to it, to open a slot on the team for him."

"Well, it turned out they were friends of his, but that's as far as it went. There was no investigation into criminal allegations. But since they were Jim's friends, naturally it gave rise to rumors."

"And what did you think?"

"I really had no opinion on the matter. I had no reason to think about it one way or the other."

"Did Turlock seem to be the kind of guy who would go that far to get on the team?"

"If I were to guess I'd say no."

"So you don't think he was responsible for Richardson's broken leg?"

"Well, that's the funny thing. Even if he was, there's no way that would have been a motive for Bill to want to kill him."

"Why not?"

"Well, it just wasn't that important to him, I mean about being on the team. It didn't seem to bother him that he was off it. I think he only joined the team in the first place to help his resume' for college entrance, you know, to look like a more interest diversified, multi-talented individual."

"I see. And what was your nonacademic interest?"

"Girls."

"Thanks for your help."

"You're welcome, Detective."

Case hung up the phone, blew out his cheeks, leaned back in his chair, rubbed his hands over his face and stared up at the ceiling. He wasn't looking forward to a surveillance detail with another day of nothing concrete. They had gotten out of the starting blocks, but in comparison, the finish line was still so far away that it seemed there had really been no progress at all. He leaned forward in his chair and looked at Rodriguez who was still on a call.

Rodriguez hung up after another minute. "Anything?"

Case asked.

"I talked to a Shirley Hernandez. She was a friend of Shawna Anderson's and read about her death in the paper. She said she was shocked by it and remembered thinking she couldn't imagine who would do that. I pressed her to see if she could think of anyone at all and she did remember when Anderson got the lead singing role in a school production; the girl she beat out was very angry and jealous. She couldn't remember the name until I read her the cast and then she picked out Sharon Olson as the girl Anderson beat."

"Did you run her down?"

"Works at a beauty salon in West Covina. I spoke to the manager there who said she works weekdays 8 to 6 and was working the morning Anderson was murdered. Olson herself claims she couldn't help because she wasn't friends with Anderson and didn't even remember her or the competition incident. Sounded like she was telling the truth, anyway, she has an alibi. I take it you haven't come up with anything."

"Only a guy with next to no motive who also happens to be a councilman." Case looked at the clock on the wall. "Almost twelve. What do say we take a half hour for lunch in the cafeteria and hit it again? We need to find a solid lead before the 5:00 briefing." But after three more hours they didn't find one. The less they accomplished, the harder they worked at it, only to get more of the same, ending up back where they started.

There wasn't much they needed to know at the briefing. Present were some officers from San Diego that Case recognized, though no recognition was exchanged. The DEA had reasonable evidence to believe two years of work on the cartels' part was ready to launch a major new supply route, stemming from the crossing in San Diego, to try and keep up with the insatiable demand for drugs in the U.S. There had already been two dry runs testing the whole operation and it was determined the first major shipment was to take place somewhere in L.A. in the next 72 hours. In place were surveillance and video all along the route, and when the bust happened in L.A., the whole route would be shut down. Timing, like in everything, was everything.

East L.A. had many blocks of quiet, dark and deserted streets of mostly unoccupied warehouses and vacant buildings that once manufactured products now imported. The area was ideal in which to conduct business of the type better conducted out of public view. One of the most crucial factors in attaining a successful conclusion to that particular type of business, was, once again, timing. That factor is what law enforcement was determined to disrupt. And both sides needed that Byrd's hit of the sixties, *Time is on My Side,* to be on their side.

From the undercover information the DEA had, they had kept a tight enough lid on' Snakebite'. The code name for the operation running the last two years had not changed, as there was no indication outside that the operation existed. On the two previous dry runs, camera surveillance showed that the drug traffickers had used 'coal mine canaries' to see if it was safe to use a particular building for a transfer. Case and Rodriguez's job was to observe one of these 'canaries', posting themselves in a general area, not a specific location. They were to observe the route and destination and report to agents farther away who would observe the same activity, as on the two previous occasions, leading into the general area Case's team covered.

After the short briefing, Case and Rodriguez stopped for sandwiches and plenty of black coffee to go, and arrived at their assigned area. Case knew black coffee, spiked with adrenaline as needed, would get him through the night.

"I never thought I'd be on stakeout." Rodriguez said as Case cruised a block.

"Get used to it."

"I mean as a grunt on loan out. There's plenty of this work on our own cases."

"It happens. You heard the Captain. Short funding, short handed, and I don't care, because you have a short timer for a partner. But right now I'd rather be working our case."

"The serial case?" Rodriguez asked.

"We're getting nowhere fast. Just lousy timing. Our perp has worked everything out so well I wouldn't be surprised if he had something to do with this."

"What could be his advantage to divert our time, when he's already leading us around by the nose?"

"I don't know. I think he just likes jerking our chain."

"But you don't really think he's got anything to do with the DEA operation?"

"I don't know. When we catch him we'll ask him."

They spent an hour just cruising and then planted themselves in a side alley. Even at 7 o'clock, it wasn't dark. But finally, after rolling around through L.A.'s scummy, chemical-filled 'air' all afternoon, the descending sun was anxious to wash the grime off in its evening bath in the clear, blue Pacific. Here amongst the depressing, useless buildings, the gloom of twilight approached.

A drunk wandered by clutching the scrunched top of a dirty brown paper bag, saw them parked in the alley, and moved on to his next preferred spot of real estate, to settle down for the evening. The occasional car drove by, having no good reason to be in this part of town.

"We'll sit here awhile."

Silence. Rodriguez looked at Case. "So, you want to talk or just watch?"

Case rolled his head, then his eyes over at Rodriguez.

"Got it, just watch."

"You're detecting better all the time."

Case took out a pack, unwrapped a stick of gum, and folded it into his mouth.

"Is it just dark or was that gum black?"

"Black Jack. Licorice gum. Wanta try it?" Case asked.

"You were chewing it in Dr. Leonard's office."

"Right."

"I'll pass."

"I wasn't offering you any. If you wanted to try it, I'd tell you where you can buy it. Nothing comes between me and my Black Jack gum."

"How does such a big heart fit into a standard issue chest?"

"It's a miracle of nature. But I don't share my gum with anyone, not even my wife when I had one."

"Did she even like licorice gum?"

"I don't know. But I wouldn't—"

"I know. You wouldn't give her any if she did. One mystery solved."

"What's that?"

"Why she left you."

"She didn't leave. It was a mutual thing. We both knew she wanted to leave."

Rodriguez thought Option #2, just watching, started to sound better and better. They pulled out of the alley, right on Franklin and parked in the middle of the block behind a car two streets away. There was silence in the car; silence on the street, lit intermittently by an occasional working street lamp. Automatic timers were responsible for the isolated lamp that came on, kids with rocks and BB guns were responsible for the ones that did not. The darkening street began to reflect alternating green, amber and red from the distant traffic lights, their monochromatic directions for the ghosts of cars long gone.

The two detectives sat in silence. Case popped another piece of black gum; it didn't keep its flavor long. Finally, his nature overcoming his discretion, Rodriguez broke the silence.

"Say, Case…,"

"Yeah."

"I was just thinking."

"Keeps the mind limber."

"Consuela and I are having an anniversary party at our house next weekend, it's our seventh and…."

"You're not playing that tune again?"

"No, it's our anniversary and…"

"Different lyrics, same tune."

"It's just a small informal get together of some friends, you don't have to bring a present, but you can bring a date. Do you good to get out once in awhile. Bring that nice lady we ran into in the hall last time."

"Thanks, but I don't think I'd be interested, and leave her out of it."

"Look, man, what's wrong wi' choo? Why ya leavin' me in the middle here? Consuela pullin' me one way, you pullin' the other."

"Why does she keep it up?"

"Because she wants to meet you, man."

"What for?"

"For such a great detective, you're supposed to know people better than that. She wants to meet my partner, see who has my back. She doesn't like to think about it, but knows it's not a job approving mortgage applications at Wells Fargo. Sometimes she worries."

"Yeah, it's not a job sitting all day in a bank on the phone or handling paperwork. It's a job mostly sitting all day in a police station on the phone or handling paperwork."

"You know what I mean. She wants to see who's looking out for me. That's natural. It would make her feel better. I tell her don't worry, but if she heard it from you too, ...I just want her not to worry every time I go to work. You are looking out for me, aren't you?"

"We're partners."

"So you can look out for me by helping me out here and let Consuela see your ugly face."

Case thought about it. He knew Rodriguez was right, but why all these complicated entanglements? He liked life when he wasn't pulled in so many directions at once. Even if he did decide to go, asking Lucy was out of the question. He didn't think that bridge survived the fire.

"I'll think about it."

Rodriguez felt he was crossing the 50 yard line. He had progress he could report to Consuela. "The kids will think it's fun meeting another policeman. I'll bet you're great with kids."

"What gave it away?"

Nothing was said for awhile and then Rodriguez noticed a man coming towards them on the opposite side of the street. It was the second one since they had been at that spot, but this guy didn't look drunk, or looked like he was going to settle in an alley, like the other one did. He looked like he had a purpose. There was something familiar about him, too. Rodriguez leaned forward and looked harder. Then he nudged Case who had leaned back in his seat for a few minutes while Rodriguez watched.

"Hey, Case. Look at this guy."

"Where?"

"11 o'clock, heading this way. Who is that guy? I've seen him before."

He passed under one of the working street lamps.

"Sure!" said Rodriguez. "The guy we interviewed in Venice, the surfer."

"Yeah, you're right."

"Right, right. What's he doing way up here?"

Case was suddenly interested. "I don't know, but I'm guessing he's the exception to the rule."

"Which rule?"

"The one about me not believing in coincidences."

"You think it's a coincidence he's here?"

"Well, there's only two alternatives, and I'd eliminate them both. I don't like him for the serial killer and I don't think he's a canary we're watching for. I can't see anyone trusting him with even that much responsibility. The people we're after wouldn't bring on board a space cadet like him."

"So what do you think he's doing here?"

"Must have a hideaway. I don't think he's cooking meth, same argument, not smart enough."

"Guys blow themselves up all the time."

"Yeah, I just don't think so. Probably has a stash here."

"This far from home?"

"I don't think he necessarily is far from home. You heard him, typical beach bum. Probably doesn't go more than 150 yards east and west, but hundreds or even thousands of miles north and south. Probably surfing at

Redondo Beach, or maybe Malibu, sleeping on the beach. A stash around here would be easy to hide. I'll bet he has stashes wherever he goes along the coast. Picks up whatever he needs to sell for cash, which probably isn't a lot."

"Looks like he knows where he's going. So what do we do about him?"

"Nothing now. Just jot down the address. We'll turn it over to narcotics. Maybe they'll follow it up, we did our duty."

Rodriguez reached for a pad and then noticed a flash of movement. The surfer ran into the building when he was a few feet from the entrance.

"He made us! He's going rabbit!" and Rodriguez jumped out of the car.

"Manny! Let 'im... Damn!" Case called in their position and took off after his partner.

Rodriguez had followed the runner, and entered the building, ten yards behind the surfer from Venice. Case was across the street and up the three steps in one bound and then inside the dusty, deserted first floor, wide entrance. There were several doors, leading presumably to offices long vacant. He was about to try the first door, his weapon drawn.

His eyes grew accustomed to the gloom, the transom over the door letting minimum light in to weakly mingle with the dark interior. He called twice to his partner, and then paused to listen. There was the sound of movement overhead and Case darted for the staircase leading to the next floor.

The next floor was just as dirty and dusty as below, but not quite so dark, with more windows to let in what was left of the light from the receding sun. The room contained rusted and abandoned equipment, along with needles and some rags that used to be clothes. The only thing alive besides Case was the retreating backside of a sizeable rat scurrying out of his immediate path. Case called again, still getting no response.

There was another stairwell across the room, directly in front of Case along the same wall he was standing next to. Case was across the room, just a few steps up the stairs when he heard a terrible crashing sound overhead and then a heavy thud to his left and behind him. He turned to look and was momentarily frozen on the stairs, staring, in disbelief. His trained mental awareness still would not accept the evidence his eyes were relaying.

Case overcame his inertia and moved off the stairs to where Rodriguez was laying. A steel pipe, at one time connected to machinery, was now protruding through his chest. One leg and his head were angled unnaturally, leg and neck clearly broken. Blood pooled in several spots, coalescing into one larger pool. Case was semi-catatonic, indecisive for the first time in his life. He couldn't leave his partner. He had to continue the pursuit. Blood was starting to reach the soles of his shoes. His partner's blood. Rodriguez's blood. Manny's blood.

Case made the 'officer down' call and knew his duty: to stay with his partner. But Case didn't need to know it was his duty. There was no way he wanted to leave Manny. He bent down and placed his hand on Manny's head for a moment. Everything was still. Everything had gone quiet. Silence. The moment was frozen in time. Case kneeled next to his partner. This was their private funeral. Another moment and then Case holstered his own weapon, retrieved his partner's, checked the load, glanced up at the gaping hole in the ceiling and headed once more for the stairs.

Case took the stairs in about four leaps. When he got to the next floor, he saw what had happened. It was a defensive trap. The floor boards were already unsafe and with a little help from a saw, they wouldn't support a man's weight, especially a charging man. The pursued man simply ran the perimeter of the room. Still yards behind, once Rodriguez reached the floor, his target would have been on the other side and Rodriguez would have headed straight towards him, directly into the death trap.

Case took the path around the room's perimeter, not pausing to look at Rodriguez lying in his own blood on the floor below. That scene would never leave the dark corners of his memory. He was intent on adding one like it, to a deeper, darker place. Again he caught the sound of running feet over head and he was up the next flight of stairs to the fourth floor. This one was dirty with more debris, like the others below, and was getting darker. And he was late again. This floor was empty, too. There was a fifth floor and then the roof.

Case wanted to stop him on the fifth floor. He didn't want a roof top pursuit at night. He started out across the room for the staircase, which alternated sides of each floor. A creak under his left foot froze him in place. He swore at himself, realizing his mistake. Case slowly and carefully slid his left foot back and then his right. He moved back, not lifting his feet, just dragging them. This might not be a trap at all; still, it was dangerous, rotting floors in these condemned buildings. He was at the room's entrance again and walked the perimeter, knowing he would come to an empty fifth floor.

Once around the fifth floor he opened the door going to the roof, leading with Rodriguez's gun. There was an eerie silence but he had no sixth sense of any presence nearby. He took the stairwell to the roof and caught a glimpse of a figure disappearing in the darkness. Without hesitating Case took off in pursuit. There was moonlight enough for Case to see a figure in the distance momentarily suspended in air and then disappear. Case ran to the spot he thought was where the figure had disappeared and saw it was the edge of the building. The figure had leapt across and Case did not hesitate to make the same leap, his right foot planted on the ledge to launch himself as his left foot reached out for the building beyond.

Case was momentarily suspended in space, the soft light breeze above and the hard concrete five floors below. The far roof was either farther than Case calculated or his right foot wasn't planted and positioned just right to give him a perfect leap. In any case, as he was bringing his right leg forward to land with both feet on the opposite roof, he knew he wasn't going to make it. He was short. He didn't get far enough to land on the roof, but he was close enough to reach out and grab on, both arms extended, hands grabbing the other side of the ledge, Case dangling five floors above the street.

Case's shoes banged on a glass pane as his body slammed against the side of the building. He hung there, five stories up, not even able to turn his head very far with his face pressed against the stone façade. Sweat began to bead on his forehead. His palms became clammy and he gave an involuntary quiver which ran a light tremble down his body, his right leg tapping on the window pane.

He tapped the pane again, and then cocked his leg back

as far as he dared and slammed his foot with all the force he could muster into the glass. He heard a crack. Another hard kick and his foot shattered the brittle, single pane glass. Case then used his shoe to break whatever pieces might be protruding from the frame. He did the same with his left foot. Satisfied the window frame was cleared of enough glass shards, Case began to lower himself, angling both feet through the open window.

It was a stretch. He had to let go of his grip over the ledge before he could get to a seated position on the window sill. As he slowly lowered himself, he got both feet inside the building, pressing down hard with both palms, now flat on the top of the ledge. As he slowly let himself slide down, his legs snaking through the window, his hands now pressed hard against the face of the building, his fingers dug into and gripped every ridge and groove. He gradually got both legs over the fulcrum and landed in a seated position on the sill, his legs dangling over the floor inside, with his upper body outside, hugging the wall. He could feel tiny pieces of glass digging into the back of his legs as he sat on the ledge. They were of absolutely no concern.

As Case slid his body forward, angling down, bits of glass tore paths through his pants, gouging his legs and leaving trickling red lines. He could just reach his left arm inside and reversed the hold, sandwiching the wall between both palms. He slid farther down, quickly reaching his right arm inside, pressing that palm against the wall next to his left, applying opposite pressure from the direction his body was moving, forcing it in and away from the window. He then let his body drop down, simultaneously ducking his head inside while his feet stopped on a metal object. The object took his weight and he saw he was standing on an old radiator, just two feet above the floor.

Case jumped down and ran along the wall on his left to the fire escape, the only exit route from the roof. He looked over the side, experiencing momentary vertigo. He kept looking down as he descended the metal ladders but saw no one. Case knew the man he was after had plenty of time to get away while he hung on the side of the building, struggling to get inside. He stopped his quick run down the fire escape, just for a second on the third floor landing, to take a fast look around the streets; see if he could catch sight of the man he was after. All was dark and deserted.

When Case got to the bottom, a lightheadedness set in which he quickly shook off. He looked for a clue for direction, knowing the man could have gone anywhere, down an alley to the next street, into a building, anywhere. Checking the dark, silent street north and south, he ran to the corner and turned right, heading west as the most probable direction the surfer would take. He ran along 2nd towards Franklin back to where they had parked. Before Case got to the corner he saw red lights blinking and reflecting off the adjacent buildings. He made the turn on Franklin and saw the response vehicles blocking the street at various angles. He could see a rear ambulance door closing and started to run. Case was 50 feet away when the ambulance pulled away, heading north, turning left and out of sight at the next corner. Case got to the police cordon and an officer let him through.

The scene commander was giving instructions when an FBI agent pointed Case out as the dead officer's partner. The commander approached Case and asked pointedly, "Where were you?"

Case was still looking in the direction the ambulance had taken, oblivious to the commander. The question was repeated, a little more harshly. Case tried to refocus his gaze on the man in front of him. And then everything in the immediate vicinity went into a strangely surrealistic distortion of overlapping patterns. Lines converged and then moved away at impossible angles. Geometry lost its sense of proportion as various objects' true spatial relativity fell into chaotic disagreement. Case watched as the sound source in his line of sight floated back, down and away, its vertical orientation becoming horizontal. This vision was almost simultaneous with other sensory nerves reporting a sharp impact and burning sensation on the knuckles of his right hand. Because of the sensory overload his brain wasn't aware of the semicircles gouging small red crescents into his right palm.

The empty shell standing on the sidewalk over the fallen site commander, lifting the back of its hand to its eyes, would be recognized as Detective Lawrence Case of the LAPD. The right arm slowly retreated to its side. Adrenaline gave out. Stamina gave out. Spirit gave out. Case fell to the sidewalk.

Chapter Seventeen

Case was waiting for Captain Murdock in his office. An officer had driven him in his car to have the wounds on the back of his legs looked at. Several splinters were removed and the area was disinfected and dressed. It wasn't serious and he was released with some antibiotics. Then the same officer drove Case back downtown. While Case was at the hospital, Captain Murdock had been called to the scene in East L.A. Case waited for twenty minutes for Murdock to arrive at Parker Center. He didn't want to think about the next forty-eight hours.

Case was up and pacing for the second time when the Captain walked in. His short hair kept him from looking disheveled in the middle of the night and except for being tieless, Murdock looked no different than any other time of the day.

"Case, why don't you sit down?"

Case didn't say anything.

"Suit yourself, but I need to, I'm tired." It was after midnight and the call came to the Captain after he had been asleep just more than an hour. "Not as flexible as I used to be sleepwise." Case continued standing.

"Listen," the Captain said, "this is tough all around. Just give me a sketch now, then after the funeral and your oblig interview with Dr. Leonard, I want you out of here for a week. I've spoken to the Feds, it's not their call, but they will need the full report for their investigation. That operation is still on, but you're out of it. The report can wait until you get back. It's not important to their bust."

When Case heard he was off the surveillance he let down and sat down, then was suddenly on his feet again.

"Not Important?!"

"You know what I mean. I told them they'll wait for the report and they didn't argue. Rodriguez will get full dress honors."

Case sat down again.

"You're alright? I heard they took you to the hospital." The Captain saw the blood on his pants when he was pacing. "I'll read the hospital report later."

Case gave an outline of the chase and the address of the building where the suspected drugs were hidden. He didn't tell him how he got blood on his pants. "The guy we were chasing, one of the people we interviewed after the Anderson killing, a surfer in Venice, but I doubt he'll go back to Venice anytime soon."

"If he's anywhere on the coast from Mexico to Canada,

we'll get him. We'll put the word out from Imperial Beach to Cape Flattery. It'll be hard for him to stay off the radar. Everyone he knows is an easy bust threat. Somebody'll flip him. Go home. I'll see you on Sunday. We'll get you the details." The Captain stood up. "Oh, and Case, there won't be any charges."

"Charges?"

The Captain walked over and held up Case's bruised right hand.

"The commander said your swing surprised him, but it was only half-speed and he ducked back out of the way. He said he leaned too far back and lost his feet. A uniform witness reported from his angle he thought you nailed him. 'Seems you clocked a lamp post instead."

Case stood up and headed for the door. He could have been a little steadier. Captain Murdock noticed the blood again. "Case, do you want someone to drive you home?"

Case shook his head and then stopped, remembering when he had to drop Rodriguez's gun.

"Look on the rooftop, north end of the building south of the address I gave you."

"For what?"

"Rodriguez's gun." He opened the door. "Don't ask."

Case crawled into bed about 1:30 A.M. but didn't sleep. He didn't want to think about how bad he felt. He would have to reenact tonight's events over and over, to others officially and to himself interminably. He got up and found not quite a shot left in a bottle. Two cans of beer in the fridge didn't help. Case decided to walk to a bar where he knew he could get served, curfew or not. He laced on some shoes, not bothering with socks, blue jeans, semi-clean t-shirt, no badge, no gun.

Case passed an all night liquor store on the way and changed his mind about the bar. All the company he really needed was his two best friends, Jack and John. The bar company would satisfy his need to hit something, but he was too depressed and tired even for that diversion. So he walked into the liquor store and the two gentlemen, Mr. Daniels and Mr. Walker, were sitting on the shelf in their usual places. He grabbed one of each around the neck. He walked to the counter, a bottle in each fist. It felt like the right balance for the short walk home. On the way to the door he stopped and thought better of what he was walking out with. Both of these guys had twin brothers. Maybe one would like to come along, just in case. A third bottle would throw off his balance, but it was only a short walk home.

Back home at the kitchen table Case swept the extraneous matter off the table onto the floor and set up his bottles and one glass. Only a couple smudges, it was fine. He poured himself half a glass of whiskey, then thought about getting comfortable. He unlaced his shoes, wondering where his socks were. When the glass was half empty he retreated to the cot, taking the other bottles with him. At least if he did suddenly fall asleep he wouldn't hit his head. He congratulated himself for this wisdom and for having the foresight to get the third bottle. He turned on his favorite jazz station and refilled his glass.

Case didn't know what time he had fallen asleep early Saturday morning and he didn't know if it was the bright sunlight outside or the radio he had left on that woke him up. All he knew was he couldn't feel his lips or his fingers or his toes. And who invited the bees in? He shook his head but they liked it in there and refused to leave. It must be early. Too early to get up after what must have been only four, maybe five hours sleep at the most.

"...that was Thelonius Monk and Erroll Garner working on that ivory for you and before that Charles Mingus coaxing some blue notes outta that bass. Now for some rare Southern gospel from Satchmo as you get all dressed up in your Sunday goin' to church clothes. Ol' Louis is gonna get you in the right spirit to go see the preacher."

"See the preacher? Who goes to church on Saturday

and...wait, it's not..." The nearly three empty bottles told him it was. He tried to get up but that just aroused and angered the cranial bees that previously were content with mild buzzing. He fell back, trying to keep his eyes open. He had to get up if this was Sunday. He knew there was something important he had to do. Holding his head tightly between both hands, so as not to let the bees inside know he was moving, he got as far as sitting up.

Case was now on his feet, in his full upright and locked position. But that didn't stop him from swaying 15 degrees from port to starboard. Case noticed that except for his shoes he was fully dressed; except for his socks. He wondered where his socks were. He went to the dining room table to find nothing but a notepad lying on it. Everything else was on the floor. He picked up the pad and squinted at it. When it finally came into focus, after several efforts at finding the right angle, he could see there was a time and location on the pad that he didn't remember writing. Or answering the phone. Or taking any message.

2:30. Rose Hill Memorial Park, Whittier. It was definitely his handscribbling. The funeral! He looked at the watch he was still wearing. 8:25. At least he didn't sleep through it. He had plenty of time to get there. Fortunately he couldn't sleep more than 28 hours, and except for the settling bees, he did feel physically refreshed.

Case went back to lie down on the cot for a little while. On the way, he noticed one shoe doing a poor job of trying to hide under the bed. He'd find the other one later. He stretched out carefully on his back, looking at the ceiling. The funeral. And he suddenly felt queasy.

What happened two nights ago was tragic. He knew he couldn't change it, maybe didn't even have control over it, but he still felt like a failure, complete and absolute. He couldn't protect Rodriguez; couldn't even catch the guy that was responsible. If he had to find him himself, he would, no matter how long it took, no matter how many heads he had to bust to do it. That part was certain. That was a promise to Rodriguez.

That was also the easy part. The funeral. And finally he had to get to the part he was avoiding thinking about, the part he wanted no part of in his consciousness. The part the bottles did their best to help him find a way out of, without a conscious decision, why he had gotten drunk. The funeral. Consuela. The kids. And in just a few hours. He desperately tried to soothe his mind with the coward's way out: something came up, some kind of emergency, he might break a leg. He stared at the ceiling. The funeral. How could he go? How could he not?

All Case wanted was to solve the case he and Rodriguez were working on. Rodriguez had done some good work. He found some statements the murders were making.

He deserved to have his work completed, if for no other reason than it was the last thing he worked on and catching the killer would bring justice and save who knew how many other people? Rodriguez deserved credit. He deserved that.

He would go nuts in the next few hours before the funeral if he didn't do something to take his mind off it. He still didn't know what he would say to Rodriguez's family. Obviously they would probably prefer he wasn't there; they wouldn't know how much blame was his. All he could do now was work. He would go to Parker Center for the murder books on the three cases and at least spend the time he had to wait, before going to Whittier, reading them.

Case peeled off the clothes he had been in for the last two days and took a hot shower. He dried off and then looked in the bathroom mirror. Pathetic. Lather and a reasonably sharp razor did a passing job of whisker removal. Bleeding was very minimal. He got dressed in fresh{?} underwear out of the top drawer, and a fresh{?} shirt on a hanger in the closet. At the left end of the closet hung his dress uniform in a clear plastic cleaner's bag. He looked at it. The funeral. He retrieved the same jeans in the living room, then remembered socks and went back to the dresser for a fresh pair. The ones he couldn't find were probably stiff enough to stand and walk on their own, which is probably why he couldn't find them. He quickly laced up his one shoe, but its partner was doing a better job of hiding.

"Come on!" He got down on hands and knees and looked under the couch, then lifted it all the way up. He looked in the empty clothes hamper, then on top of the refrigerator in case he had chucked it. "Come on," he said again. "There aren't that many place it could hide." His mouth felt like the dry Santa Ana winds had sucked all the moisture out and left a couple tumble weeds behind. He poured himself a glass from the kitchen faucet, but there was nothing approaching cold about it, which is what he wanted. Doubting, but hoping he'd find some ice in the freezer, he opened it, and, lo and behold! His other shoe! "How did that... Don't ask."

Case's stomach told him in no uncertain terms food was not on its mind, so he didn't waste his time trying, but went straight downtown for the murder books and also the high school year books. Back at his duplex, Case just began reading, starting over, from the beginning, and reading again. Rodriguez's discovery of the causes of death fitting the talents of the victims certainly had to mean something, but didn't give a clear motive, the one thing Case needed to understand.

He found and studied the ten year old school pictures of Shawna Anderson, Stephanie Dodson and Jim Turlock; all smiling, seemingly happy, decent looking kids. Somebody wanted to kill them, and bad enough to wait ten years if it took that long. Who, and why? With that kind of determination, if there were more intended victims, Case was sure there would be more actual victims. If this guy wanted to kill someone, they wound up dead. Case had to get ahead of him, and he didn't have a clue how. It was all about motive, and Case couldn't explain it, but he had a real serious feeling he was all out of time.

It was time to get dressed and leave for the funeral. Case felt like he was going to his own funeral. He took the 10 east to 605 and then south to Whittier. At Rose Hill Memorial Park Case found the gravesite and blended in with the crowd gathered around. He couldn't avoid looking several times at Rodriguez's widow and two young children. The day gave all the appearance of being bright, with a cheerful sun winking between puffy white, drifting clouds in a clear, pale blue sky. That appearance was all a false overlay to the darkness in the hearts of the mourners, especially Consuela Rodriguez, in a black veil and dress, and her two small children, Pedro 6 and Maria 5, who missed playing with their father on this Sunday. It would be the first in a string of missed Sundays that would go on for years.

The full dress honors ceremony was somber and impressive, with all the pomp and circumstance the Los Angeles Police Department affords one of its own fallen comrades. The thirty minute ceremony ended with people milling around for another twenty minutes. Case waited for most of them to leave before approaching his partner's widow. With her appeared to be a parent and perhaps a few close relatives. His feet and legs were willing to move, but it took all his will power to get them to go in his intended direction. She saw him approach and stop a few feet away.

"Ma'am, I'm Lawrence Case. I was Manny's partner."

She looked at him briefly. "Manny told me he asked you many times to our home, because I asked him to, but you never came. Because of this for you I am 'ma'am' and not 'Consuela'."

"I'm sorry, um…Consuela. Yes. He asked me to your anni--, I …I was planning on coming very soon. I'm very sorry for your loss."

"Yes, you are very sorry. Everyone is very sorry. I am very sorry. I told Manny I did not want him to be a policeman, but he says it is important. He wants to make it better for our children. I said it is not safe. It is dangerous. He said not to worry, he has a good partner. He said he liked you very much. I told him I want to meet you. Hello, how are you?"

Case couldn't say anything. He knew under the circumstances, if she wanted to, she could cast blame on him. He had watched her maintain a stoic demeanor throughout the service, determined to stay strong, he guessed for the children that clung to her. At that point he knew it was better to keep his mouth shut than to open it for any reason. He watched her walk away.

Case felt rotten enough. He didn't know if it was more rotten than he expected he would feel or just as rotten as he expected he would feel. All he knew was he wanted to kill something. That was all, no big deal, just kill something, anything, it didn't matter what, just so long as he was killing and something was being killed: a mailbox, a car, a wall, an ATM machine, himself. He balled up his fists. K-I-L-L something.

It was nearing 4 PM. What should he do, where should he go? He could go jump in the ocean and see how far he could get before a shark thought he looked tasty. No. He thought of an even better torture. He could go visit his brother, the one with a wife and four kids, 4, 5, 6 & 8. That was it.

Not often, but sometimes, like now, if Case wanted to lose himself in a chaotic cacophony of conflicting chatter, he went to his brother's house in Downey. He called his brother, said he was coming by, and his brother said okay. It wasn't far west of Whittier and Case took the surface streets.

Once in Downey, Case was positive of his brother's location, but knew he could just follow the sounds of mayhem and destruction. Once on his brother's block he recognized the 3 bedroom stucco track home right away. It wasn't the only house with toys strewn on the front lawn, but it was the only one with the front door open and kids and a dog chasing each other in and out. Case couldn't see the backyard but he knew it wasn't as tidy as the front with an additional wading pool that needed changing.

His brother Jerry was in the living room when Case walked in. The door was open and he was just kind of carried along with the tide of small bodies.

"To what do we owe…" He stopped when he saw his brother in full dress uniform.

"I was in Whittier. It was my partner, but I didn't come here to talk about it. In fact, being close by, I just didn't want to go home right now, and…"

"Sure, no problem. You're staying for dinner, right? Meg's in the kitchen. Have a seat. Do you want anything? Meg!"

Case found a place to sit just as another herd made its way through the living room and he managed to get his feet out of the way just in time.

Jerry was a few inches shorter than Lawrence and a few, actually several, pounds heavier. He was getting regular home cooked meals for years. He was only three years younger than Case but got married late, accounting for the young children. Jerry's wife Meg came out of the kitchen, wiping her hands on an apron tied around her plump waist.

"Hi, Lawrence. My, don't you look nice. Are you staying for supper?" Meg was an inch shorter than Jerry and had the happy look of a hen with her brood.

"Yes, he is Hon. Is there any lemonade in the 'frig? I'll make some if not, if you're busy with dinner."

"I can make it. Sit sown and visit with your brother. It's been a long time since we've seen you Lawrence. I'm glad you came over." She gave him a hug.

"Nice to see you, too."

"Kids are all getting pretty big," Case noted. "I don't know if they were all walking last time I was here. And so far I don't think all four, right?, have been through yet."

There were four kids, two boys and two girls. They never stopped in any one spot, just kept travelling through. Their parents tried but failed to get them to stop long enough to say 'hi' to their uncle, but they would accomplish that when they corralled them all at dinner.

The boys accepted their instinctive responsibility towards each sister, a duty they performed with gusto and without prejudice. The sisters, four and six, were convinced their parents didn't really love them. Why else would they keep those two monsters around to pull their hair and make terrible faces at them?

Meg had come to a stopping point in the kitchen and came out into the living room to visit with their guest for a few minutes. It wasn't long before the four year old girl, Jennifer, came running in the house, crying,

"Mommy, mommy! Jeremy is being mean to me! He's real mean!"

"What did he do?" Meg asked.

"We were playing outside and we were playing what would you want to be, like a dog or a cat or a fish or something, and he said he would want to be a horse so he could run real fast and nobody could catch him and I said I would want to be a bird so I could fly real high and look around and see everything and see for real far and he started laughing and said birds don't wear glasses and then he called me a nerd bird because if I was a bird and I was wearing glasses all the other birds would call me a nerd bird and he's real mean." She had to stop crying to get all that out, then she started crying again.

"Did he hit you?" Her mother asked. "Do you have an owie?"

"N--n--no." She managed to get out between sobs.

"Do you have a bruise?"

"N—n--no."

"Then he didn't hurt you. If he hit you with a rock or a stick, that would hurt and you would cry a lot. You might have to go to the doctor at the hospital. But words can't hurt you. You don't even feel them. You don't have to go to the hospital from words. Do you know what to say next time he says something you don't like or calls you names?"

"W—what?"

"Say: Sticks and stones can break my bones, but names can never hurt me. Then you can just walk away. When someone calls you a name you don't like or teases you, they just want to see you cry."

"But they're being mean."

"So all you have to do is say 'Sticks and stones can break my bones but names can never hurt me' and walk away and don't play with them anymore until they stop being mean. Then that person will have to find someone else to play with and you don't have to cry because he didn't hurt you. See? You don't have to have a band aid, or medicine or anything like that. Now go find something else to do until supper, but don't go far because it's almost ready."

Jennifer ran back outside not to miss out on any playtime. Thirty minutes later the family and Case were all seated at the dinner table. Case put his uniform jacket on the back of his chair. He was mildly surprised that the two girls and the two boys didn't sit next to each other, but they arranged themselves in age order. Jennifer and Jeremy were the two antagonists from before but they didn't seem to make any effort to separate themselves.

During the meal, if the bedlam receded, it wasn't to any perceptible degree. But that's why Case was there. He wanted to be out of the world of teenage drug OD's and criminals escaping justice and wasted lives and in a world of tempests in teapots. Little Jennifer was trying to negotiate some corn kernels onto an adult size fork when she dropped the fork on the floor. Ever ready Jeremy sitting next to her laughed and said:

"The nerd bird dropped her fork!" He hesitated a second and then said, "Now she's a dork stork! The dork stork dropped her fork!" And he rocked back and forth laughing harder and harder in self-admiration of his cleverness. Jennifer immediately broke out crying as hard as her brother was laughing.

"You're mean!"

This exchange had no effect on the rest of the diners, it was just absorbed into the overall ambiance of the dinner. Case observed how Jennifer had not mastered her earlier lesson and was still on square one in dealing with her brother. He also noticed Meg wasn't going to use dinner time for lesson reinforcement, therefore not mixing pleasure with business.

After dinner the kids wore themselves out with more activity and were soon off to bed. They all said goodbye to their Uncle, mostly shy, because he was practically a stranger to them. Case felt a little guilty about that. His brother didn't give him any 'You need to come over more often' because he knew his brother was going to do what his brother was going to do. Case put his jacket on, not buttoning it, thanked them for the meal, gave Meg a little hug, and was back in his car. He jumped on the 710 heading north and home.

Chapter Eighteen

Case thought back over the evening as he cruised north on the freeway. It went well he thought; uncontrolled mayhem. Just what he needed to clear his head after the previous days' events. But now he had to delve back into his world and figure a lot of things out: what he was going to do with the serial killings case he had on his hands, what he was going to do with the job, what, if anything, he was going to do with his life.

He pulled into his driveway and turned off the ignition, crossing mental fingers with his routine little prayer for the next time he needed it to start. Inside, he carefully hung up his dress blues, not that he wanted to be careful about it, but so that next time they'd be ready with no last minute surprises. At the fridge he decided tonight was just a one or two beer night. Snapping back the pull top, a little foam immediately bubbled out the top as if happy to be released from the confinement of the Genie's bottle, in this case, can. Case's one-beer-a-week limit was temporarily suspended.

Case sat heavily on the couch with his can of beer. 'What's it all about, Alphie?' he thought. He downed the first can and thought maybe the answer was in the second. When that can of beer had no more wisdom than the first, he decided to stick to his plan and call it a night.

Case was awake early Monday morning. This was the first day of his week off? That's what the Captain said. Case didn't see how that would work in real time. He showered, shaving could wait; he got dressed and in his car, thanked the spark plugs, or coil, or whatever it was that was responsible for his car starting again, and picked up something in a drive-thru on the way downtown. He was at his desk forty-five minutes when Captain Murdock called him into his office.

"What are you doing here?"

"I'm supposed to see Dr. Leonard today, right?"

"That's not for hours, not until two this afternoon."

"I thought I'd..."

"Look," the Captain interrupted, "I want you away from it for awhile."

"What about the shortage of manpower?"

"When I want your help allocating resources you'll be the first to know. Records indicate you've put in almost twenty months without any vacation, except the week I had to cut short."

"I have nothing to vacate to, and this case has got to get worked."

"I'm putting Detectives Young and Fuller on it, at least until you get back. I want you to give them your notes."

"Young and Fuller? They couldn't find penguins in Alaska."

"Neither could you. There aren't any penguins in Alaska."

"No? What happened to them?"

"They all took a cruise ship to the South Pole."

"So what am I supposed to do for a week?"

"Not my problem. Go to the beach. Speaking of the beach we put out an APB on Derek of Venice. Since you're here, go see the sketch artist and we'll send out an update attachment." Case headed for the door.

"And Case," the detective stopped and looked around, "we'll get the guy, one way or another."

Case turned again and the Captain said, "Wait a second. Sit down." He did.

"It's tough about Rodriguez. You know the family will be taken care of, survivor's benefits, memorial fund."

"That doesn't fix anything."

"I know. That's why you have to take a little time. You can't carry that and still do your job. You can't get there from here: honor him by finishing this thing, if you haven't got it 100% together. It's still too early, but you're going to have to let it go, at least in the short term. I'm mainly talking about the guilt you're wearing. You want it? Fine. At least put it off for later."

"Is that what Dr. Leonard is going to tell me?"

"Maybe."

"Then I don't have to go?"

"Go on. Get out of here. Go see the sketch artist."

Case was finished giving his description, based on his one-time memory of Derek, to the artist. His memory was accurate and so was the drawing. He decided to kill the next couple of hours at his desk trying to identify leads, the Captain's orders notwithstanding. A woman was walking in his direction from a few offices away. At first he didn't recognize her. Then he did. It was Lucy. She didn't seem surprised to see him as she approached.

"Lawrence, I'm really sorry about what happened. I came down to see you, but you weren't at your desk so I asked the Captain and he said I could find here. Your partner seemed like a very special person. Of course, I only met him that one time, but I could tell."

"Yeah. He was a good cop." He knew she meant it, but sympathy was just an emotion. It couldn't actually *do* anything.

"It's just so terrible. I know you must feel horrible. I really wish I could help in some way."

"Yeah, so do I."

Lucy didn't know what else to say, or do. "Do you need a hug?"

And that's when he lost it. He went off like a pyrotechnic show. His face suddenly looked like a cherry bomb and his arms flew up like Roman candles. He was a 2 liter bottle of pop shaken so hard the cap blew off with 80% on the contents exploding out the top. Somewhere in the back of his mind a regret was being formed that it was Lucy he was about to unload on. But he couldn't stop himself and that regret would play out later, although much sooner than he thought.

Case hit the wall with his right fist, turning around, his back to Lucy, yelling at the ceiling:

"A hug?! A HUG?! Yeah, that's what I need! That'll fix everything!" His voice increased 50% in volume. "You were at the funeral. You saw his wife and kids. They can't even get that he's gone. I was his partner. Do you even know what that means?" Case was shouting. "Why don't we get some marshmallows, all sit around a campfire, hold hands and sing Kumbaya? Then we can have a group hug. Wouldn't that be nice? A hug! That's the most stu--."

He had unconsciously turned back around, facing her, and then he focused for the first time on her face, and stopped. She looked like she had been slapped as she was staring at him. She held her breath; her eyes wide and her mouth hung half open. He stood there for a moment looking at her and his show was over.

"I...I...I'm..."

Lucy took a step back, then another, retreating, as if from a crazy person, then turned slowly, walked back down the hall and disappeared around the corner. Case just stood there. A minute before he was six foot two. Now he was three foot two. He suddenly had a clear idea of where he wanted to be at that moment: someplace else. And that someplace could only be the Blue Sow. His feeling of mayhem and needing to kill something awoke from its dormancy with renewed vigor. It was only Monday afternoon, but if he was lucky he would run into two or three of his buddies that wanted a piece of him.

When Case pulled into the side lot there were only a

couple of cars parked there and the inside was, as he should have expected, pretty deserted. The bartender/ owner gave him a nod when he walked into the cool, compared to the outside temperature, and dim interior.

"Draft," Case said. There would be no servers on duty at this time. Case took his dripping glass of beer to nurse it in a booth not far from the door. There were two retired cops at a booth a couple spaces away and one at the bar. No one paid any attention to him. He knew he wouldn't be lucky enough to find McCulley there, or O'Rourke, whom he was sure he could engage in a heated enough conversation to push him to the breaking point. He just wasn't having any luck.

Case was halfway through his beer. This place was worse than a morgue. He decided to put a quarter on a few platters before somebody put the juke box in a museum. Case finished his beer just as Joe Cocker finished *Cry Me a River*. He was going to have another beer, why not?, he had no intention of keeping his appointment with Dr. Looney, when the guy at the bar started complaining about something. This was just too boring. He had to get out of there.

As Case neared the front of the bar he heard the bartender say: "They're pretzels, what do they look like?"

"Where are the other kind?" the customer groused.

"What other kind?"

"The ones that look like faces."

"They must have been out of them. These are what they delivered."

"But I like the twisted kind that looks like faces, not these...sticks."

"It's all pretzel. What's the difference, twist, sticks?"

Case stopped half way out the door. He suddenly turned around and rushed to the bar.

"Let me see that." He grabbed the bowl and looked. Pretzel...*sticks.*

"Hey! What's the matter with you! Get your own pretzels."

The bartender said to Case, "Tell this guy it's all the same stuff."

Case rushed out without saying a word, thinking of his little niece Jennifer. He headed back downtown, barely turned off his car in the underground garage before he was back in the building, taking the stairs two at a time and started flipping through his notes at his desk without even sitting down. He finished looking at what he wanted. He was sure. He had a motive. It was crazy, but he was sure. He checked his watch then headed upstairs to keep his appointment with Dr. Leonard.

Case rapped on the door of Dr. Leonard's office.

"Come…"

And Case was inside.

"…in."

"Doc. Sorry. I'm a little early, but I want to run some - thing by you, see what you think."

Dr. Leonard was about to ask Case to sit down, but the shock of what he was hearing from Case, so many foreign ideas, left him dumbfounded and he just motioned for Case to take the seat in front of his desk, but Case couldn't sit. Case knew he hadn't ever exactly shown any interest in what the doc had to say, so he decided to spread a little butter.

"Doc, you're the finest Police Pscy…, you know, whatever, I've ever worked with. I need your opinion of something that just seems crazy."

Still disoriented by what he was hearing from this detective he asked: "How many Police Psychologists have you worked with?"

"Just y…, it doesn't matter. Look, this serial killing, the three murders, we haven't been able to find a motive."

Case didn't know where to begin, his head was still spinning.

"Detective, please sit down."

Case did so, pulling out a pack of Black Jack, and gestured to Dr. Leonard, who declined ("What was I thinking?" Case thought). Dr. Leonard took a pack of menthols out of his coat pocket and lit one up.

"What happened to the carrots?" Case asked, surprised.

"Don't tell anyone. I fell off the produce wagon. Maybe nicotine isn't as good for eyesight as carrots, but I've stopped kicking the dog. So, you wanted to run something by me? Something turn up with the same case you came in with before?"

"Yes, Manny...he found something, an interesting connection between the victims and how they were killed."

"First, Detective, I want to express my sympathy for the loss of your partner. It's a horrible tragedy. I believe it is important to talk about it when you are ready."

"Thanks, he was a good cop. We're going to get the guy responsible. It wasn't related to these murders. I know that's what I'm supposed to see you about, but right now I don't want to talk about Manny's death. I want to finish the work we were doing while he was alive."

Case explained all three murder methods and how they related to the talents and skills of the victims. He also related that Rodriguez found the Simi Valley High School alma mater for all three.

"That is interesting. The Supreme Irony."

"What's that?"

"I just call it the Supreme Irony when someone is killed using their own method against them, like when a man is hanged on the gallows he built to hang an innocent man."

"My big brother used to grab my wrist and hit me in the face with my own hand and say 'Why are you hitting yourself?' "

"Something like that. The killer is using the same means to kill his victim as that which the victim used against him in some sense."

"We thought that might be what was going on, but ruled it out. All the victims were in the same graduating class. It points to one killer, especially considering the style of the killings, even though the methods were different. If the purpose was to get back in the same way that he was wronged, it doesn't fit. If he lost to someone for a position, maybe he thought they cheated for it. Maybe he was just jealous. The problem is there are multiple victims, each killed using different methods. It didn't make sense one person needed revenge for wrongs he suffered in multiple fields."

"Paranoia could explain it. He might think every time he's disappointed, there's a conspiracy against him."

"We thought of that but eventually ruled it out. We did search for a single suspect, connected to all three victims, and having something in common with each one that illustrated the way they died."

"But you couldn't find any."

"No, we couldn't."

"So, the killer was making a statement with the way he killed them, but not why he killed them."

"Right. The methods do not reveal the motive. We needed a single motive that applies to each victim, and I think I found it. But that gives me two problems."

"First, what did you find? We'll worry about the problems if you're right about the motive."

"You remember the pretzels at the first scene? At the other sites we found other items, definitely planted by the killer. At the Dodson shooting there were candy pebbles and at the Turlock gassing there were Zagnuts, a crunchy candy, used to be called chicken bones."

"And?"

"And that's it. That's all I have."

"Which is what?"

"Which is crazy. That's my first problem. If I'm reading it right, I don't buy it as a motive. But if it is the motive, which means there could still be more victims, my second problem is: what was all the effort about with the different methods; what do they mean? Why did he kill them in those particular ways?"

"So what do you think the killer is saying with the items he planted?"

"Pretzel...*sticks*   candy   pebbles...*stones*   and chicken...*bones*.   Sticks and stones can break my bones..."

Dr. Leonard crushed out his cigarette."... 'but names will never hurt me'."

"Crazy, right? Somebody killed three people over a nursery rhyme, from maybe getting teased in school?"

"It might not be crazy." Dr. Leonard countered.

"Everyone gets teased sometime about something. That's no reason to kill. No one would wait, plan and carry out a serial killing, over name calling. Kids are taught to ignore it. That's why mothers teach their kids that rhyme, when they're young, that names don't hurt. I was just at my brother's house last night and..."

"Detective Case," Dr. Leonard interrupted. "...I must stop you right there. You've just hit a hot button so forgive me if I launch into a tirade. I don't know how, nor do I think it is possible, to put it more strongly. 'Sticks and stones can break my bones but...', though well-meaning is the most misdirected, ill conceived, worst possible advice a mother can possibly give her child.

Yes, on a physical level the meaning is obvious, but the damage done by physical objects to the body: bruises, scrapes, cuts, even broken bones mend and heal and are soon forgotten. But the damage done to the psyche, to the sense of individual value, to the feeling of worth as a human being, the sense of acceptance and equality among peers could take years to, or may never heal, as a result of belittlement, humiliation, disrespect, derogation and ridicule. The idea that the recipient of such abuse is 'not hurt' is ludicrous in the least and tragic in the extreme. Essentially telling her child to "ignore it and go play", instead of replacing the negative the child received with positive reinforcement, is the worst possible approach. She is in effect supporting the bad message the child is receiving of negative self value when she does not deny it, simply saying to ignore it. Claiming the child cannot be hurt by names since words have no outward physical impact is shallow, one-dimensional ignorance at its worst."

Dr. Leonard spoke evenly, calmly and never raised his

voice; then apologized for his outburst. Case accepted his apology. Dr. Leonard continued:

"At best, ostracized children will find a very small group that accepts them, but never lose the sense of rejection, because they are driven out of the "main herd". At worst, their physical bodies will continue growing, demonstrating no outward appearance of abnormality, but their psyche has been stunted. It grows, too, but blocked from a normal healthy path, in what direction it grows is unknown and of unlimited, unpredictable possibilities."

"OK, you're the doctor, but it just seems to me that no matter how bad someone had it in high school, after ten years?, would carry out a triple homicide? It just seems like most people would move on and put it behind them."

"Of course, statistically speaking, most people would. But depending on the individual, the nature, the degree and duration of the circumstances we can't make categorical predictions. Like the planet, most of the human mind is yet unexplored. Yet compared to the human mind, we know everything there is to know abut the planet. The mind is truly the last great frontier. That said, there have been great strides forward in the study of the brain."

Case felt a lecture coming, but he was in a rare,

accommodating mood.

"And you're going to explain some of them."

"If you want to hear."

Case gestured for him to continue. The doctor took out another cigarette, but didn't light it.

"It was once thought that the brain was undifferentiated. But we now know different parts of the brain are specialized for different functions, although different areas do work together and rely on each other. There are continuing studies of the various parts of the brain and their functions. The hippocampus is a part of the brain …"

"The what?"

"Hippocampus. It's Latin for seahorse."

Case raised his eyebrows, wondering if the doctor were serious.

"Never mind. It doesn't matter. The hippocampus is just below the cerebral cortex, found in the medial temporal lobes. It's an area of the brain that specializes in learning. Another specialized area in the temporal lobes is the amygdala. It deals with fear and anxiety and aggression.

This will sound a little technical, but it goes to the point. The brain consists of neurons that communicate with each other across synapses, which separate the neurons. One form of communication is chemically, by means of neurotransmitters, the most effective of which is glutamate. Are you with me so far?"

"Right behind you."

"Excellent. Now, when there is sufficient glutamate it opens the second receptor in the post synaptic neuron, resulting in LTP, or learning. This area is also where memory takes place. When the amygdala gets involved, you'll remember, that's the area that deals with fear, anxiety and aggression..."

"Of course, I was just going to mention it."

"When the amygdala gets involved it releases a chemical that partially blocks the second receptor in the post synaptic neuron and since glutamate is made from a single amino acid, partially altering it, disrupting learning and memory at that point. These are in the limbic system concerned with emotion."

"Is there an English version of the lecture?"

"Sorry. When these two different areas of the brain are working at the same time, basically against each other, the fear/anxiety affecting the learning /memory, a third area, dealing with reason and rational thinking, has the effect of lessening the impact the anxiety region has to disrupt the learning region. Usually, it lessens the disruption to such a degree there is little impact discernable at all in the hippo...learning, memory area."

"What kind of anxiety can cause this?"

"Good question. You're paying attention."

"You're so riveting."

"It varies from brain to brain, dealing with neuron receptors. What triggers anxiety and fear? It can be any stimulus from mild to severe, depending on stages of development."

"So what does this mean to me?"

"Since these processes are converted from electrical to chemical impulses elsewhere in the brain, it means we don't have enough experience in the field of learning/memory disorder, which symptoms can lie dormant for years, when the rational area fails to function in an effective way, at the time of anxiety disruption, to the learning area. We just need more experience to know that happens when that rational area fails to override the disruption in that area of the limbic system."

"Any guesses?"

"If the area of reason fails to do its job, there is speculation the dormant symptoms can be triggered by another area dealing with an entirely different emotion."

"And that is?"

"Hostility."

Case paused to let the implications sink in.

"So the bottom line is, what you're saying is, even something as minor as harmless teasing, can lead to unpredictable results, even, what appears to be, pre-meditated, calculated, cold-blooded murder?"

"Well, as I said, a lot has to do with the intensity of the stimuli and the development of the brain, but at a certain degree of both, then yes."

Case still didn't want to believe it. "Given that's true, and I can't argue it on the scientific level, argue it?, I can't even understand it, but, given that's true, it does give a motive that can tie all the victims to the same killer. There could be more on his list, or Jim Turlock could have been the last. The only option is to find him. The question of why he killed in the ways he did may or may not help identify the killer, but knowing that might help me understand what type of person I'm looking for."

"Good work, Detective. There's real reason to believe you have your motive. All that remains is to identify the killer."

"That's all. What does your crystal ball say about the

reason he would have done it the ways he did?"

Dr. Leonard looked at Case for a moment without answering. He lit the cigarette he was holding and leaned back in his chair. He turned and glanced out the window, thinking. He turned back to Case.

"That would take some hypothesizing, but I think we can come up with a pretty reasonable idea. It appears there are two things going on here: the motive for the killings and the methods of the killings, as we've established. Since the motive seems to be provided in the message the killer left behind, then I still think there's a strong reason to believe he did employ irony, just not in the way I at first thought. However, I think they are closely related.

Assuming we're reading his message correctly, his motive is revenge for abuses he suffered. He was probably completely vulnerable. So his methods of killing provides the irony in that he's turning the circumstances around 180°. He must have been vulnerable and defenseless. He's demonstrating that now, not only is he in complete control, because he can kill in whatever manner he chooses, but the manner he chooses also demonstrates he is even superior in his victims' own strengths, by using those strengths against them. He is no longer the helpless victim, but the complete master. This is the important piece of the puzzle that Det. Rodriguez found that should help identify the killer, as not being in the victim's own circle, but outside it.

I think, detective, you have why he killed them: revenge from abuse; and you have how he killed them, in various ways, and perhaps, now, why he killed them how he killed them: demonstration of control. Now all you need is who killed them."

Case considered that. "If all that's true, it's telling me this guy is not too worried about getting caught. He could certainly have gotten his revenge without telling us anything."

"But revenge in secret is not as satisfying as being able to claim the victory."

"Life in prison or worse is a stiff price to pay for bragging rights. And if this guy can wait and plan for ten years in cold blood, then he's a human reptile."

"Meaning what?" the doctor asked.

"Meaning he believes we'll never catch him." Case got up to go. "Thanks, Doc. Go back to carrots; they're better for you. The next bag's on me. I've got to go now and start searching through haystacks for a needle."

"Quit smoking again? That would be one for and one against."

"Who would be against?"

"Freud."

"Freud?"

"My dog."

"Get a goldfish."

"Since you're here, I could offer a couple more thoughts if you'd like."

"Sure, Doc. I'm always willing to hear what you have to say." Case sat again.

"Ah...yes...of course. Well, if what we surmise is true, that the individual you are seeking was subjected to an extreme amount of pressure over an extended period of time, then evidence suggests he would have constructed for himself what they now call a 'happy place'. A place where he could retreat, mentally, to escape unbearable realities. Prisoners have done that, as well as people in terrible pain. Somehow they put it away and exist, mentally at least, in an entirely different reality, in a different place."

"What kind of place."

"Any kind to the subject's liking: peaceful, the typical desert island with warm breezes, or a place evoking happy memories of the past. It could even be a symbol, just a simple object, like a baseball, if the subject had his best times playing ball. It could be an entirely random object the subject saw once, and associates with a good feeling, and has become his talisman. I know that's clutching at straws in your haystack, but if something like that exists, it could be a lead."

"And the other thought?"

"Well, according to the ditty, I don't think you're actually in much of a time constraint."

"Oh? Why not?"

"Because everyone knows the ending. He gave the first three parts; the last is like a pregnant pause. No one really has to hear it to know what the end is. So he has no need to demonstrate it."

"Assuming it is a man." Case countered.

"Yes. There's really nothing to support that assumption, but assuming it is a man. The final shoe doesn't have to drop."

"You may be right."

"But you don't think so."

"I don't think it's a matter of symmetry between victims and phrases in a nursery rhyme. I think it's a matter of he's not going to quit until he's finished, if we're reading this right. Nothing I'm getting is telling me this is all over. I can't say why, but after everything you've explained, all

I have is my gut telling me the next thing to drop is not going to be a shoe, but another body."

Chapter Nineteen

Case went directly to his desk, gathered everything he had on the case, and headed out the door. He wasn't leaving anything for Dets. Itchy and Scratchy, wherever penguins liked to vacation. Back home Case literally hit the books. It wasn't just that it was getting late in the day, a little after three, but somehow the feeling was strong that the hour was late. He felt sure another body would drop, and soon. Indications were that the killer he was looking for was arrogant, but not stupid. The police could make lots of mistakes, but the killer only one, and the longer he went, the greater the likelihood was that he would make one. Even if there wasn't going to be a fourth victim, the killer already had three to answer for, but Case couldn't shake the feeling he was on a head-on collision course, and soon. He just hoped it would be soon enough to prevent a possible fourth.

The kitchen table was covered with interview notes, the murder books for each homicide and the SVHS year books. Case tried to get them to fit together somehow in his mind. He arranged them and rearranged them hoping they'd point to the killer on their own, become a complete picture if put in the right order. He had read them enough times that he could quote most of it from memory.

Case wasn't at it twenty minutes when the phone rang.

"Yeah."

"Case!" It was Captain Murdock. "Get back here with those files! I have Detectives Fuller and Young here ready to get started."

"I had a good meet with Dr. Leonard about the case. I think I might be getting close. I need to follow up on a couple things."

"I told you. Until next Monday you are to give it a rest. Fuller and Young can handle whatever you've got. Now bring those files in right away. That's an order!"

"But…"

"Should we make it two weeks?"

"OK, Captain, I'll bring them in."

"Right away means now. If I have to send someone out to get them, they'll get your badge and gun, too."

"I'm on my way." Case knew the Captain couldn't see behind his back. Now his time was *really* short. He had to find something immediately, and he had no reason to think he would, or at least get out of there and find somewhere else to work. He figured he had at least an hour, half that time before the Captain realized he wasn't coming in with the files, and as much time to get someone out there. If he had agreed too easily the Captain would have known he was lying. He probably knew anyway, which meant he probably didn't even have an hour. But that was most likely a bluff. The Captain wouldn't waste manpower on an errand like that. Most likely, Case assumed, he'd just get another insub in his jacket. But he might send Dets. Heckle and Jeckle, they weren't doing anything anyway.

Case decided to start one more time from the very beginning. He started with Shawna Anderson. First he studied the crime scene photos. Then he read his notes about her, brief as they were. Finally, he went to the school year book for the senior class and read everything he could about Shawna Anderson, the bio under her picture and then the section about the groups and clubs that she belonged to from the information in her photo bio. He and Rodriguez had checked out many of those people and he reread those notes. He did the same thing with the other two, Stephanie Dodson and James Turlock.

He had done this so many times that he knew he should approach it from another direction. And then it hit him. From the angle of the killer's motive being jealousy for losing a position, or anger for being cheated out of one, he was following the direction that the killer was someone in their group. Someone in their circle. But he had already decided that didn't fit the one killer theory, which he was convinced of.

It also would not fit if Dr. Leonard was right about the reason for this sticks and stones message the killer was so intent on leaving. Teasing in one's on group would be more of a good natured variety. Teasing leading to murder, crazy, but...would be anything but good natured. It wouldn't be teasing; it would be bullying and abuse of a vicious nature. He wasn't looking for a student the victims hung out with, he was looking for someone the victims would have considered merely an object of ridicule.

Case checked his watch. Twenty-five minutes since the Captain called. This was going to be close if he didn't bail out of there soon. But he didn't want to leave without something to go on. He would have to find somewhere else to work, maybe check in somewhere for the night, doable, but inconvenient. He started over again, this time to see if he could get a vibe from the student photos and bios. The victims were all of the athletic and performing type. An 'outsider' would probably be an academic, a bookworm; not be in the victim's natural circles.

He started with the first student in the senior year book, really just glancing at faces and scanning bios. Several pages went by along with ten minutes. Then several more pages and ten more minutes. And then he saw... and then he knew. About half way through the class Case stopped looking. He stopped at one student and couldn't look away. It wasn't the face, although that would draw one's attention, but it wasn't the face that froze Case. It was the eyes. That's how he knew.

When Case could pull his eyes from the picture he read the name: Paul U. Kirby. Chess club, Science club, Math club. Not surprising. So he was a nerd. But that in itself wasn't conclusive about anything. He wasn't, obviously, the only student in those clubs. What was conclusive, and he looked back again to the photo, was those eyes. Paul U. Kirby's had a strange, mesmerizing look Case had never seen before. They belonged to a hunted, cornered animal. But not to a defeated one. They looked vulnerable and damaged, having suffered years of hurt and pain. At the same time those eyes also looked back with a challenging intensity of absolute resolve.

Case involuntarily shivered. He would not want to be on Paul U. Kirby's short list. Eyes are supposed to reveal vast emotions and meanings. Those eyes revealed a determination for revenge, total and complete. Eyes might be the windows to the soul, but not the eyes of Paul U. Kirby. It was obvious behind those eyes there was no soul. Behind those eyes was a deep, dark, bottomless pit of void. From that pit issued a shadowy, black cloud of dark matter, rising like smoke, laced with jagged red bolts; the jagged bolts of red had one purpose: to cause maximum pain. Case heard a knock at his door.

Captain Murdock wasn't bluffing. Tweedle Dee and

Tweedle Dum were early. There was no hesitation; at the first knock Case was up and moving. He had to react. No time to plan, just to move. He grabbed all the materials he was working with, picked up a shallow box he kept in the corner with magazines he hadn't yet decided to throw away, dumped it on the floor, dropped the materials in the box, turned around, turned the radio on medium volume, ran to the bathroom, turned on the shower, pulled the shower curtain closed, left the bathroom door half open and was out the back before the detectives sent to retrieve the books had knocked for the third time.

Case knew any second one of the Bobbsey Twins would use a skeleton key to open his door. With the car out front, the radio on and the shower running, they'd be convinced he was home, at least long enough for Case to get away. They'd easily be convinced Case was at home and in the shower because they would already assume it. They could search the living room, and bedroom if necessary, grab what they came for, and leave before Case got 'out of the shower'. When they didn't find what they were looking for, they'd be forced to wait until Case got 'out of the shower', buying him a few more minutes before they finally went into the bathroom and realized they'd been duped. That should be enough for a clean getaway. He hoped they would turn the shower off.

Case ran around the back of the duplex past his

neighbor's side carrying his box. He saw Mutt & Jeff's unmarked car parked behind his at the curb. He opened his driver side door, threw the box on the passenger seat and slid in, quietly closing the door. He turned the key in the ignition, forgetting the little 'start' prayer, his mind elsewhere. The car made several noises, but none of them a starting noise. He tried again. Same set of noises, still missing the one he wanted. He slammed both open palms on the steering wheel. "Not now!" Of course he had to try again; same results. The car was not going to change its mind this time. He grabbed the box and jumped out, quietly closing the door.

That's it. He wasn't taking his car to his brother anymore. He'd find a new mechanic, even if he had to pay him. Case, carrying the box, made a wide berth towards his neighbor's half of the duplex, all the time looking at his own front door. Ruff 'n Ready were inside. He just hoped they hadn't checked the bathroom yet. Case knocked on his neighbor's door. Clearly surprised to have a visitor, Eugene opened it right away.

Eugene Bledsoe, 38, had just moved in earlier in the year, the first time out of his parents' house, on his own. Eugene had an impressive sports card collection, a really nice comic book collection, many first editions that cost him over $100. each, and a collection of action figures of which he was especially proud, all in the original packaging. What he did not have, or ever had, was a date with an actual girl. This lack might not be hard to understand, except for what he had in the garage: a cherry 1969 lime green Ford Shelby Mustang fastback. He only took it out of the garage to give it a bath. The odometer didn't click many tenths from the garage to the driveway and back again.

"I'm from next door," Case blurted.

"Yeah. Hi."

"Quick. I need to borrow your car."

"Why?"

"Police business."

Eugene wasn't much for standing up to authority, but, his car? That's where he drew the line. No way. He wasn't going to let anybody drive his car, police or not. *He* didn't even drive his car.

"Sorry, no way."

"Quick I need it." Case glanced over at his door. "Quick. Give me the keys."

"No way."

"C'mon, hurry up. Give me the keys."

"Why should I?"

"You know how you been trying to get a date with the

mail lady, uh, Julie, right?"

"How do…"

"But you know how she'd rather join the Army; even though she's a member of Peace at any Price, than go out with you?"

Sourly, "Yeah."

"I'll get her to go out with you. Gimme the keys."

"How?"

"Don't worry, I'll do it. Gimme the keys."

"How?"

"I'll tell her you love cats and donate to Help Homeless Hummingbirds. She goes for sensitive-guy crap like that. Gimme the keys." He looked at his door again.

Eugene thought about it; thought about his Shelby, thought about Julie, thought about Julie in his Shelby, went inside and then came out and tossed Case the keys. "Don't scratch it."

"Don't worry." Case hit the garage door opener on the key ring, jumped in and backed the Mustang out of the garage.

Eugene ran out in the street and yelled at the back of the speeding Shelby: "Tell her Friday!"

Speeding away Case looked in the rear view mirror and thought, "She'll never go out with him." He leaned back against the seat, getting comfortable. "Nice wheels, though."

He stayed on surface streets since he didn't have a destination yet. He just needed an unobtrusive spot to stop and make a call that hopefully would point him in the right direction. He turned right onto Cesar Chavez Ave., heading north, before it turned into Sunset Blvd. He pulled onto a quiet residential street and parked. Case called a Sgt. in R & I he knew he could count on. A few, especially the older crowd, respected Case for what he did. Case just hoped it wasn't general knowledge that he was on ordered vacation. With this Sgt., though, he didn't think it would matter. The guy would probably run a few things he needed even if he didn't owe Case some favors.

Sgt. Williams picked up on the second ring. "R & I, Sergeant Williams."

"Williams, it's Case."

"What's up?"

"I need an address."

"Any special hurry?"

"No hurry. Ten minutes ago will be fine."

"That important, huh?"

"The usual life and death. Seriously. Start with an address. Call me back no later than the second you get it. Then keep looking for whatever else you can turn on the guy. His name is Paul U. Kirby. I don't know what the 'U' is for. You know the drill. Start with DMV, then check IRS, SSA, DOD, voter and property tax roles, even INS if you have to. Whatever you can find. But call me on this number with the address first. How's Betty, good? Great. Call me back." Case broke the connection.

Case stopped for a second to let his mind refocus, then looked around in the car, almost noticing it for the first time. He wasn't used to such luxury. Eugene had not updated it with GPS or a CD player or anything like that, still it was a thing of beauty and Case admired it. He owed Eugene that much. You know, he thought, it's a good thing I couldn't get my car started. It seemed bad at the time, but it was meant for good. This way Bert and Ernie don't know what I'm driving and can't put out a watch-for alert. He felt so good about that, he decided to give his brother another chance and not find a new mechanic. If he had, he would have had to drop Johnny Black label. This way everybody's happy: his brother still gets his business and Case could stay with the quality scotch.

Everybody but Frick and Frack. He wondered what they were going to tell the Captain when they came back empty. He'd love to see them standing there, sweating on the carpet in front of Murdock's desk. Served them right; at half Case's age or less, they were always dropping retirement home brochures on his desk and putting him on senior care mailing lists. Youth had some things going for it, but experience wasn't one of them.

He grabbed the SVHS year book and looked again at Paul Kirby's picture, studying it. What made you kill three people? How many more? Who's next? With that thought in mind, he turned to the club photos again to study the groups with the previous victims. Logically, Kirby's next victim should be in one of those group photos. Of course, Case realized he had no definitive proof Kirby was the killer, no evidence at all. Just his detective's sense, and those eyes. Even without anything solid to work from, Kirby was as good a starting place as any other, and Case was convinced better than most.

It didn't take long for Cases' phone to ring. It was Sgt. Williams with Kirby's address. Case didn't think it would be far, but he was surprised how close it actually was. He was already heading in that direction.

"Thanks. I'm on my way. What else?"

"His car, a black 2007 Ford Focus, California vanity plate N-V-R---"

"H-R-T."

"Right! How did you know?'

"Lucky guess."

"OK, I'll keep digging. Call me back if you need anything else," Sgt. Williams said.

"Count on it."

Case had an address in N. Hollywood. It was an apartment building on Moorpark St. west of Vineland Ave. He got on the 10 a short distance and then 101. Taking a right at the Vineland Ave. exit, it was only a couple lights to Moorpark St. He turned left and drove three and a half blocks, almost to Lankershim Blvd., before he found the apartment building he was looking for. It was a three story affair covered in a light colored stucco. He parked out front, then, once in the lobby, buzzed the manager's unit.

The manager appeared after a second buzz. He was about 5'6" Case judged, late 50's, very short hair on the sides, bald on top, a half-smoked cigarette hanging from the right side of his mouth, wearing open sandals he probably just slipped on, baggy sweat pants and a clean or dirty t-shirt, Case couldn't decide which. He looked to Case like an ex-fight manager who never had a title bout. Case told the manager his business with a tenant on the third floor.

"I'll take you there. Gotta take the stairs, elevator's temporary out of order."

Case wondered how temporarily it had been out of order. The second flight let them out at one end of a hallway running the length of the building. The walls looked freshly painted. It couldn't have been too expensive a job: they were painted one consistent bright white, floor to ceiling, end to end. Case wondered if they were covering up old paint, graffiti, etc., or if that was the finished product. There was no color; no pictures, designs, signs or anything else to break the consistent white, floor to ceiling, end to end. And no doors. No doors opened onto the main hallway. At regular intervals were short, branch hallways with a facing door, near the end, on either side. Each door displayed its apartment number in black painted numerals on the identical tan doors.   The manager lead Case to the apartment Case requested. Case rapped loudly on the door.

"Police!"

There was no answer. Case knocked again and counted to five.

"Open it." He told the manager.

"Don't you need a warrant?"

"Don't you need a fire, safety and health inspection?"

The manager grudgingly got out his pass key and unlocked the door.

"Go back downstairs. I'll let myself out." The manager left without saying a word.

Case took out his gun and turned the doorknob, opening the door an inch. He held the gun in both hands, pointing at the door and listened. Then he pushed the door hard open and stepped to one side pointing the gun into the apartment. There was no sound at all, no indication anyone was there. Case stepped cautiously inside, lead by his outstretched arms, his gun pointing the way.

On his left was an open kitchen area with an adjacent table and two chairs. On the right was a small living room. So far it was all open to view. The apartment was small. There was only a bathroom beyond the kitchen on the left and the single bedroom across from the bathroom on the right left to check. He stood with his back to the wall before the bathroom door and pointed his gun at the bedroom door. Quickly glancing around his left shoulder he saw the bathroom was empty. Just the bedroom now. If Kirby was there, he was in the bedroom.

Case looked at the bedroom door. It might all end here. This guy could have an intruder trap. Case repeated his actions at the front door: pointing the gun with both hands he pushed the bedroom door hard open and stepped to one side. Looking quickly in he saw no one. He stepped to the other side of the door and pointed the gun ahead of him at the cross angle. No one. Case cautiously stepped into the bedroom. He was going to proceed very carefully.

The bedroom was almost square. There was a closet on Case's left as he stood looking in the room. It had sliding wooden doors. Both were slid all the way to the right. The bed was next to the wall on the right, unmade. A book was on the floor next to it. Opposite the closet was a small desk under the single window facing the street, and opposite the bed was a long workbench occupying nearly the whole length of the wall. There was plenty to look through. He just didn't know if he was going to be able to make sense of any of it. There were journals, notebooks and loose papers, seemingly in no particular order amid brain teaser puzzles to take apart, other scientific mental challenges and even the ubiquitous Rubik's cube and swinging metal balls. Some of this was on the desk under the window. There were papers and journals on the floor next to the wooden chair in front of the small desk. The rest of it was on a long work bench in front of the third wall. Case figured Kirby spent most of his time working at that bench. It had a comfortable chair on casters. Strangely there was no computer in sight.

Case started with the closet on his left. There were a few shirts on hangers, and a pair of shoes had been tossed on the closet floor. A single shelf above the clothes hanger rod was jammed with books. Case took a closer look, but so far, had not touched anything. If he was impressed with the subject matters, then he was impressed. The books were all science, math, anatomy, metaphysics, astrophysics, particle physics, and many specialty branch studies. Einstein was, of course, represented by his general and special theories of relativity. Case guessed Kirby's favorite authors were Carl Sagan and Stephen Hawking. He must have every book they wrote.

Did he really read all this stuff? He wondered if he ever engaged in lighter, bedtime reading. Case looked over at the unmade bed against the wall at the right. He slipped on tight fitting plastic gloves and walked over to pick up the book on the floor lying next to the bed. The gloves were SOP. If he left his prints a defense attorney could claim any evidence was planted. But any evidence he might find linking Kirby to the killings wouldn't be admissible in court anyway. The manager was right, he needed a warrant to search the apartment, and no judge would issue a warrant based on nothing more than his hunch from a ten year old picture in a school year book. He knocked on the door to question the individual, but he had no right to enter.

In any event, Case wasn't there to find evidence on the prior murders; without Kirby there, he was looking for a possible clue as to his present whereabouts, for questioning, and possibly prevent another death. Case looked at the book and got his answer about Kirby's reading habits. A Sgt. Burke novel. Case used to read those. They were fun. Sgt. Burke did pretty much whatever he needed to get the job done. He usually got shot once or twice in each book, but it never seemed to bother him. What Case liked the most about them was, other than in real life, justice was always served in the end. Sgt. Burke always 'got his man'.

So Kirby did enjoy lighter, bedtime reading. Case guessed everyone needed a break from all that egghead stuff once in awhile. Case looked at the cover and laughed. *Sgt. Burke Gets His Man.* The title pretty much told it all, but it was fun to follow his predictable exploits. Case started to look around the room when his phone rang. It was Sgt. Williams.

"What d'ya got?"

"Not much," Sgt. Williams answered. "There's not much on this guy. Born Feb. 29th, 1984, graduated …"

"February 29th?"

"That's right."

"Hmm. Unusual. First time in my experience. I guess they're out there. Doesn't mean anything, but unusual."

"It comes every 1,461 days, every four years. Just one-fourth less often than every other day. Statistically there's got to be a lot of people with that birthday."

"Sure, but how many people do that you know? You'd

have to have 365 acquaintances just to know one person with your same birthday. I don't like coincidences, and I don't believe the Zodiac controls peoples' lives, but that is an odd day and this guy seems like a pretty strange bird. Anyway..."

"Yeah, so, he graduated Simi Valley High School, 2002, top of class academically, no known criminal associations, not apparently a member of any fringe group, no record: local or Federal including Homeland Security."

"Employment record?"

"Haven't dug that far yet. Most likely some high tech firm in Silicon valley."

"I don't know. I'd guess he has the ability, but by the looks of it, hasn't put it to use, at least not professionally. Thanks, let me know if you find anything else."

"You got it."

Case continued searching the room. He was determined to be very methodical. He didn't want to miss the tiniest thing that might indicate Kirby's next move, or where he might be, or risk setting off some kind of trap. Under the bench were file draws. Case opened one and then another. They contained mechanical drawings of a variety of objects. It would take hours to study those now, hours he didn't want to spend. He was sure they probably had a lot of useful information; probably tie Kirby to the murders. He wanted to come back with a warrant so they could be used as evidence once he could convince a judge of probable cause for a search. Right now, he just needed to find the tenant of this apartment. Where was he, out planning his next murder? Doing a dry run to perfect his timing? Maybe he was already at the execution stage. And who would that next victim be? Then Case knew what he needed to find, to answer at least one of those questions.

He started again, this time at the bed, looking under it and under the mattress. It obviously wasn't on the small desk. He pulled open the shallow drawer. He opened the file drawers again under the work bench and checked thoroughly between all the manila folders and technical manuals. He checked each drawer. It would not be hard to find. Not there. The closet was the last place to look. Nothing could be concealed between the tightly packed books that disappeared out of sight behind the sliding doors. He slid the doors to the left revealing the rest of the shelf. Two books near the end were sticking out slightly, with their spines tilted towards each other. He pulled on them and could tell there was something wedged between. Sliding one book carefully out, and then the other, and there it was, now sitting on the shelve in plain view: Paul Kirby's copy of the Simi Valley High School Senior year book. Case's murder books were in the car. He had a feeling this was Paul

Kirby's own murder book.

He took the book down and sat at the work bench. If Dr. Leonard's assessment was right about the meaning of the items Kirby left at the murder scenes, then he didn't save his year book for nostalgic reasons. Case turned to individual student photos and there on the first page was the picture of Shawna Anderson. Or at least Kirby's version: he apparently used a pin to poke out both eyes and there was a stitched 'X' over the mouth done with a black marker. A death's head. Case would definitely replace this book where he found it when he was finished.

Case lifted a group of pages to flip through from the back with his thumb. He flipped two pages and there was James Turlock's photo, defaced exactly like Anderson's. He flipped more pages, slowly, one after another, and found no similar altered pictures. He hoped if there was to be a next victim he would find the defaced photo indicating who that would be. Maybe Kirby only did that after the fait accompli. He continued flipping pages until he was near the front, almost through. He then found Dodson's altered photo, eyes poked out and stitched black 'X' on the mouth, like the others. He could see there were no small holes in the facing page. He flipped it and then the next. There it was. The second photo from the end of the row, one row from the bottom.

Case read the name. Max Bruner. Eyes poked out, 'x'ed

mouth. He called Sgt. Williams who answered immediately.

"Home, work address," Case said into the phone. "Max Bruner, same class as Kirby, Simi Valley High. First, get a black and white out to his home. He's the killer's next target. If Bruner's not there, and anyone else is, wife, family member, whatever, have the officers get Bruner's current 20. They're to get whatever information they can. If he is at work, call him, have him stay put and send another black and white there. Call me right back with everything you get. I'm still searching the Kirby apartment..."

"How'd you get a warrant al---"

"...until you get back to me and then I'll proceed to Bruner's 20. Out." Case cut the connection. He then looked again at Bruner's photo. Did that mean he was already dead? In that case, where was Kirby? Case's gut told him no. He read the bio under the picture. "Left guard." He flipped to the group photos and found him with the football team. "Wrestling team." Case found him in the wrestling team photo. Back to the bio photo. "Champion weightlifter." Case wondered what Kirby had in store for Bruner. What was he going to do, hang him from a goal post? Unlikely and didn't fit. Strangle him in a wrestling hold? Better, but the three previous killings were apparently not by Kirby's own hand, and besides, he would certainly be no match for Bruner. Weightlifter.

Champion weightlifter! That had to be it. Dominate and kill him by his own strongest trait. But that was still a long way from knowing where.

At this point, until he heard from Williams, Case could only wait. But not idly. Something there could still provide valuable details. Case realized what apparently didn't belong, that seemed out of place, was often a telling clue. The Sgt. Burke novel was like that. It didn't seem to fit the surroundings, but he was satisfied with his own explanation for it being there. Case looked on the small table. He flipped through a cube desk calendar; it was a *Far Side,* all previous pages torn off to the current date. Nothing on the desk held his interest. He then stepped back to the door to give the room an overall scan, looking for the incongruous.

In the far corner, something on the long workbench caught his eye. It was a cheap, plastic Hawaiian souvenir of a hula girl with a green grass skirt and a curving palm tree with a brown trunk and green branches. The guy had been to Hawaii? Case doubted it. He liked hula girls? Why not? Palm trees? He remembered what Dr. Leonard had said about a mental escape place. It could be triggered by an object.

Case had to admit the interview with Dr. Leonard didn't do any harm. Detectives worked with fragments. The more fragments a detective had, the better. Some were the nuggets that held the key. Others were just as they appeared, of no meaning whatever. So far, he wasn't discarding any fragments. As Case wondered if that fragmentary detail, the Hawaiian souvenir, was of benefit or should be scrapped, he knew it was a fragment he would not have been looking for. His phone rang.

"Case."

"Sergeant Williams. I have a Maxwell S. Bruner in Montebello; married, two children, 8 and 11. The officers on scene spoke to his wife. He's at work. He's a personal trainer at Body & Fitness just a few miles from their home. The officers are staying with the wife until contact is made with Bruner. Another black and white should be at the gym any minute."

"Give me the number there."

Case called the gym and asked for the manager.

"This is Tom Weston."

"This is Detective Case, LAPD. I need to speak to Max Bruner. Is he there?"

"Max? Uh, yeah. Just a sec---oh, wait a minute. I'll need to check his schedule."

"Make it fast. This is very important."

Weston was back in half a minute which seemed like ten

to Case. "Max's last appointment of the day is an off-site. He'll go home after that."

"Off site?"

"Yeah. Some clients prefer to work out at their own weight rooms where they live, usually apartment houses. They pay more for that, but then they can work out on their own any time between sessions."

"Where was this appointment and who was the client?"

"I can't tell you that. How do I know…"

"It doesn't matter. They won't be there anyway. Just tell me, this is a first time client, right?"

The manager checked. "Yes, it is. How did…"

"Here's LAPD's number. Tell the operator you want to speak to Sergeant Williams in R & I. Tell him what you told me and answer any questions he asks." This guy had a suspicious nature. If he thought there was some kind of scam, it wouldn't do any good giving him Williams' direct number.

Case knew he was running out of time. He had to find Kirby and he still didn't have a clue how. He stepped back again and looked the room over. Then he stood in the middle to turn a complete 360°. Before he got half way around he noticed the travel poster on the wall to the right of the closet for the first time. In big letters across the top it said South Seas. Below that were two large palm trees arching to the left above a blue sea and just a hint of beach below.

That certainly tied to the souvenir. What was he planning, an island getaway once he finished with his victims? Or was it just the palm trees that were a mental trigger to something happy. There were certainly a lot of palm trees in and around the L.A. area. They were a striking feature. It always seemed to Case that they didn't belong there, but they were a nice touch. It gave an otherwise sprawling metropolis some character. But how can they have any positive meaning to Paul Kirby? What good memories could he have from living here, if this is what his life has come to?

Case made a quick call to Sgt. Williams. He answered again on the first ring.

"Did you talk to Bruner's manager?" Case asked.

"Just hung up. He tried to contact Bruner. No luck. He has no idea where he could be; neither does his wife. You turn anything?"

"My only hope is to find Kirby and Bruner. It's probably already too late, but I have to try."

"His wife says he's a big, strong guy. Your guy must have a gun if he's nabbed Bruner."

"Maybe. Can't speculate now."

"Watch yourself," Sgt. Williams cautioned.

Case was still looking at the travel poster when he noticed the calendar on the wall next to it.

"Keep me posted," Case cut the connection.

He walked over and took a closer look. It was hanging on the wall by a green push pin. Strange. It was still showing February. The cube calendar on the desk was up-to-date, but the wall calendar was several months behind. It was a current 2012 calendar. The days stopped at 29, or, rather, went up to 29, being February. 2012 was a leap year. He just had that discussion. February 29 was Kirby's birthday. Did he leave that page up because his birthday appears so infrequently on a calendar he seldom gets to see it?

Everyday was marked off like some people do. Some draw an 'X' on each square. Kirby used a, what? Case looked closer. Some kind of little rubber stamp. The stamp was struck at random angles on each square of the month. Case leaned in closer. Palm trees!? They were little palm trees made with a rubber stamp and ink pad. Case went over to the desk and thumbed the cube calendar again. Nothing unusual. He opened the drawer and rummaged through it, finding an old style ink pad with a metal lid. Continuing to look he found the small rubber stamp with the little palm tree design.

But was this supposed to mean anything? He went back to the wall calendar. So he liked looking at his unusual birth date. On a hunch he lifted the February page and looked at March. Clean, no stamps on the squares of March. He looked at April and May. Nothing. He released those pages. Only February had its days stamped with the palms. Why? The rest of the months aren't stamped. Only February, right up to his birthday, and then stop. No other months, just February stamped with its 29 palms.

Wait; 29 palms. *Twentynine Palms?* That's out in the desert, east of San Bernardino. East of Yucca Valley on highway 62. Case went shooting out there with friends a couple times when he was in school. Could that be it? Did Kirby somehow take Bruner out to Twentynine Palms? His first thought was: crazy. But that's what he said about the rest of this case. He shouldn't be surprised. It fit with the way this guy seemed to think.

Case had to make up his mind. If he was wrong, and he went on a wild goose chase, he could be losing his one chance to save Bruner, if that were still possible. It was even possible Kirby expected him to find what now seemed like a too obvious message, only to send him in the wrong direction. Instead of going southeast, maybe he should be going northwest, to Palmdale.

Chapter Twenty

Case left and locked the apartment, ran down the two flights of stairs and jumped in the waiting Mustang. When it roared to life he retraced his route back down Moorpark St. to Vineland Ave. and jumped on 134 east until it became Interstate 210 at Pasadena. Now he just had to fly straight as an arrow past Azusa, a little dog leg past Upland and then a straight shot to San Bernardino. That was about half way. It was about 60 miles to San Bernardino and another 70 to Twentynine Palms as the crow flies. He was no crow, but he was flying.

He gambled on Twentynine Palms because deception didn't seem to be Kirby's style, at least not with the police. Maybe, probably, he used it with his victims, but his attitude with the police was arrogance, 'catch me if you can', believing they really can't. If the police were smart enough to get what he was saying, fine; if not, too bad for them. Either way, it didn't matter. Kirby was going to complete his plans.

At 4 PM now, Case guessed his ETA would be somewhat before 6. Even though it was rush hour, when wasn't it in L.A.?, out here on 210, there wasn't the solid L.A. traffic. He was cruising in the fast lane doing 70 mostly, occasionally having to drop back to a frustrating 60. Now he was feeling the disadvantages of Eugene loaning him the Mustang: no ball light to put on the roof, no siren, which meant if he didn't want to get pulled over, he had to keep his speed somewhat reasonable, although 80 seldom drew attention, if he could get up to it. And no police radio. It wasn't Eugene's fault, but Case felt a little more justified in not getting him his date.

As Case cruised along, his normally disciplined, analytical, single-focus detective mind began to wander. Sgt. Williams raised a pretty good question: if Kirby did grab Bruner and take him all the way out to the desert, how did he manage it? Case almost skipped that thought as soon as it came up. Did it matter? If he did, he did. Although Kirby probably could have been a rocket scientist, he wasn't exactly dealing with them. Case doubted he threatened him with a gun, preferring to use brain over brawn. Any number of ways he could have convinced Bruner to 'get in the car' or 'get in the trunk'. He could have had photo–shop pictures of his kids as hostages, threatening their harm by his "partner", if he refused. It didn't make any difference.

Case kept shifting his eyes back and forth between the dash clock and the speedometer. He could be going in the wrong direction; he could be too late. He pressed the accelerator as hard as he dared. Case thought about Kirby's high school senior picture. He wondered if he still looked like that. Probably not. There was no forced entrance at the three murders. Either: all three recognized him, in which case they might have asked him in, but he doubted that, or: they didn't recognize him because he had altered his appearance, and he talked his way in. Case was talked into one of his high school reunions, never again. What made the biggest impression on him was how people looked: some of them had not changed in the least, maybe a couple of year lines, others he would have sworn he had never even met before, that's how different they looked.

210 breezed past San Bernardino and then dipped south past Highland and Redlands and became I-10. Interstate 10. It was tempting to just stay on it all the way to its end in Jacksonville, Florida at the Atlantic Ocean. Maybe he would do that when this was over. Just drive; hundreds of miles followed by hundreds of miles and followed by hundreds of miles more until they became thousands of miles followed by thousands of miles. No shot or strangled or stabbed bodies to look at, no crimes to solve. No boss to please, no widow's grief to feel guilty about…"Everybody's talking at me, can't hear a word they say…" That's right. He'll be the Midnight Cowboy, but cut out New York and just head straight for Florida.

He was coming to Hwy 111 that turned south for Palm Springs, another 'palm'. And if he had stayed on 10 in about 15 miles he would have come to a little town called Thousand Palms. But his money still on Twentynine Palms. That exit, Hwy 62, was coming up in just a few miles, turning sharply north. After a while it made its bend towards the east and then at Yucca Valley headed due east, straight for Twentynine Palms, just 25 miles away.

His trip out there so many years ago was coming back to him; the memory aided by the dry desert air and the heat, rising from the desert floor, to return to the sky form whence it came. He remembered leaving the highway to bump along in the open desert, looking for a good place to do some target practice. There were four of them. The two lucky ones that got to sit in the front, on padded seats, weren't tortured like the two in the back, holding onto the roll bar in the open Range Rover and landing hard on the metal box seats with each bump and jostle. He remembered, too, an abandoned mine out there in the desert. It was shuttered up, and they just drove by it, not interested. They were anxious to do some shooting.

Just a few miles from his destination Case thought of Paul Kirby. Either he was very close to him, or he guessed totally wrong and they would never meet. His dependable gut said they would meet in Twentynine Palms. The Mustang sped east.

Case's mind was about to go on high alert real soon and for a few minutes he allowed it to drift. He speculated on how palm trees could have become a symbol for Kirby. They did connote an island paradise, but growing up around them, how would he get that association?

Twentynine Palms might give the sense of desert isolation "away from it all". But he grew up in the city. He would have seen palm trees many times before thinking of them in terms of desert islands. Case was sure he would never know. Again it didn't matter. ...Who knows? Maybe the one happy time in his life was a car trip to Disneyland and, as a kid, he sat in the back seat, looking up at the palm trees as they went by.

He was nearing the town of Twentynine Palms, a blip in desert. If he guessed right, the desert didn't hold too many options where Kirby and Bruner might be, and the town itself didn't seem too likely. Anything he was planning would have to be away from other people and in a setting completely controlled by Kirby. He had to think like Kirby. Simple murder wasn't the issue. It was style that was important to him, his statement of superiority over his opponents. Case had already decided the method would be something to do with weights. Max Bruner was a champion weightlifter. He doubted there was a fitness center in Twentynine Palms like there was in Montebello where Bruner worked. He couldn't do it there anyway. Too exposed, he would need a cave.

The mine! He remembered again the boarded up, abandoned mine he had seen years ago with his friends. Still guessing, but that's all he had been doing, and again, it fit. Case had one small problem: he had no idea where the mine was. All he remembered was they had left the main road to take a dirt road, and then had left that for open desert. He didn't even remember which direction it had been, off to the left or off to the right of 62. There was probably only another hour of light and he knew he'd never find anything out there in the dark. He was going to need directions.

Case drove another couple miles until he came to a roadside diner. He had passed one dirt road on his left leading out to who knew where, and not long after that one on the right. He probably passed more before he started to notice them. The parking in front of the diner was gravel and Case raised dust as he pulled in, a little too fast. He went inside. It wasn't air conditioned.

"You must be awful hungry, mister, or heard we got the best grub around," said the Gabby Hayes look-alike behind the counter.

"Just need some information."

"Must be pretty important. Seems to be you're in an awful hurry."

"Yes, I am." Case showed his ID. "L.A. homicide."

"L.A. homicide! Driving a fancy rig like that? You undercover?"

"No. I just need to know if you can tell me where there's an abandoned mine somewhere around here."

"Abandoned mine? Don't rightly recall anything about

an abandoned mine in these parts. 'Course, I've been behind this counter near forty years, and if there is one, must be a long time ago. I don't remember hearing any talk of a mine. Are you sure about that?"

"I saw it thirty years ago. I just couldn't say if it was a mile from here or ten miles from here. Do you know of someone that might know?"

"Doris in county records could help you."

"Where's that?"

"Same direction you're heading. Mile up the road."

"Thanks." Case started to leave.

"There's a motel a ways on, nothing fancy but clean. It'll do you for the night."

"I'm not staying the night."

"Oh, you'll have to."

"Why?"

"If you want to see Doris over at county records. County records closes at five." 'Gabby' glanced over his shoulder at the clock over the cook's window. County records had been closed for just over an hour.

Case walked back to the counter. "Look. I just drove from L.A. on the trail of a killer. He might be holed up out at that mine or he might be in your town and he might kill again. Can you think of anyone else who would know where it is?"

"I don't know," he mused, pulling his whiskers. He looked at a man hunched over a beer near the end of the counter. Case looked in that direction. The man looked homeless, but out here, Case thought, how could you tell? His jeans and near colorless shirt had the layer of desert dust in common with everything else around.

"Charlie. Know anything about an old mine out in the desert around here?"

Charlie answered without looking up. "Reckon I do."

Case walked to where Charlie was sitting. "You know about the abandoned mine?'

"I'd be repeating myself if I answered that ag'in."

"Why didn't you speak up before?"

"Why didn't you ask?" Charlie said over his beer.

"I did. You heard me ask the man at the counter."

"Reckon it pays to ask the right person."

Case was in no mood for games and just about out of patience, and he could feel his temper ready to fill that void. The day, the drive, and everything else were starting to take their toll. But he couldn't risk a mistake here. There was no one to play "good cop" against his "bad cop", so he was going to have to play "good cop". He just wasn't sure he knew how, he had never done it before.

"What are you drinkin'?"

Charlie was about to answer when Case thought better of it.

"Yeah, I see. Want another?"

"Well, I was just about to order dinner."

Case motioned to the counter man, who came over. "Take his order, get him what he wants." Case pulled out a twenty. "Give him some pie when he's done and another beer."

"That's mighty neighborly of you." Charlie looked up.

"My pleasure. Do you mind talking while you eat?"

"Never bothered me before. 'Course Joan, she was my first wife. She was never all that pleased about it. Said my Ma shoulda learned me better. Ma did all she could to put food on the table, without givin' a mind as to how we et it."

"What about the mine? Do you know where it is?"

"I better. Used to go out there sometimes with my daddy's brother. He used to work out there. That would be Al… no, wait, that was Daddy's youngest brother, Uncle Al. We used to call him the fun Uncle. Liked to have his fun, my Uncle Al did. No, he wasn't the one worked the mine. It was Howard, Daddy's older brother. That would be … most over fifty…gotta be more than that, 60 years or more ago. Doris over at County records could tell you for sure. But…"

"Right. Closed. That's okay. I just need to know how to get there."

"Which way did you…oh yeah, sure, you come east out on 62. Well, you passed the road on the way here. 'Bout two miles back there's a dirt side road, be on your right goin' that direction."

"Yeah, I saw it."

"So follow that coupla three miles. Road comes to an end. Can't say why it don't go all the way to the mine, never did. But at the end of the road, off to your right you can see some small hills, mebbe half mile off. That's where the mine is."

"Okay, thanks. Enjoy your meal." Case got up to leave.

"Wait! How you planning on getting out there?"

"Driving."

"In that fancy rig you come here in?"

"That's right."

"You don't want to take that out in the desert. You'll ruin it. Put a hole in your oil pan if you try an' do more'n 15 miles an hour."

"It'll be fine. It's a loaner."

Case back tracked 2.2 miles until he came to the dirt road heading into the desert east of highway 62. It would be easy to miss if you weren't looking for it. He cut his speed in half, then slowed some more. It took less than ten minutes to come to the end and he could see the hills the guy in the diner told him about, off to the right. With no road at all he had to carefully pick his way, bouncing in places and scratching brush. Now wasn't the time to worry about the Mustang, but Case did feel he at least owed Eugene a car wash when he got back.

At the crest of a small rise, Case saw the boarded up mine and the black Ford Focus. He rolled slowly to a stop and shut off the engine five yards to the left of the killer's car. He checked the clip in his gun, flipped off the safety and got out of the car, holding the button below the door handle in, and then releasing it after the door was closed so as not to make any unnecessary sound. He could feel sweat running in several places under his clothes, not sure if it was the heat, tension, or both. He entered the mine, stepping carefully past the torn down barricade. He fought back a momentary panic, knowing he was exposed, light behind him, nothing but blackness in front, as he had to wait for his eyes to adjust to the dark inside. Case moved out of the entrance to stand against the wall to his left, minimizing his exposure.

This precaution was his undoing. But he was doomed from the start. He couldn't stop in the entrance, silhouetted in the outside light. But in moving inside, before he could see well, he tripped the hidden wire, releasing a mallet he never saw in the dark. Even if he had caught the quick motion, it was too fast to duck. The mallet slammed him hard on the side of the head. A second mallet, two feet lower, designed for the same purpose had he entered and crouched, bruised his rib where it struck. Case saw a magnificent light show; a galaxy of stars set in a backdrop of pure black, and as fast as the stars appeared, they were gone, leaving only the black.

Case was unaware of a man standing over him, taking a moment to look at the rabbit he snared. He was also oblivious to being drug thirty yards along the dirt mine floor and then being handcuffed to the wheel of an enormous iron bucket.

Case awoke to a terrible headache, made worse by the intermittent, but regular, heavy thud that pounded in his head. He opened his eyes a little too quickly and got a sharp stab of pain for his effort. Light wasn't the cause of his discomfort, as there was almost none leaking in from the outside and there was no artificial light inside. The pain came from his eyelids slamming open at the top, like a runaway garage door hitting the top of the garage. He would have to open them more gently. He wasn't sure if it was his eyelids or that consistent thud in his head that was the problem. He was also reluctant to open his eyes, because that would mean they would have to adjust to the dim interior, and he didn't like the results of the last time he tried to adjust to the dark.

If only that pounding would stop. Case then experienced a momentary spatial confusion when he realized the pounding, that intermittent thud, was not in his head but coming from the outside, nearby, but definitely not in his head. It was somewhere up above. Turning his head and trying to look up was a mistake. An excruciating one. Case relaxed and waited. It was pleasantly cool in here, out of the desert sun. His eyes did start to make out objects, without causing another clunk in his head, when he opened them. He was seated, arms behind him, constrained, he found, after a tug. Cuffed. His back was against a flat, hard surface. He was sitting on rough ground, in an uncomfortable position. A cave. Walls nearby and overhead. Not a cave, the mine. The last thing he remembered was stepping inside to get out of the entrance light. And then...stars. He had obviously been knocked out. He wondered for how long.

It all came back just as a man stepped into view. The man's appearance was unremarkable: 5'8", sandy hair, very ordinary looking. He wore hiking shoes, jeans and a button short sleeve tan shirt. He had a pocket protector with two pens. C'mon, Case thought. You can't be the master mind, scary killer. Well, master mind he could be, why not, but scary killer? Again, killer maybe, why not? But not scary. So looks alone would suggest none of those things, but for all that, here he was. A murderer with a trail of three dead bodies. Yes, here he was. What was he doing here? Where was Max Bruner?

Case looked up at the unintimidating man in front of him. "Paul Kirby." Case said. A simple statement.

"Congratulations, detective, albeit a hollow accomplishment on your part. Don't you find it interesting? Here we are two professionals in what could only be described as a contest of the highest order: survival. You pitting your skills as a detective against my skills as an ad hoc inventor of applied mechanical engineering techniques to attain specific results. Tailor made specific results, designed to achieve, I wouldn't call it revenge, but retribution, attained in an almost poetic way.

They focused on me for no reason but their own amusement. In the end, it took careful planning and a lot of time, the time being of no consequence; in the end

I proved who had the superior intellect. They thought they were so clever and creative. I showed them true cleverness and creativity. In the end, they became amusement for me. I was the amused."

Paul Underwood Kirby was in a spotlight of his own making. "What I find interesting is that all your skills as an experienced professional accomplished nothing. In fact, here you sit, my captive, your fate a factor of my whim, and I, embarking on this career for the first time, am supremely successful. Granted, you're always playing catch-up, can only react, but I helped you all along the way, help, without which, you would still be chasing butterflies. And your job is to at some point stop reacting but start preventing and apprehending. Even spelling it all out for you, you are helpless. As we speak, you are two feet from my latest, and last I should point out, personal project, happening in real time; a man dying, or perhaps already dead, in your very presence, and there you sit, restrained by your own handcuffs, helpless to prevent it. Don't you see the poetry of it? We three, all closely connected in purpose and space, here together: the architect of the drama, the purpose of the drama and the intended spoiler. All three tightly knit together, me in complete charge, a total success, you, on a hero's mission, on what you probably consider the side of right, a dismal failure."

A megalomaniac, Case thought, loves the sound of his own voice.

"A dying man, you said? What dying man?"

"Don't you realize, it's happening right behind you? The other three deaths you had to infer the processes because I left no indication of the method used. This fourth and final act in the small play, in your presence, is actually happening as we speak. You can't actually see it in your position, but it is taking place right behind you. The man you're here to save is dying while you sit there. You can't see it, but you can hear it."

"That constant thumping? I thought that was going on in my head. What is it?"

"Ah! My latest creation. There have been four to date, each special in their own way. 'Which is my favorite ', you're probably wondering? I hear parents don't pick favorites, they 'love' all their children the same, which is, of course, rationally impossible, so, yes, I do have a favorite, but we won't go into that now. To your question, that thumping is the life being crushed out of Max Bruner's body, one weight at a time. You are cuffed to and leaning against a very old, rather large bucket on two wheels, used in the mine for hauling out ore. Mr. Bruner was convinced to position himself at the bottom of the bucket."

"How did you get him here?"

"THAT'S NOT IMPORTANT!" Paul Kirby did not like being interrupted. He struggled to control himself.

"Child's play. What is important is the mechanism created to test Mr. Bruner's strength and endurance. It is a creation of my own design: a continuous moving belt of buckets dropping large rocks into the bucket containing Mr. Bruner, from a considerable height, much as corn is fed into a grain elevator. This belt is feed by a conveyor belt, at a right angle to it, accessing a more than adequate supply. The rocks dropping at a steady rate, a kind of Chinese water torture, is the thumping sound you hear. In the Chinese water torture, it takes a considerable amount of time for each drop of water landing on the subject's forehead to feel like a boulder. My device provides that experience right from the start.

I then added my own variation. It makes the experience, that is, my experience, more interesting. Mr. Bruner assured me that he could bench press 250 lbs. So for a challenge I provided him with a half inch sheet of plywood to cover him and told him I would set the device to stop at 340 lbs. If he could maintain that weight for 30 seconds, he would be released. That bit of hope gives him incentive to go beyond the limit of his endurance. His feet are secured to a bar inside the bucket so he couldn't use his legs to help support the weight."

"Did you think he might be able to hold the weight for that long?"

"It didn't matter if he could or not. That's a one point

one ton bucket, twenty-two hundred pounds. My calculations, give or take, since, of course, the rocks are not all the same weight, is that it would take approximately eighteen minutes to load 340 pounds of rock. It's been running for, let's see, uh, almost 35 minutes, so that's about 700 pounds, right around one third full. Each struggling second would get him closer to meeting the 'goal'. Giving false hope was a refinement I had not thought of at first."

"It adds an extra touch of cruelty to their deaths."

"Thank you. That was the intention. When practical, I wanted to find out, for my own curiosity, just how long they could hold out, what the limit of their human endurance was under the circumstances. This time I won't get that information. But that's purely academic." Then Kirby added, "I remember reading somewhere: 'dead is dead'."

The automatic loader continued dropping rocks over the back of the large bucket, landing now on the completely buried sheet of plywood. The bucket had two large wheels at the rear of center, and it tilted back, resting on the ground, behind the wheels, under the weight of the rocks. As the pile grew, the rocks began to slip forward, moving towards the front end, which was a large, forward protruding lip.

All the while Kirby was talking Case had been intently

looking at him.

"You seem to be staring at me, Detective. Am I that unusual looking to you? Am I not what you expected in a serial killer?"

"Quite the opposite. Not unusual looking at all. I was wondering, was it worth it?"

" 'Was it worth it?' Am I happy, satisfied? Save the trite, clichéd questions. You ask if I'm satisfied with what I've done as if I had no justification. You have no idea of what it would take for me to be satisfied."

"I ask because I saw your school picture. You know I'm only here because I was at your apartment. How did I find your apartment? You gave no indication of that. I picked your picture out of hundreds and knew it was you. The meaning of the objects you left at each scene told me what It was all about, not the specifics, but enough. I'm staring because you look nothing like your picture ten years ago. I would not know you were ever in that class."

Kirby nodded his head. "I did that not as a validation of their prejudices, as people would think, but to suit my own purposes. It was really pretty easy: braces, speech therapy, hair color, minor plastic surgery. That's what gained me the access and it killed them in the end."

"I ask if it was worth it because of just that. You could

have moved on with your life and been successful in any number of fields with your academic record and intelligence. That has all been sacrificed."

All Case had was the typical ploy of buying time, but he didn't know for what. He didn't expect the cavalry to save him. He did want to know what this guy's next move was. He'd just have to play the situation out as it unfolded.

"Flattery won't save your life, if I was planning to kill you, which I'm not."

Case couldn't help showing the slightest relief at that welcome information.

"That's right; you'll get out of here. I'm not going to kill you. I don't commit senseless murder. I have great regard for the innocent, even though, in this case, it would seem logical to kill you to protect myself. And if I answered your leading question, what I plan on doing with my life, then ordinarily I would have to kill you. But lucky for you, it makes no difference whether you know or not. By the time you get out of here I'll be long gone. And you and all your colleagues will never find me, will never see or hear from me again, no more than you would have this time had I not allowed it.

So, Detective, 'Was it worth it?' Instead of what I could have done with my life, where is it heading? And the sacrifice? That all fits together in one answer. At first I wasn't totally satisfied. You could say I was still perfecting my method. What is truly satisfying is justice, and in this country we don't get true justice, I mean in the punishment of crime. We set an arbitrary sentence of time to compensate for crimes. Apples and oranges. The Bible has it right: true justice is an eye for an eye. Make the causer of harm experience that same harm as closely as possible."

"But you're alive and they're dead. How was murdering them 'an eye for an eye'?"

Paul Kirby rolled his eyes to the ceiling, and shook his head as he turned away. He was struggling with whether it was worth the time and patience to try to explain a simple idea to a small child.

"How could you get this far and be so wrong?"

"Wrong about what?" Case played along.

"Just about everything."

"Like?"

"Like trying to get free. Those are cop cuffs. You're cuffed to the wheel of that ore car. Like: It would seem by now, *Detective,* that you would grasp the point that these were not simple revenge killings, as if killing was even the point. You're here! You see! And yet you don't understand. With all of them, killing was not the point at all; the method, that is the only thing that is important, to get them to experience what I experienced."

"But still, you did kill them, and as you pointed out, 'dead is dead'.

"Yes. Collateral damage. Acceptable? Of course. Desirable? Mox nix. But the equivalent, compensatory punishment? Not at all."

"They had to suffer in the same way you did."

Kirby clapped his hands twice. "Bravo, Detective."

"So, just killing them wasn't enough, or even the point. After prolonged suffering, according to the M E, you reveal your true identity and your revenge is complete."

"Well, I can see why you would think that. That's the typical cliché: Just before they die 'Guess who? It's me! I got the last laugh!' I even thought that myself at first; even did it that way the first time. And now we finally arrive at the real point, which is why I said I wasn't totally satisfied in the beginning.

Shawna died knowing her killer, and in the last moments, undoubtedly, understood why. That's when I realized the truth. It would be a terrible torture to die without knowing who their killer was and especially why. To think it might be a totally senseless, random killing, as if it could have been anyone else; that they were simply in the wrong place at the wrong time; in short, to have died for no good reason; that, Detective, is torture to accept. At the very last moment, when they knew they were going to die, but not why, is the ultimate psychological torture. Shawna Anderson, of course, didn't want to die, but she knew there was some justification in it. The others died without a clue, feeling an utter unfairness about it. Presumably their deaths might have been marginally easier to accept had they been given a reason. That's why my physical change was doubly beneficial. They died *not* knowing.

The false hope refinement was an added touch of sheer brilliance, as you noticed. Making them believe they had a chance to live; giving them false hope, a nice touch I must say. So with the process complete, yes, I'm totally satisfied with he results. And now," Kirby paused, closed his eyes, relishing his achievement, "it's ready; I can take it to the next level."

"The next level? I thought you said this was the last."

"I said it was my last personal project."

"How many more victims do you have?"

"Me? Personally? None. But all my work can't end here. The next level is for the benefit of society."

"The benefit of society?'

"Yes, I'll be offering my services to the public."

"Offering your services to the public?"

'What, is there an echo in here?" Kirby looked around. "Yeah, there probably is."

Case didn't like the sound of where this was going. Up until now he thought how all this was going to end would be anticlimactic. "What are you talking about?"

"Do you like a good irony, Detective? The rest of your question, about was it worth the sacrifice of where my life could have gone and where is it now heading? True, the course of my life has changed, but in a good way. That's the irony. They changed it by giving me a real purpose in life, filling a heretofore unfulfilled need. It's the American way: I identified a need and now I'm going to fill it. I'll be an entrepreneur. I'm going to right the imbalance. It's really quite simple. I'll be a pioneer in a field of great public service: sticking up for the underdog, saving the innocent."

"You're going to save the innocent?"

"That's right."

"How?"

"By offering my process."

"Offering your process?"

"It's really tiring for you to keep repeating everything I say. I have come to the side of the underdog, the helpless…" As Kirby talked, Case knew he was right about never being able to break free. "…the innocent in the classic struggle."

 The loading belt continued picking up, moving, and dropping rocks into the ore car, as if enchanted, mindlessly and endlessly doing its task. The interval between each falling rock was as silent as, and actually was, a tomb. Kirby took a step, during a silent interval, towards Case as he warmed to his subject. The crunch of gravel under Kirby's foot drew Case's glance and he noticed the protruding bar at the base of the car, a few inches above the ground. Although Case could not see it, there was also a bar on the other side of the car. A chain would connect to the bars and attach to a tow motor to haul the car out once full.

"Just maybe…" Case thought. And to Kirby, "What struggle?"

"C'mon, Detective, there's no reason to play dumb. Everyone knows about the division of the two classes: the classroom academics, the 'A' students, and the school yard bullies, the classic brain versus brawn." Kirby liked analogies. "Like the Morlocks and the Eloi."

Case avoided looking down at Kirby's feet again, but he wanted him to step closer as the loader continued its unvarying work.

"The who and the what?"

"From *The Time Machine*. Not a direct comparison, but the concept is the same. The Morlocks lived under the ground, the Eloi above. The Morlocks were brutes who controlled the weaker, innocent Eloi. Inside the classroom..."

It seemed to Case that Kirby had never progressed a day beyond high school, he was still living it.

"...brains got the acclaim and all the attention. Brawn was out of their element and sat in class looking out the windows, planning to get even. Outside the classroom..."

The conveyor belt continued loading the car and the pile grew higher as the killer built his theme. The rocks started to peak and began spilling to the front of the car.

"...the academically inferior could feel superior. Stronger of body than mind, they dominated the weaker by whatever cruel and brutal way their weaker minds could conceive." He moved closer to Case, near the large protruding lip of the front of the car. "All that will change; and you're going to help me." The rocks were cascading more and more towards the front. The killer looked at the seated Case, hands cuffed to the wheel.

"I'm going to help you? How?"

"I'm getting to that. You made it this far and you're getting all of it. You need all of it."

Case wanted all of it, but maybe one or two steps closer. He also needed to keep the other's focus. "It looks like you got your ultimate revenge, but wasn't there anyone to help; your parents? This was the only solution, devoting your life to revenge? Can you live with four murders?"

"My parents? My Mother was embarrassed and my father wasn't getting involved in kid stuff. He told me to man up for myself. I guess I did. And 'can I live with four murders?' They were prototypes. They will eventually be honored as critical to developing my process. My perfected and proven method will be used to benefit thousands."

Case kept his eyes on the killer's while watching the rocks cascade to the front of the car with his peripheral vision. He blinked to look at the killer's feet. Just a couple inches closer... The car started to creak, beginning an almost imperceptible tilt. What was that about benefitting thousands?

"I can see you're confused, but you have to understand, for when you give your final report to the police and the media. That's how you're going to help. By letting them know the motive and the effective retribution of my method, the media will let my public know, and they will understand. They will reach out to me for help. They will find me. You never will.

You see, I knew there were thousands of others that suffered. The suicides prove it. Do you know how many teenage suicides there were last year because of hazing, bullying and harassment? 1,480-83. Three of them could not be definitively confirmed, but were highly suspected. That was up from the year before; in fact, it's been going up every year for years. I tried to find a network out there that I was sure must exist. But none did. So I created the solution myself. It was like when someone gets a great idea, they can't believe no one thought of it before.

I was astounded to realize, I just couldn't believe, that all of these brilliant, tortured people believed they only had two options open to them: suicide or school shootings, which also ended in either suicide or being shot. I couldn't believe that no one had developed my pro-active, proven method that I will first offer as a service and then franchise across the country."

And then Case knew he was insane.

He took a final step forward and looked down at Case. "No longer do the innocent have to take their own lives because they can't tolerate the abuse any longer, and believing there's no way out. They can subscribe to my proven method of patiently studying..."

There was a loud crunch and snap of bone followed by an ear-splitting shriek as the iron tow bar at the bottom of the car rolled forward, landing on and breaking Kirby's left foot, trapping him in place. The ore car had finally become front end heavy and fell forward, resting on the ground. Paul Kirby fell back into a seated position, then grabbed his left shin, groaning in pain.

Case looked at him. "Interesting arrangement, the three of us: victim, killer and cop, in such close proximity. One dead, the other two trapped by the very object that killed the third."

"Shut up! You're going to get me out of here!"

"Not likely. You know I can't release a prisoner in custody. Besides, I can just wait you out and you'll never get out of here."

"I can just shoot you and you'll never get out of here." Kirby pointed Case's gun at the detective.

"It seems we have a standoff." Case said.

"No ...we don't." Kirby was really feeling the pain. The broken foot was agonizing. "I have ... I have the... gun. That's the trump."

"And how are you going to use it?"

Kirby thought about it. "If I shoot you, I won't get out of here. If I don't shoot you I won't get out of here. So

...shooting you would not ...affect the outcome ... therefore be pointless."

"So you can't shoot me, because as you pointed out, it would accomplish nothing. If you do shoot me, you will be caught, and if you don't shoot me you will be caught. There's no way out for you."

"In that case...de...tective, shooting you...would make no...no difference...either." Even in the cool interior, Kirby was sweating heavily. "The only way...for me...is the credible threat that I will...shoot you. You...don't want...to die. You...have to believe I will do it, right...up until I do."

"But the threat is not credible. Because shooting me won't get you out."

Kirby fired the gun. The bullet struck the ore car at the right side of Case's head, ricocheted off, hitting the stone wall in front of them and ricocheted again, imbedding itself in the ground six inches from Case's left leg.

"One shot...almost hit ...you twice. You have... to ask yourself: 'did I ...miss on purpose...or be...cause...of the pain ...affecting...my aim?' "

"What about the innocent?"

"I have...to deal...with present cir...cumstances. Four have died...one more...for the greater...good. So...I believe you...are ...con...vinced I will...kill you." Kirby lay back and rested, closing his eyes. Case waited, hoping for some kind of opportunity. Kirby was breathing slowly, fighting the pain, not wanting to go into shock, trying to gather his strength.

"OK, when I ...take the cuffs off, don't say...anything...don't...move. Any attempt...if you move towards the front...I think I won't miss." Kirby took another minute and then leaned forward and opened the handcuffs. Case rubbed his wrists. Kirby kept the gun on Case.

"Pickup...the cuffs and drop... them ...over here." Case did so. "Now...stand at the front... of the car." Kirby kept the gun on Case.

"Put this around... your ankle."

Case locked one of the cuffs to his right ankle. Kirby locked the other cuff to his own left wrist.

"Walk...around to the ...front and shut off the generator."

Kirby lay stretched out which caused an even sharper pain in his broken foot. Case could get just far enough around the front of the car to shut off the generator on the other side. The belt stopped just as one more rock fell onto the car and the feeder belt stopped as the rocks it carried could no longer fall to the loader belt.

"Now...push the ...front up."

"I can't lift a ton of rocks!"

"DO IT!"

Case strained, unable to even budge the car. Case kept straining. Kirby finally realized the futility of the effort.

"Stop...come back around...this side...where you were... by the wheel and start...pushing rocks ...off the back...of the...car." Case complied and Kirby sat up, giving Case the slack he needed. He pushed one rock off the back of the car.

"Faster!" Kirby managed to yell. "More rocks! Faster!" Case kept pushing rocks off the back. Kirby watched him work, trying to ignore his smashed foot, his face contorted in pain and dripping in sweat.

"OK. Stop. Now...come back...the front ...push rocks to ...the back."

They reversed their movements and Case was at the front of the car, taking weight off the front by moving rocks to the back.

"Now...try...again."

"This is crazy. I couldn't lift it if it were empty. The car itself probably weighs a ton."

"DO IT!"

Case strained and still couldn't budge the car.

"Go back...more rocks out."

Once again, Case went to the back of the car and rolled more rocks out. He looked inside and could see shards of plywood, crushed, blood stains, beneath which he knew was the crushed body of Max Bruner. He probably was never able to sustain any weight. The falling heavy rocks probably split the wood on impact and then crushed him.

"This is your ...last chance. Stand still." Kirby unlocked the cuff from Case's ankle. "Twenty yards...further back...there's some old equipment. Go back...long iron...bar." It was getting more and more difficult for Kirby to speak, sapping his strength. "Bring...the bar. Look at me."

Case got the message. Kirby was pointing the gun at him as if to say, "I'll shoot again."

Case found the bar and dragged it back to where Kirby was leaning back on his elbows. He indicated to Case that he wanted him to put it beneath the rod trapping his foot. Waving his arm forward he wanted Case to slide the bar farther underneath.

"Now...lift."

Case still was unable to lift the car off Kirby's foot.

"Stop," Kirby said. "Need a ...fulcrum. Put a rock on ...the other side."

Case put a rock behind the car's towing bar.

"Too big," Kirby said.

Case got a smaller one.

"Now...slide bar under... again...and over rock."

Case was able to slide the long bar next to the car, under the tow bar trapping Kirby and over the rock he positioned as a fulcrum. He was surprised how he could then lever the front of the car up enough for Kirby to grab his pant leg and slide his foot aside and free. He screamed with pain at the jerking motion he made on the pant leg, desperate to get his foot clear. There was just enough room. Case didn't tilt the car all the way back, but let it back down, resting on the front.

"Sit down." Kirby said. He never stopped pointing the gun at Case as he unlocked the cuffs from his wrist.

"Stand up and walk slowly around and stand at the wheel, facing the back of the mine," he ordered. Kirby drug himself backward, grabbed the front end of the car and hauled himself to a standing position, on his good right foot.

"Put your wrists together, behind your back." Standing now, and free, Kirby felt tremendously better. He had suffered a minor setback, but that was inconsequential. He was still in complete command and would continue as before. He cuffed Case's hands behind his back and then, with his left hand, grabbed hold of the cuffs, leaning his weight, which pulled on Case's shoulders. With the gun still in his right hand, Kirby stuck it between Case's ribs and Case could feel the metal barrel against bone.

"Now, turn around and walk. Slowly."

Case started moving towards the front of the mine with Kirby hopping along beside. He was still looking for an opportunity, but knew this wasn't it. Not with a gun in his ribs. Near the entrance Case glanced at the spot where he had been knocked out. "This guy has been pretty lucky," he thought. "Even a serious mistake resulting in a broken foot hasn't been a total game changer."

Once outside the mine, even with the sun down, the desert air was a sharp contrast to the cool interior. It wouldn't be long before that would change very rapidly. It was much lighter outside than the gloomy interior as the moon and stars gave plenty of light. But it was just as quiet as the inside, once the loader had stopped. They were miles from any semblance of civilization. One could easily imagine there was no civilization, anywhere.

Kirby let go of the cuffs and used the barrel of the gun to push Case away. "Move over there." Then he rested against the hood of his Focus and noticed the Shelby Mustang.

"Nice car."

"It's a loaner."

Case was facing the open desert.

"Back slowly towards me. Stop. Lift your arms up. I've got the gun pointed at you. When I unlock the cuffs, let your arms fall slowly to your sides and walk away. Okay, now stop. Turn around. I said you'd never catch me. This way I'll be sure. Sorry." Paul Kirby pointed the gun at his victim and fired.

Chapter Twenty - One

The sound of the loud gunshot rolled across the desert. Small desert dwellers were startled by it and scurried into their underground burrows or crouched beneath cacti. An instant after the shot there was an explosion and a hiss of escaping air. The Shelby Mustang landed heavily on its right front wheel. Paul Kirby's latest victim was the right front tire of the Mustang. He opened the driver side door of the Focus, sat on the seat, swung his good right foot in and gingerly lifted his left foot inside. There was no position he could rest it that it wasn't a stab of pain. He started the car, backed it up, driving past the injured Mustang, and off into the desert. The bumping would hurt his foot all the way until he could get to the paved highway, miles away.

Case stood there and watched him go, thinking how cautious Kirby was. He shot out the tire but he still had Case's keys anyway. As if reading his mind, Kirby stopped after forty yards, stuck his hand out the window and dropped the keys on the desert floor, then continued lumbering away across the uneven ground.

Case tried to keep his eye on the spot where Kirby had dropped the keys. As the tail lights were already disappearing in the distance it was hard to make out the exact spot. He ran the forty yards, following the tire tracks, knowing the keys would be on his left, still not easy to find in the brush and dark. Case couldn't get this close and let the killer slip away. If there was any chance at all, he had to stop him. As he frantically searched for the keys, Case started to get a sick feeling in the pit of his stomach, the thought that he had already lost. Why had Kirby left the keys; for that matter why did he even un-cuff him? Kirby never intended on killing Case; Case was part of his plan, insane as it was. But he wouldn't have died out there. He could have walked out, even cuffed, in not much more than an hour.

What was with the cat and mouse? Case's mind raced from one thought to another as he scratched and jabbed his hands on needle sharp Agave. Kirby's arrogance, thinking he still was so smart he would never get caught? Case couldn't know Dr. Leonard would say that was part of it, but it was more subtle than that. Paul Kirby had validated his own self-worth for the last ten years with the idea he was intellectually superior. Freeing Case might be construed as arrogance, but Kirby was keeping intact his own validation through intellectual superiority. He was proving it by freeing Case and remaining in control.

Case couldn't stop his mind from racing but he was only interested in finding the keys and apprehending a killer. He hoped he might catch a reflection off the keys, but he saw none. Then a few feet away something glinted in the night. He ignored it, probably an old can. The keys couldn't be more than twelve inches from the tire tracks; he saw the keys fall straight down. He couldn't go wandering off chasing beer cans or pull tabs. He stopped and looked around; must have gone too far. He looked back, and then he saw the keys lying in the open. They did reflect a little light from that angle looking back.

Case ran back to the car now, worried about time. He knew if Kirby got to the highway, even a minute ahead, Case would not know which way he went, back towards the city or further into the Mojave Desert. He was no mathematician but it was pretty simple: At 60 mph Kirby could go the half mile to the dirt road in half a minute. At 10 mph, which is what he was probably doing, it would take him three minutes. Then at 30 mph he could drive the three mile dirt road to Hwy 62 in six minutes. That would give Case five minutes to run eighty yards, find the keys, change the tire and four minutes, driving 60 mph, to catch him at the highway, before Kirby was gone, with no indication which way he went. Even worse, the dirt road might be less than three miles and Kirby might do 40 instead of 30 on it, cutting that time in half. Knowing more than five minutes were already spent, Case ran.

But Case's mind refused to help; it just kept coming up with more bad news. It pushed out what little hope Case was trying to hold onto. It told him, for all that, even squeezing out the minutes, it wouldn't be that simple. And then Case was sure none of that really made a difference. From what he had learned of Paul Kirby, he wasn't leaving the difference of a mile or two as the determining factor of his successful planning. Certainly, breaking his foot was not figured in, but then it didn't ruin his plans, he was still free. No, Case was sure Kirby was way beyond this stage in his schemes. He was right about one thing: there were probably thousands of people like him out there. He might even already have willing like-thinkers in place, waiting to 'initiate phase II' of his grand design.

As Case got to the Mustang, he just couldn't help getting one bad thought after another. He suddenly realized he most likely still wasn't going anywhere. He doubted Eugene had a jack, lug wrench and spare. After all, there wasn't much chance of getting a flat on his driveway. Case opened the trunk and was surprised to find all three. He guessed Eugene wanted to keep everything original, to maintain the value of his mint Mustang. Case looked at the car; that ship had sailed. It was going to need a little detailing to be called 'mint' again. By the time Case was ready to change the tire, over ten minutes was gone and so was Paul Kirby.

Setting up the jack presented its own problem. Rather than the jack lifting the car, the weight of the car would drive the jack into the dirt. He had to find a flat rock to set the jack on and then work slowly and carefully to maintain the balance. If the car slipped off the jack he could damage the axel. Taking fifteen minutes to finish the simple change, Case threw the lug nut wrench, wheel and jack back in the trunk, slammed the lid, jumped in the car, started it, backed up hard, gouging the desert surface, spraying rocks and charging away in a cloud of dust, in futile pursuit.

At the highway, Case watched as a semi went past, heading for L.A., and a passenger car went east, into the heat of the night in the Mojave. Case had no choice but to turn east for Twentynine Palms. He drove the short distance, and once in town, found the sheriff's office. There were two deputies on duty, one sitting at a desk on the phone. The other asked Case, "Can I help you?"

Case showed his ID. "Detective Sergeant Lawrence Case, L.A. homicide."

"Well, there hasn't been any homicides around here in some time. You just visiting?"

"There was one tonight. I need to speak to the sheriff. I'm in pursuit of an escaped killer. We need to set up a road block. Is the sheriff in his office?"

"No. He's at home. Just me and Frank on duty tonight, and Bill, out in the patrol car."

"Can you get the sheriff on the phone?"

"Well, he doesn't like us to call him unless it's really important."

Case didn't want to lose his temper; he needed co-operation. "This is extremely important. Would you call him, and I need to call my Captain in L.A. Is there another phone I can use?"

The deputy gestured to an empty desk. Case called Capt. Murdock's private line. The Captain answered right away.

"Captain, this is Case."

"Case! Where are you? I sent Fuller and Young out to your place and they said you gave them the slip."

"I know. Listen. I'm in Twentynine Palms out in the Mojave."

"Twentynine Palms! I know where it is. What are you doing out there?"

"Captain, listen. There's not much time. It's probably already too late. I know who the killer is; I've been to his apartment and I trailed him out here. I was too late to stop his fourth killing."

"Another one?"

"That's right. Listen. I'm at the sheriff's office. Hang on."

Case turned to the deputy. "Is that the sheriff on the line? Let me talk to him." Case identified himself and briefly explained the situation. Sheriff Oberg said he would be there in under two minutes.

"Okay, Captain? The sheriff will be right here. You need to coordinate with Highway Patrol to set up a roadblock. The guy's name is Paul Kirby; he's injured and has my gun."

"WHAT?"

"Here's the sheriff. I'll fill you in later."

The sheriff walked through the door, a man in his 50's, stocky, 5'9", 190 lbs., completely bald, and wasn't wasting anytime. He walked over to Case.

"You're the detective from L.A.?"

Case dispensed with all formalities. "I've got my Captain on the phone." He handed it to Sheriff Oberg and Captain Murdock gave him a quick run down of the situation.

"I haven't got all the details from my detective, so he can fill you in with what you need for CHP. Thanks for your help, Sheriff, and tell Detective Case I'll be waiting here for his call when he's clear."

Sheriff Oberg hung up, told his deputy to get the California Highway Patrol and turned to Case. He told the other deputy to take it down.

"Alright, give me what you've got."

Case described Paul Kirby as he last saw him.

"He's driving a four or five year old black Ford focus, California license NVR HRT. He has a broken left foot; happened about one hour ago. He's armed with my gun."

The sheriff's eyes widened at that. It was a hard thing for Case to say, but he had no choice.

"He killed three people in L.A. over the last two weeks and he brought one here from L.A. tonight. Killed him in the abandoned mine northwest of here."

"I know the place," the sheriff said. "Give me time and direction and I'll get CHP out there. We'll also notify all clinics and ER's in the area. He'll need medical attention."

"I left the scene thirty minutes after he did; shot out my tire. I figure I could travel faster on the desert because of his injury and gained five minutes, so he got to 62 twenty-five minutes ahead of me and it's been ten minutes since I hit the highway."

"Meaning he's been on it thirty-five minutes."

"Right. And I have no idea which way he would have gone, so you need to block east and west fifty miles in both directions."

"Except for one problem. There's a cut off, 247, twenty miles west of here. If he went there, it's too late for a road block, he's already on it."

Case wasn't surprised. "Where does that go?"

"120 miles through bare desert, a couple small towns, then a major hub where 40 hits 15 at Barstow."

"Then we'll need three sites."

The sheriff shrugged his shoulders. "I'll give it all to the Patrol, they'll make the call."

"Give them Capt. Murdock's number for any clarification."

"If that's all you can tell me, he wants you to call him. Use the phone over there."

"Thanks. Oh, sheriff. You'll need to send the coroner out to the mine. A Max Bruner. He's buried under a ton of rocks in an ore car."

Case sat down heavily at the desk, his energy rapidly draining as his adrenaline started to fade.

Case called Capt. Murdock.

"Murdock."

"It's me. I'm heading back. The sheriff is working on the road blocks."

"How does it look?"

"Not as easy as I first hoped. They could catch him easily on 62, but he might have turned north for Barstow. If he did, he would have left 62 before I even got to town here."

"This guy, Kirby,? he's injured and he has your gun?"

"I'll give it all to you right now and then I'm heading back."

"Listen. That's a two hour drive. Spend the night there and I'll see you tomorrow. The investigation is over; you can make your report and then still take the rest of the week. Just think, Case…"

"What?"

"You completed this investigation and you weren't even supposed to be on the case. Just think how many you'll clear when you actually *are* on the cases."

"Yeah, just think." Case made up his mind. "Captain, I'm not staying out here in the desert. The drive back will do me good. Let me rough it out for you so I can get it off my mind for now."

The Captain just waited.

"This guy Paul Kirby picked his victims for a reason. I discussed it with Leonard this afternoon. You can go over the psych stuff with him. After talking to him, I rolled the dice, betting on Kirby. Turned out he was our guy. His apartment led me here. But the guy's smart. I don't know how he got Bruner out here.

There's an old mine in the desert. I remembered it from when I was out here once, years ago. I guessed that's where he'd be, but it was the only logical place he could be. He was prepared; had it rigged with a trip wire. I was knocked out. He got my gun, cuffed me, and murdered Bruner in my presence."

"You were knocked unconscious? For how long?"

"That's right. I don't know; couldn't have been too long."

"Listen to me. I want you to go to a clinic right now and get yourself checked out. You can tell me the rest in the morning."

"Later. I couldn't stop Kirby. I was sitting right there while Bruner was being murdered, buried at the bottom of an ore car, under a ton of rocks."

"For all you know he was dead when you got there."

"The car got front heavy and fell forward, crushing his foot. He was trapped. Trapped! I had him. There was no way he could get free. He would be in custody right now." Case was reliving it. "I helped him! I helped him get free and I let him go. I even helped him out of the mine and get away. I should have left him there."

"He threatened to shoot you. You had no choice."

"Shooting me would have gained him nothing. He couldn't afford to. He would be in custody right now."

"So with nothing to lose, he would have shot you. He killed four people. You must have thought he would, too, or you wouldn't have released him."

Case considered where they were with the whole mess. "No warrant or reasonable cause for the search; we can't convict, the evidence in his apartment is inadmissible. Releasing a prisoner, allowing a murder suspect possession of my firearm; I'll be suspended for that."

"We'll get him for Bruner's murder, and don't be so sure about the rest."

"Yeah, we'll get him for Bruner's murder. First we have to get him."

"And if the guy's a head case as Dr. Leonard seems to think, he reported to me after you left, the guy will probably want to confess to the other three."

"One can only hope."

"Look, Case, you stopped him. He might not even get far enough to find treatment. He could be passed out in his car right now. Either way, we'll get him. Don't worry about that. Right now I'm telling you to do something. It's not an option, it's not a maybe; I'm TELLING you to do it. Go somewhere to have yourself checked out. If they want to keep you overnight for observation, stay overnight for observation. If they release you, check in somewhere, spend the night; drive back in the morning. DO NOT drive back tonight."

"Right. See you." Case put the phone in the cradle.

"Case... Case!"

Chapter Twenty – Two

The heat had left the desert. The night air started to cool. Case got in the Mustang and headed west back to L.A. He was in no particular hurry. There was time to drive and appreciate the landscape. Used to L.A.'s blacktop and pavement, people and buildings, traffic and smog, Case felt like he was on the surface of the moon; dry, barren and deserted. Miles of empty, full of nothing. Case did not appreciate the landscape.

His adrenaline had run its course and the tension of the last two hours was gone. They had taken his mind off his throbbing head. That throbbing now was back, and with a vengeance, for being ignored. His ribs hurt and his arms and shoulders felt the strain. There was dried blood on his hands from the cacti needles and it felt like there were nettles on and under his skin. But nothing serious; overall he was in very good shape. He was still alive. Case only ever concerned himself with physical OK-ness. Now he knew the difference between that kind and the psychological: he had nothing to complain of he wouldn't be over by morning, but he never felt worse in his life.

Everything had gone wrong. On the drive back he had plenty of time to dig himself a deep hole to climb into. Murdock was so sure Kirby wouldn't get far, especially because of Case's brilliant police work in slowing the suspect with an injury; not to mention that he was now armed and dangerous, armed with Case's gun. Murdock was sure 'he can't get far'. Case wasn't so sure. As he drove west through the night, there was almost nothing he was sure about.

Past Yucca Valley, 62 made the sharp turn south where it ended at Interstate 10; Interstate 10, non-stop from the Pacific Ocean to the Atlantic Ocean. It cut straight across the country, all the way from Santa Monica, Ca. to Jacksonville, Fl. That's a good start. If he really wanted to get away he could jump on 95 in Jacksonville and take it all the way down the coast, the whole state of Florida. Leave the mainland, picking up Hwy 1, and drive out into the Gulf of Mexico, along all the Florida Keys, from Key Largo to Key West, until you can't go no more. Case sat there looking at the interstate. He could turn left and drive away. Naw, not yet. He wasn't ready to leave yet. He could do that later. He still had things to do. He looked to the right; back towards L. A. For one thing, he had to return Eugene's car.

Case wasn't happy about his decision not to go to Florida. It did nothing to improve his mood going back to L.A. He drove through the night. He had made some lucky guesses: identified the killer, caught up with him, but he was too late and he was coming back empty handed. The Captain felt certain they'd get him. Case wondered.

Case drove Interstate 10 west. It became the San Bernardino FRWY., then the Hollywood FRWY., 101. He didn't know where he was going. He got off the freeway on Santa Monica Blvd. There was plenty of traffic and people out, a sharp contrast to the desert just a couple hours away. He took a right on Highland Ave. and then another right on Sunset Blvd., having no idea where he was going. At Western Ave. he took a left, heading into the hills above Hollywood. When he finally stopped he found himself in the parking lot of the Griffith Park Planetarium, overlooking the city. He pulled into a parking slot, facing south, where he could see the whole L.A. basin. It was all lit up, the lights of the endless boulevards stretching away forever. One long boulevard, a bright scar, cutting diagonally across the landscape.

Alphie came to mind again; the song ran through his head, "What's it all about?" The question of the ages. What's it all about. Looking out at the lights of the city below, he couldn't see one, but knew there were millions and millions of people, doing what? Doing whatever millions and millions of people do. Do they know what it's all about? Do any of them? Does even one of them? From his vantage point all he saw was an enormous city lit from horizon to horizon, filled with unseen people trying to figure out what it's all about. Or maybe not. Maybe they didn't care.

Case used to care. And he knew he still did, just in a

different way. He never thought any more about when he was young and new on the force. He had wanted to get rid of all the bad out there. Years convinced him to lower his sights. After all, unachieved goals only lead to frustration. So he wanted to get rid of enough bad to put the good/bad ratio in the good's favor. More years convinced him to lower his sights more. His new goal was to eliminate enough bad so that good could narrow the gap and catch up.

Years convinced him to lower his sights. If he could keep bad in check so that it didn't gain ground...By then it was about the force; too much bad blood and disillusion. He was once proud to be on the force; more than just a job, it was a job with a higher calling. But that didn't work out so well for Case. The force left him behind. Not officially of course; officially it was still all about the higher calling, as it should be in Case's thinking. But that wasn't the reality. Politics and all the rest Case didn't want to think about left him no longer proud of the force. It was only his means to battle the windmills of injustice; his weapon against those that steal, cheat, kill and prey on the innocent, weak and defenseless for their own gain just because they can. He realized how melodramatic that sounded and Dudley Dorightish, but it was all he had.

What really bothered him was how low his sights had fallen. The Kirby case was supposed to be a success. Four murders, a killer identified but still on the loose with a 50-50 chance of catching him. And for him it was over. Case closed. Solved, or nearly so. 'We'll get him' Murdock said. He was a cold blooded, maybe sadistic, murderer. He certainly deserved whatever justice society deemed appropriate. Society would put a big hurt on Paul Kirby. All to the good. Case wondered. Big success. That was supposed to give him a feeling of accomplishment. Most cases didn't even turn out that well. No wonder he drank. And Manny...

Case looked at the city. It was spread out before him; and as far as he could see, which was far on this starry, cloudless night, the city lit up like a Hollywood premier. It was a beautiful sight from where he sat, extending endlessly to the east, south and west. Maybe the only beautiful thing about it. The sprawling beast. Did it have a soul? Case didn't think so. The sum of its parts totaled zero. Case identified with it at that moment. The sum of him seemed to total zero, just like the city. A pointless existence. That defined him and defined the city. If the vastness before him lost one of its nonentities, would it notice? If one flickering light out there were extinguished, would it matter?

Did any of the people out there wonder what it was all about, or did they just want what they could get today, and not care about tomorrow? He suddenly didn't care about tomorrow either; he wanted no part of it. Case got out of the car and climbed the 20 or so steps to the outside observation deck. He was absorbed by the behemoth below. He left his feet and floated, slowly gliding through the night air, out, over the city, hundreds of feet below. Case stood there on the observation deck and watched himself float up and away, far above the tall buildings. Then he watched as he slowly dissolved, turning to ash, then dust, then to a fine mist, finally to molecules as his essence was absorbed by the city. And then the sum of the city remained constant. Zero plus zero is zero.

Case started the car, backed around and headed down the mountain. He made a right on Los Feliz Blvd. It made a sharp turn to the south and became the single, longest surface street in L.A., Western Ave., running for 35 miles, straight as an arrow, without a turn or a bend, from just above N. Hollywood, crossing Sunset Blvd. and, when it could go no farther, ending in San Pedro.

Western Ave. suited Case. He just wanted to drive and not stop. So he drove Western from one end to the other. At first he drove between a few tall buildings; then it turned into neighborhoods. He drove through the night, past stores and playgrounds, schools and residences; partly seedy, partly middle class, on and on; on and on through the night. He drove past Culver City, through Inglewood, Hawthorne and Gardena. He drove past Carson and Torrance and Lomita. Finally, there was no more to drive. He was at the end, San Pedro.

Case liked Western Ave. because there were no decisions to make, just stay on it and drive. Now, at the end, the only thing in front of him was the Pacific Ocean and he had to decide: left or right. He just sat and stared ahead at the ocean. Behind him were miles of undulating sparkling points, lights, like off a thousand shot glasses. He looked through the windshield. Undulating waves of water. A person could drown in either one of them. Case sat there between the world behind and the ocean in front: between the Devil and the Deep Blue Sea.

Left would send him into a 'U', back the way he came, but on Normandie Ave., to Vermont Ave. and back to Hollywood. That was out. He turned right onto Palos Verdes Drive. It toured around a great jut of land, protruding form California's southern sweep of coastline, interrupting its smooth arc to Mexico. Case drove north around the high bluffs of Portuguese Bend, under the watchful eye of The Wayfarer's Chapel, or the Glass Church, as the locals called it, on the bluffs high above. Palos Verdes Drive became Sepulveda Blvd. A short distance was Torrance Blvd. where a left became Highland Ave., running along the coast past Redondo Beach, Hermosa Beach and Manhattan Beach. He drove on and on.

Case stopped at Marina del Rey. People strolled the walks past the hotels and tackle stores in the warm night, even this late. Case, not knowing why he stopped, took the road around the marina and came to Lincoln

Blvd. He turned on it, vaguely wondering where he was going, but not really caring. He knew it wasn't important and didn't want to think about it. He arrived at Venice Blvd., turned left and stopped on Pacific Ave., Venice Beach, where he and Manny had been before. He didn't want to think about that either.

There were more people about on the Venice Boardwalk. Case only wanted to drive and keep driving, so he did. He took Pacific Ave. up to the Santa Monica Pier, and the beginning of one piece of Hwy 1, or the Pacific Coast Highway. Lincoln and Sepulveda Blvds. connected that end of the Pacific Coast Highway to its other end at Palos Verdes where it continued its run south, all the way down the coast to San Juan Capistrano.

Case stopped at the Santa Monica pier. He looked at the ocean, getting the same morbid thought. His trail could end just a little further than Route 66 did. He was suddenly tired. Fatigue overcame him; it was palpable, there with him in the car, a companion in the night. Together they watched the ocean. The full moon lit a brilliant yellow runway across the water from the shore to the horizon. Do you want to take a ride on the yellow brick road? Fatigue voted yes; Case was neutral, so it wasn't unanimous.

Case left Santa Monica behind and followed the Pacific Coast Highway as it followed the Pacific coast. There was a great, sweeping bend as the land curved to the west, heading for Malibu. Somewhere after Topanga Beach before Case got to Malibu he pulled off the highway and drove up to bluffs overlooking the ocean and shut off the engine.

From the rise Case could see the Pacific Ocean out there below him. It was living up to its name tonight. It was peaceful, even soothing. Gentle breakers on the beach, gentle ripples on the black surface. It looked like an immense water bed, inviting, for someone as tired as Case. He could crawl out onto the surface and sleep forever.

Not one to be introspective or reflective, nonetheless, he began to wonder what the sum of his life was. Still at the bottom of that deep hole he had dug for himself driving back from the desert, he presumed if someone could read his thoughts, they would think he were in a pretty black mood; as black and deep as that ocean out there. Case felt a pity party coming on and he didn't want to go there. He hated parties.

Pulling back from that brink, Case still wanted to ask Alphie: 'what's it all about'? Was anyone happy? Who was happy? Was Paul Kirby happy, the guy with the broken foot that would heal and the broken life that never would? His victims weren't happy, neither were their families. Was Manny happy? Were Consuela and the kids happy? He had never accepted their invitation, had never been to their house. Now he never would. A chill ran down his back when he remembered predicting they would meet at Manny's funeral.

Case sat and looked at the ocean; so peaceful. He could sit and look at it forever, just watching the gentle waves, focusing on them and nothing else. But his mind wouldn't let him. It wanted answers that meant something; something that mattered. He started the car. After the desert it could really use a bath. Then he laughed. He had promised Eugene he wouldn't scratch it, but he hadn't promised it wouldn't get shot.

Case put his hand on the gear shift knob and put the car in gear...Consuela and the two children mattered. Case didn't worry about Consuela. She was young and pretty and the way Manny spoke of her Case knew in time she would find someone. But what about the kids? What could he do? He wanted to do something for the kids, but what could he do? Then he remembered years ago he had been talked into signing up for some kind of savings or investment program through the city. He only agreed because it was easier than arguing. Something called a 401 Ross, or K Ross? He wasn't sure what it was called, but he didn't need it whatever it was, and telling the Captain to sign it over to the kids would be one less paper hassle to worry about. He'd tell the Captain to say it was for their future education, part of the department's survivor benefits and leave Case out of it.

That decided, there was nothing left to think about, least of all tomorrow. He didn't want to think about tomorrow. He wasn't interested in tomorrow. Case dropped the gear indicator to 'R' and backed around to drive down the road. At PCH he made a right and continued driving north. As long as he kept driving he didn't have to think about tomorrow. He needed to keep driving. He passed Malibu, and then, the Mustang seemed to know where it was going, because suddenly, he knew where he was going. He wasn't driving aimlessly anymore. He had been going in the right direction, north, all night, ever since leaving San Pedro. And he hoped the offer was still open. He was going to Ventura. He needed a hug.

Made in the USA
Charleston, SC
12 December 2014